Halfhyde
for the Queen

Historical Fiction Published by McBooks Press

BY ALEXANDER KENT
Midshipman Bolitho
Stand Into Danger
In Gallant Company
Sloop of War
To Glory We Steer
Command a King's Ship
Passage to Mutiny
With All Despatch
Form Line of Battle!
Enemy in Sight!
The Flag Captain
Signal–Close Action!
The Inshore Squadron
A Tradition of Victory
Success to the Brave
Colours Aloft!
Honour This Day
The Only Victor
Beyond the Reef
The Darkening Sea
For My Country's Freedom
Cross of St George
Sword of Honour
Second to None
Relentless Pursuit
Man of War

BY DOUGLAS REEMAN
Badge of Glory
First to Land
The Horizon
Dust on the Sea
Knife Edge

Twelve Seconds to Live
Battlecruiser
The White Guns
A Prayer for the Ship

BY DAVID DONACHIE
The Devil's Own Luck
The Dying Trade
A Hanging Matter
An Element of Chance
The Scent of Betrayal
A Game of Bones

On a Making Tide
Tested by Fate
Breaking the Line

BY DUDLEY POPE
Ramage
Ramage & The Drumbeat
Ramage & The Freebooters
Governor Ramage R.N.
Ramage's Prize
Ramage & The Guillotine
Ramage's Diamond
Ramage's Mutiny
Ramage & The Rebels
The Ramage Touch
Ramage's Signal
Ramage & The Renegades
Ramage's Devil
Ramage's Trial
Ramage's Challenge
Ramage at Trafalgar
Ramage & The Saracens
Ramage & The Dido

BY ALEXANDER FULLERTON
Storm Force to Narvik

BY PHILIP MCCUTCHAN
Halfhyde at the Bight of Benin
Halfhyde's Island
Halfhyde and the Guns of Arrest
Halfhyde to the Narrows
Halfhyde for the Queen
Halfhyde Ordered South

BY JAMES L. NELSON
The Only Life That Mattered

BY V.A. STUART
Victors and Lords
The Sepoy Mutiny
Massacre at Cawnpore
The Cannons of Lucknow
The Heroic Garrison

The Valiant Sailors
The Brave Captains
Hazard's Command
Hazard of Huntress
Hazard in Circassia
Victory at Sebastopol
Guns to the Far East

BY R.F. DELDERFIELD
Too Few for Drums
Seven Men of Gascony

BY DEWEY LAMBDIN
The French Admiral
Jester's Fortune

BY C.N. PARKINSON
The Guernseyman
Devil to Pay
The Fireship
Touch and Go
So Near So Far
Dead Reckoning

BY JAN NEEDLE
A Fine Boy for Killing
The Wicked Trade
The Spithead Nymph

BY IRV C. ROGERS
Motoo Eetee

BY NICHOLAS NICASTRO
The Eighteenth Captain
Between Two Fires

BY FREDERICK MARRYAT
Frank Mildmay OR
  The Naval Officer
The King's Own
Mr Midshipman Easy
Newton Forster OR
  The Merchant Service
Snarleyyow OR
  The Dog Fiend
The Privateersman
The Phantom Ship

BY W. CLARK RUSSELL
Wreck of the Grosvenor
Yarn of Old Harbour Town

BY RAFAEL SABATINI
Captain Blood

BY MICHAEL SCOTT
Tom Cringle's Log

BY A.D. HOWDEN SMITH
Porto Bello Gold

The Halfhyde Adventures, No. 5

Halfhyde
for the Queen

Philip McCutchan

MCBOOKS PRESS, INC.
ITHACA, NEW YORK

Published by McBooks Press, Inc. 2005
Copyright © 1978 by Philip McCutchan
First published in Great Britain by George Weidenfeld & Nicolson Limited
First published in the United States by St. Martin's Press, Inc.

Cover painting: *Coaling a Warship* by Norman Wilkinson in *The Royal Navy,*
1907. Courtesy of Mary Evans Picture Library.

Library of Congress Cataloging-in-Publication Data

McCutchan, Philip, 1920-
  Halfhyde for the queen / by Philip McCutchan.
    p. cm. — (The Halfhyde adventures ; no. 5)
  ISBN 1-59013-069-3 (trade paperback : alk. paper)
  1. Halfhyde, St. Vincent (Fictitious character)—Fiction. 2. Great Britain—
History, Naval—19th century—Fiction. 3. Victoria, Queen of Great Britain,
1819-1901—Assassination attempts—Fiction. I. Title.
  PR6063.A167H314 2005
  823'.914—dc22

                                                            2004018229

Distributed to the trade by National Book Network, Inc.
15200 NBN Way, Blue Ridge Summit, PA 17214
800-462-6420

Additional copies of this book may be ordered from any bookstore
or directly from McBooks Press, Inc., ID Booth Building,
520 North Meadow St., Ithaca, NY 14850. Please include $4.00 postage
and handling with mail orders. New York State residents must add
sales tax to total remittance (books & shipping). All McBooks Press
publications can also be ordered by calling toll-free
1-888-BOOKS11 (1-888-266-5711).
Please call to request a free catalog.

Visit the McBooks Press website at www.mcbooks.com.

Printed in the United States of America

9 8 7 6 5 4 3 2 1

Chapter 1

IT WAS PITCH DARK by now, with an increasing wind blowing through the strait from the Atlantic. A dirty night out at sea: water washed aboard, swilling over *Vendetta's* turtle-decked bows as course was altered towards the coast of Spain on the signal from the flotilla leader, bringing wind and sea abeam. In accordance with orders issued back in Gibraltar, all the navigation lights went off as the five vessels of the Fourth Torpedo-Boat Destroyer Flotilla formed in line ahead behind Captain Watkiss and headed towards Point Calaburras to the south-west of Malaga. On *Vendetta's* navigating bridge, last of the line as junior ship, Lieutenant St Vincent Halfhyde stood, bracing his tall, angular body against the wind, telescope lifted to watch the stern of his next ahead as the flotilla pushed on through the restless sea. At any moment now, the final orders should come from Captain Watkiss, by shaded signal lamp trained astern. The weather, dirty as it was, had proved kind to their as yet undisclosed mission: they should be nicely screened from the view of any hostile eyes along the Spanish coast.

St Vincent Halfhyde, still watching closely and ready to caution his officer of the watch should the gap between his ship and the next ahead narrow too much, thought fleetingly of the Great Armada that some three hundred years before had sailed out of Spanish waters against England. He thought of Nelson and his captains who in these very waters had fought the French and, again, the Spaniards. The ancient enemy! And enemy again, though Great Britain and Spain had been these many years at peace? It was inconceivable, surely; yet the urgency with which the TBD flotilla had been ordered out in secret from Gibraltar seemed scarcely to speak of peace. Halfhyde paced his narrow bridge, as restless as the sea itself, as he waited for the orders to come through.

Only the morning before there had been no thought of action movement, of a sudden dash to sea. Halfhyde, in tonight's cold and wet, reflected upon yesterday's awakening from a whore's bed. The day had been fresh and bright, clean and invigorating before the sun was fully up, though there had been a promise of a Mediterranean scorcher to come. Halfhyde had stood bare-chested at the window of the square, white-walled house, breathing deeply to dispel the previous night's fumes of whisky and tobacco, looking down on the harbour and the sparkling, sun-gilded blue waters of Gibraltar Bay—or Algeciras Bay as the Spaniards preferred it. High up to the north-west, beyond the isthmus that connected the Rock of Gibraltar to the Spanish mainland, stood upon its mountain eminence the old Martello Tower known as the Queen of Spain's Chair. In this Queen Isabella had sworn to sit until the Spanish flag was hoisted over the fortress of Gibraltar, her release from this self-imposed vigil being chivalrously given by the action of the British garrison in hoisting the standard of Spain for long enough to allow a dignified descent . . . and Isabella's chair still commanded a fine view of the small white town of La Linea and of the frowning, light-brown hills of North Africa across the strait.

Below, in the harbour and the dockyard, the long day's routine had already begun; the rousing bugles of the Royal Marine Light Infantry had already sounded throughout the mess decks and flats of the great battleships and cruisers of the Mediterranean Fleet and of the Channel Squadron assembled in the bay for the spring exercises and combined manoeuvres. Boats were crossing the harbour—duty steam picket-boats and boats under oars heading in towards the steps below the signal tower. Anchored separately from the rest of the warships lay the vessels of the Particular Service Squadron; from the flagship, Her Majesty's battleship *Revenge,* flew the flag of the rear-admiral in command: a white flag with a red St George's Cross, defaced in the quarters nearer the mast by two red balls.

Halfhyde sighed; fresh and clean the day, but for him and all his ship's company it was to be spoiled: Her Majesty's ship *Vendetta,* junior ship of the Fourth Torpedo-Boat Destroyer Flotilla, currently secured to a mooring buoy in the waters of the harbour, was under orders to shift at six bells in the morning watch to the North Mole for coaling, a filthy task. The previous day, when the rest of the flotilla had coaled ship, *Vendetta* had been ordered to sea to the assistance of a merchant vessel in distress; today she alone would fill her bunkers. Halfhyde turned from the window and his contemplation of natural and maritime beauty and surveyed the girl still asleep in the rumpled bed. Halfhyde, bent a little against the ceiling's constriction, grimaced. In truth the girl, though passable enough, was less beautiful than she had appeared the night before; nevertheless the bedding of her had been satisfactory, and as Halfhyde looked down on her nakedness he felt desire stirring again, and urgently.

Getting back into bed beside her, he spoke her name. "Carla . . ." His touch, running down her body, caused her to open her eyes. They were deep brown, lazy and voluptuous. She welcomed the awakening, trembling a little with memory and anticipation; St Vincent Halfhyde had proved a capable lover, one who could respond to her passionate Spanish nature, a man of muscle and hard body and of no paunch or flab. Once again satisfied, Halfhyde rolled over and stood up. "Time to get back to my ship, Carla."

"No. Please stay."

"Impossible. Her Majesty is a hard taskmistress."

The girl pouted through damp strands of black hair. "She is a terrible old woman, your Queen Victoria."

Halfhyde sat on the bed, reached out and took the small, oval face in his hands. He said solemnly. "As a loyal officer I should thrash you for that."

"But you will not?"

Halfhyde chuckled. He shifted his grip, rolled her over till her buttocks stared him in the face, and gave her a resounding smack. She cried out and squirmed away.

"English devil! Be a little late. Your Queen Victoria, she will never know."

"Carla, I am not an ordinary seaman, I am the captain. There's a difference." Halfhyde got to his feet and went across to the wash-stand where he washed and shaved in cold water. As the razor scraped across his face efficiently he said, "I shall come ashore this afternoon. You'll be here?"

"For you, my love, yes."

"Good." Shaved, Halfhyde dressed in his plain clothes, a suit of white sharkskin, and took his leave with a kiss planted lightly on the girl's cheek: to do more might well have delayed him, and he was a punctilious commander, as punctilious as he expected his officers and men to be. Leaving the room he walked along a cool corridor, down a flight of stairs and out into a small square from which he descended into Waterport Street with its shops and stalls, bars and eating places, picking his way past the droppings of the goats from which the town and garrison of Gibraltar drew their milk, past small boys who even at such an unpropitious hour tagged along at his elbow with descriptions of their sisters' bodily charms until driven away by a roar of impatience. "Away with you, *niños!* Sell your sisters to the soldiers, who are here for longer than sailors and will produce more profit in the end."

Halfhyde strode on, swinging a silver-topped cane. He walked past the naval picket-house, returning the salute of the sentry, on past the small cemetery where lay so many of the heroes of Trafalgar, their bodies landed in honour from the old wooden ships that had brought victory to Lord Nelson, on down the hill to the Ragged Staff Gate and through the dock-yard to the Tower steps where his boat should be awaiting him. And was, he noted with a captain's satisfaction as he cast a critical eye over the turn-out of the ratings manning it. Seeing his approach, a barefoot leading-seaman, wearing three blue good-conduct badges on the left sleeve of his white uniform, climbed nimbly from the stern-sheets and stood at the salute.

"Good morning, Parslow."

"Good mornin', sir. A fine day, sir."

"Shortly to be sullied. Is the ship ready to shift berth, Parslow?"

"Yessir, I think so, sir. I'd not speak for the first lieutenant, sir."

"Quite right, indeed." Halfhyde, about to descend the steps, paused and looked across the harbour. A galley was approaching; in the stern-sheets sat a rotund officer with a red face beneath a blue-puggareed white helmet. From the face, fire reflected: the morning sun, caught by a monocle. Halfhyde said, "Captain Watkiss is coming ashore, I see."

"Yessir."

"I'll wait." This was a wise decision; even as he made it, a hail came from the approaching galley and an arm was waved vigorously.

"*Mr Halfhyde!*"

"Sir?"

"May I ask where you're going?"

"Back to my ship, sir."

"No you aren't." The galley swept up to the steps, and the senior officer of the flotilla disembarked, telescope in hand. Captain Watkiss mounted the steps and returned Halfhyde's salute. The sun reflected in golden glory from the four stripes on either shoulder, from the shining brass buttons of his white uniform. Pompously Watkiss cleared his throat and said: "I've been bidden to wait upon the rear-admiral commanding the Particular Service Squadron, who is currently conferring with the captain-in-charge ashore."

"An early summons, sir."

"Quite. Something in the air—must be!" Captain Watkiss, nose raised suspiciously, moved closer. "Where did you spend last night, Mr Halfhyde, may I ask?"

Halfhyde shrugged. "Quietly, sir."

"Very quietly! In a barrel of whisky by the smell of your breath." Watkiss flourished his telescope. "You appear sober, however—"

"Very sober, sir—"

"Which is fortunate for you, since I don't like drinking officers. I—"

"Sir, I dislike having my movements questioned in front of lower-deck ratings—"

"Then you must get accustomed to it, Mr Halfhyde," Captain Watkiss said energetically. "I am a post captain and your senior officer, you are merely a lieutenant-in-command, are you not? And you'll not answer back, d'you hear me? Now, I wished words with you, which was why I hailed you." Watkiss lifted the telescope and waved it in front of Halfhyde's face. "Be ready—have your ship ready—for anything that may happen. Admirals do not hold conferences before breakfast without good cause."

He turned his back and walked away in a curious bouncing motion, his sword clutched in his left hand clear of the dockyard stone. Halfhyde, grimly furious but impotent, swung on his heel and went down the steps to his boat. Captain Watkiss was not a comfortable senior officer under whom to serve, and the relationship, since Halfhyde had been temporarily appointed to the command of the *Vendetta* by the vice-admiral commanding the Inshore Squadron at Malta, had been largely a sour one. No one had been more astonished than Halfhyde when, following upon the successful cutting-out of the sailing ship *Falls of Dochart* from under the noses of the Russian Black Sea Fleet in Sevastopol, his appointment had been made permanent by

the Admiralty. Someone, somewhere, must obviously have overcome the diplomatic storm that had threatened as a result of
his, Halfhyde's, actions on that occasion; and equally as astonishing as the confirmation of his appointment had been the
comparative meekness with which Captain Watkiss had received
the news of it. But there were many sides to Captain Watkiss,
Halfhyde reflected as, still seething, he came alongside his ship
and was piped aboard. Captain Watkiss could be both a
chameleon and an overblown balloon, and like any overblown
balloon was mightily susceptible to the prick of a pin . . .

Reaching his quarterdeck, Halfhyde returned the salutes of
the gangway staff and received his first lieutenant's report: "Ship
ready to shift alongside the coaling berth, sir. Buoy-jumper
standing by and starboard anchor ready to let go."

"So I noticed, Mr Prebble. Thank you." Halfhyde paused. "I
am advised by Captain Watkiss to stand by for possible orders,
but have not been told what those orders might be. In the
meantime, pipe the hands to stations, if you please."

"Aye, aye, sir." The first lieutenant motioned to the bosun's
mate and the pipe began shrilling its message through the ship.
Halfhyde went below to change, and when properly dressed in
white uniform proceeded to his bridge. Shortly after, *Vendetta*
cast off from the buoy, got under way and made across the harbour to secure alongside the coaling berth. All hands were piped
to shift into coaling gear, and emerged from the mess decks
looking like tramps and vagabonds. The officers were no less
sensibly attired. With all ports and non-working hatchways
closed tightly against the clouds of coal-dust to come, the operation started. Up the brows from the wharf came a constant
stream of Spanish dockyard workmen supported by ratings of

all branches—deck, engine-room, cooks, stewards and supply ratings—bearing bags of coal for tipping down the chutes into the bunkers. Almost within minutes, everything and everyone in sight was black. Sweat poured, tempers flamed, language grew foul and then fouler. A light breeze coming through the strait from the Atlantic only made matters worse, blowing the dust into every nook and cranny, laying it against the canvas-shrouded six-pounder guns and against the covered torpedo-tubes. The bridge took on the aspect of a pit-head housing, and Halfhyde longed to hear the wash-deck hoses in glorious cleansing action. To get away from this appalling filth, the recurrent hell of a seaman's life since sail had vanished from the seas, would be close to heaven. Halfhyde's mind wandered towards the girl of the night before: more bliss awaited him, but the clock moved only slowly.

Some eighty minutes after coaling had started, Captain Watkiss was seen coming off in his galley, in which a certain confusion appeared to be taking place: a canvas dodger was being rigged alongside the senior officer, who rapidly became invisible behind it as the galley came within coal-dust range. Fifteen minutes later the expected happened: aboard the flotilla leader a signal lamp began winking out *Vendetta's* pennants and was read by a blackened duty signalman and reported to Halfhyde.

"From *Venomous*, sir. *Do not make so much dust.*"

"Thank you."

The signalman coughed into a hand, discreetly. "Reply, sir?"

"Any reply would be unwise."

"Yessir." Grinning, the signalman turned away. Halfhyde glared towards the leader, his long jaw out-thrust. All post captains in Her Majesty's Fleet had their idiosyncrasies, and must be allowed them, but Captain Watkiss had many more than most. Halfhyde sat firmly upon insubordinate thoughts and ten minutes later another signal, this time general to all commanding officers, was received from the leader: *You are to report aboard immediately.*

Halfhyde swung round upon his first lieutenant. "Mr Prebble, I am bidden aboard *Venomous*—immediately. Call away my galley, if you please." He paused and lifted an eyebrow. "What are you staring at, Mr Prebble?"

"I beg your pardon, sir. Something tells me you have it in mind not to clean first."

"You are told right, Mr Prebble. The signal says immediately. Captain Watkiss is a stickler for obedience to orders. Now, my galley, if you please."

"You are insolent, Mr Halfhyde, in good keeping with your reputation." Captain Watkiss flapped at his immaculate uniform, its whiteness now sullied by coal-dust shaken from his visitor. "Damn it all, man, no other commanding officer has seen fit to attend upon me in such a state!"

"No other commanding officer is coaling ship, sir."

"Don't argue, Mr Halfhyde," Watkiss said in a distant tone. "I have a mind to order the hoses turned upon you. However, time is short and I must put up with you. I have received orders from the rear-admiral commanding the Particular Service Squadron, gentlemen." Captain Watkiss, seated at the head of the ward-room table with his commanding officers placed to right and left, drummed his fingers on the wood. "I am entrusted with a most important mission—a mission that is to remain a close secret, known only to such persons as must of necessity know, both now and after it has been successfully carried out. I am permitted to tell you little. Indeed I am permitted to tell you only our destination at this stage. Further orders will be passed later, as and when it becomes necessary." The voice became almost reverent. "I can add only this: much is at stake, gentlemen. The honour and safety of the realm is involved, and there is to be a need for diplomacy—" Watkiss broke off, staring haughtily at Halfhyde, and angrily too. "You seem anxious to speak, Mr Halfhyde. What, for God's sake, is it now?"

"With great respect, sir, you have *added*—to use your word uttered—without any indication as to the original proposition."

"What the devil are you talking about, Mr Halfhyde?" The senior officer bounced in his chair, his face reddening. "Kindly do not talk to me in damn riddles!"

"Our destination, sir. You said—"

"Yes, I know what I said, thank you. You will not be impertinent—"

"Sir, I—"

"Hold your tongue, sir!" Captain Watkiss seized his telescope and flourished it. "Now where was I? Oh yes. Our destination." He paused, screwing his monocle into his eye the better to stare importantly round the table. "Gentlemen, the Fourth Torpedo-Boat Destroyer Flotilla under my command has been temporarily attached for duty with the Particular Service Squadron. I am ordered to proceed to sea with my flotilla independently, leaving the capital ships here in Gibraltar. I am to proceed immediately *Vendetta* has finished taking coal. Mr Halfhyde?"

Halfhyde sighed inwardly: the girl would feel slighted, but

might, perhaps, understand the call of duty. He said politely, "Sir?"

Watkiss drummed his fingers on the table. "At what time will that be?"

"At noon, sir."

"Very well, noon. Course will be set to clear Europa Point easterly and this course will be followed until the flotilla is out of sight from the coast of Spain. Once out of sight I am ordered to heave-to and wait for darkness. At dark I am ordered to close and lie off Point Calaburras, steaming without navigation lights." Watkiss sat back at full arms' stretch and stared at each officer in turn, weightily. "Do your duty well. For now that is all I have to say, gentlemen. Go back to your ships and make ready, and await the signal to weigh." His voice became even more solemnly portentous as he added: "Remember that England and Her Majesty put their trust in each of you."

Chapter 2

AHEAD NOW, Point Calaburras loomed: behind it, as Halfhyde knew from peaceful journeys into Spain in past years, ran the rough road, little more than a track, that served as the main highway between Granada and Malaga and Gibraltar itself, by way of the motley collection of buildings that formed the frontier township of La Linea. Away to the north-west of the headland lay Malaga, and in between lay great sandy beaches washed, gently for the most part, by the warm waters of the Mediterranean. Halfhyde looked ahead through his telescope; but they were still some distance off and he could pick nothing out.

"Leader's calling, sir."

The voice of the yeoman of signals, dropping into a virtual silence, for the engines had been ordered to dead slow by now, was almost startling. Halfhyde swung round as the yeoman read off the leader's message, addressed as a general signal to all ships: the two letters, FD, meaning *Stop Engines.*

Halfhyde spoke to his officer of the watch. "Make it so, Mr Sawbridge."

"Aye, aye, sir." Sawbridge passed the order to a seaman boy who manipulated the telegraph to the engine-room. Bells rang below and a couple of seconds later were repeated on the bridge. "Engines repeated stopped, sir," Sawbridge reported.

Halfhyde nodded and once again brought up his telescope. The vessels drifted, inching on under what was left of the now stationary propellers' thrust. They wallowed a little in a slight swell; the wind had left them by now, cut off by Point Calaburras itself, and the sea was smooth apart from the gentle lift of the swell. The darkness was intense, could almost be felt, the low-slung stars of the Mediterranean sky obscured by a heavy over-cast. The ships ahead were no more than deeper shadows in the blackness, could almost not have been there at all had it not been for the hint left behind of the stench of funnel smoke. Then Captain Watkiss manifested his presence once again: the leader's shaded blue signal lamp flashed astern down the line, to be read off by Halfhyde's yeoman.

"General from *Venomous*, sir. You are to repair aboard immediately."

"Mr Prebble."

The first lieutenant materialized at his elbow. "Sir?"

"Sea-boat's crew and lowerers."

"Aye, aye, sir—"

"And Mr Prebble—pass the order by word of mouth. The bosun's call might carry too far."

"Aye, aye, sir." In the darkness Prebble saluted and hurried away down the ladder. In double-quick time he was back to report the sea-boat swung out and lowered on the falls to the upper-deck level: for which intelligence he received a rebuke.

"Mr Prebble, I am not an invalid nor of advanced years either. I shall go down the falls. Lower to the waterline, if you please, and be ready to slip the moment I'm aboard."

"Aye, aye, sir."

Prebble clattered down the bridge ladder to pass the order and Halfhyde, a few moments later, followed him aft to the sea-boat's davits. "I trust I'll not be long, Mr Prebble," he said, and without ceremony grasped the rope falls, swung himself out, and slid down into the boat. As soon as he was seated the order came to slip, and the disengaging gear was knocked away. With a jerk and a splash the sea-boat took the water and was borne off the ship's side plating by the boathooks. The oars went out and Halfhyde was pulled strongly ahead towards the leader, in the wake of the other commanding officers also bound for their orders.

Stepping aboard *Venomous,* Halfhyde was struck by the strange quiet of a warship hove-to on the ocean's bosom: there was a total lack of engine sound, and only the gentle movement to the swell, and the creak of woodwork as a side-boy led the way below to the ward-room, gave any clue to their being at sea. Once again Captain Watkiss was seated at the head of the table, with a look of import about him, and this time with a gold half-hunter watch held ostentatiously in his hand.

"Ah, Mr Halfhyde! Mr Halfhyde at last! Wonders will never cease, I suppose." Watkiss waved a hand around the table, indicating the other captains of his flotilla. "Mr Halfhyde, as junior ship you should have reached me first, so as not to keep your betters waiting. You are aware of that, I take it?"

"I am, sir."

"Then what is your excuse, may I ask?"

"I had further to come, sir. Or should my betters have delayed their own arrival, lying off so that I could arrive first and thus not keep them—"

"Oh, hold your tongue, sir! Damn your impertinence! Sit down." Captain Watkiss's words were as strong as ever, but his tone was mild; he appeared preoccupied with other matters and was in fact undergoing one of his chameleon-like changes. "You're here, that's the main thing. And as it happens you're to be the chief actor in this affair."

Halfhyde lifted an eyebrow. "I am, sir?"

"Yes." Watkiss pulled at a black silk toggle and his monocle rose from his ample stomach. He fixed it in position. "However, I'll come to you in a moment. You could pass well enough for a damn Spaniard," he added, staring Halfhyde up and down through the monocle. "Long face, long chin, sallow, dark hair, skinny. Now then." Watkiss looked around impatiently. "The shore maps. Where's my damn clerk? Oh, there you are," he added as a nervous-looking young officer approached, bespectacled and wearing a white cloth stripe below his single gold one. Watkiss drummed his fingers on the table in long-suffering fashion while the clerk laid a map before him with fumbling hands. "Now, pay attention, all of you, particularly Mr Halfhyde." Watkiss jabbed with a pencil; the sleeve of his uniform tunic rose up his forearm and the tail of a highly coloured tattooed snake became visible. "There's Gibraltar, there's Point Calaburras, and there's my flotilla. Now—follow me round the coast. D'you see? Fuengirola, Torremolinos, Malaga. Malaga's a fair-sized town and port, the other two are no more than fishing villages and tiny at that. A hut, a bar, a boat, two men and a cat. I understand you're aware of all this, Halfhyde, my dear fellow?"

"I am, sir."

"Which is why you're the number one man as it were—

except for our principal, of course, but I assume that's obvious."

"Principal, sir?"

"Yes." Once more Watkiss looked around. "Where's my damn clerk again? Coffee. See to it."

"Yes, sir."

"Not yes, sir—aye, aye, sir. What I said was an order."

"Aye, aye, sir."

"Well, don't waste time, get on with it." Captain Watkiss turned back to his commanding officers. "Our principal, now. Colonel Stanley, late the Royal Horse Guards—the Blues, don't you know. A good regiment. I know him myself, as a matter of fact—rides to hounds."

"As far as Spain, sir?" Halfhyde asked with his tongue in his cheek.

"What?" Captain Watkiss reddened dangerously. "I dislike your humour, Mr Halfhyde, dislike it intensely, so be pleased to hold your tongue." He paused, lips compressed. "Colonel Stanley is a Queen's Messenger, and he has met trouble with the damn dagoes, they're a shifty lot, wouldn't trust 'em with my grandmother's honour. Colonel Stanley is by way of being *persona non grata* currently with the blasted King of Spain, what's his name, er—"

"No name, sir," Halfhyde said.

"Oh, don't be impertinent, he must have a name!"

"No, sir, since he does not exist. King Alfonso—"

"*Alfonso!*" Captain Watkiss interrupted scathingly. "There's a name for you! Nancy-boys the lot of them!"

"King Alfonso XII died in 1885, sir. Since then there has been a regency, which will last until Alfonso XIII is of age, and the Regent is Alfonso's widow, Maria Cristina, originally of Austria—"

"All right, all right, I was about to say all that myself until you were rude enough to contradict me, Mr Halfhyde. Do let us keep to the point, shall we?" Captain Watkiss replaced his monocle, which had dropped out under stress, and glared round the ward-room table. "Colonel Stanley, at present in disguise, is coming south from Madrid with the Spanish police upon his heels. I am not precisely so informed but I assume he has with him his diplomatic bag. Ponder upon the importance of *that,* gentlemen! The diplomatic bag! Why, there could be all manner of secrets in the diplomatic bag, important concerns that are to be known only to Her Majesty and Whitehall." Captain Watkiss thrust his jaw forward pugnaciously, as though about to attack the Queen's enemies personally with fire and sword. "I am ordered by the rear-admiral commanding the Particular Service Squadron to land a boat and bring off Colonel Stanley before those buggers get their hands upon him." He studied the intent faces and interpreted correctly the anxious expression upon one of them. "Yes, Mr Beauchamp, you look as though you have something to say. Say it."

"Yes, sir." Beauchamp, a senior lieutenant bearing a thin gold stripe between the two thicker ones, was Watkiss's first lieutenant and wore the harassed air that might have been expected of the holder of such an appointment. "The diplomatic bag, sir. It has Foreign Office protection, as you know, of course—"

"Yes, I do. I dislike unnecessary words, Mr Beauchamp, they are verbal diarrhoea, and it is verbal diarrhoea to tell me what I already know. The diplomatic bag's supposed to be internationally honoured, but do you imagine for one moment that a set of damn dago pimps will take the slightest notice of that? Come to that—*any* blasted foreigners? They're all tarred with the same brush, they're not British. No, Mr Beauchamp, it's up to me to get *my* hands upon it, then it'll be safe for Her Majesty."

"But—"

"No, Mr Beauchamp, not but. The diplomatic bag's in peril and with it its secrets and given half a chance the scoundrels will rip it open; that's fact—I said it. Mr Halfhyde?"

"Sir?"

"Ten minutes after all the commanding officers have returned to their ships, I intend to move the flotilla in towards the land—not far, but far enough. When I make the signal to heave-to, you will embark in a boat under oars and be pulled inshore. Muffled rowlocks, no lights, no talking, slow strokes so as not to cast up spray. You will be landed and your boat will return promptly to your ship."

"Where shall I land, sir?"

"Here." A finger was jabbed down upon the Spanish coast-line a little way inward from Point Calaburras. "From there you will make your way into Torremolinos, where Colonel Stanley should be awaiting you."

"And if he is not?"

Watkiss rustled irritably. "I've said he *will* be—"

"Your pardon, sir. You said *should* be."

"Don't play with words, Mr Halfhyde, you know very well what I meant. Argument will get us nowhere, and could be dangerous for your career if you persist. Colonel Stanley will be there."

"And his whereabouts, sir?"

"How the devil should I know?" Watkiss stared blankly, light blue eyes wide.

"A rendezvous, sir. I must know where to meet him."

"There is no precise rendezvous so far as I know, Mr Halfhyde. I've already said, haven't I, Torremolinos is small enough. You should have no difficulty at all in making contact."

Halfhyde inclined his head ironically. "I take your point, sir. A Colonel of the Blues, a Queen's Messenger with a diplomatic bag, will contrast strongly enough with the *hombres* of Torremolinos and the donkeys—"

"Hold your tongue, Mr Halfhyde," Watkiss broke in peremptorily. "Colonel Stanley will be acting the role of a visitor from England, so much I have been told." He added with distaste, "I understand they call them tourists, a dreadful word to be sure. He'll be known as Smith, plain Mister. *John* Smith."

"And the diplomatic bag, sir? Has that also been put into disguise? The royal cypher will surely—"

"Yes, Mr Halfhyde, that has been taken care of, you may be sure. Colonel Stanley is not a fool." Watkiss paused. "Now what is it?"

Halfhyde said, "It's true I know this part of the coast well, sir, but my Spanish is sketchy, mere kitchen-Spanish picked up from the *hombres*. It'll not pass, although you made the point that my person would. I see a discrepancy, sir."

"Well, I don't. My earlier remark was a mere observation, not an instruction. The admiral feels, and so do I, that cloak-and-dagger pretences are all balls and bang-me-arse, Mr Halfhyde. Too many pitfalls in trying to assume an unnatural nationality. No, you'll go in as a British seaman, a merchant seaman who has swum for the shore after his ship went down eastward of the strait. The steamship *Ellabank*—an explosion in her boiler-room. Your name is Albert Thompson, able-seaman. Your story will be supported as to this sinking—word will have been leaked through La Linea. You should," Captain Watkiss added with complacent pomposity, "have no difficulty."

"I trust not, indeed, sir."

"But, as always, Her Majesty's Service holds its dangers, as we all know, and you must take great care. Now then. Just in case Colonel Stanley's *not* yet there—delays can occur—you'll wait until he is. When you make contact with him, you'll escort him to the point at which you landed and if it's still dark you'll signal direct to your own ship by means of a flare—you'll take a tarred rope's-end with you, and some spunyarn, and lucifers wrapped in oiled silk. You'll be picked up the moment the signal's seen, and after that I shall take my flotilla to sea and enter Gibraltar. You may ask why Colonel Stanley cannot enter Gibraltar through the land frontier. The answer is, I think, quite clear: it is in that precise area that the dago police will be waiting to cut him off. Are there any questions, gentlemen?"

"One, sir." This was from the captain of *Venus*. "If Mr Halfhyde's delayed and has to wait, what will be the orders for the flotilla?"

"A proper question, Mr Cholmondeley-Ross. I shall go to sea, and heave-to out of sight of the land, returning nightly until one hour before dawn to await Mr Halfhyde's flare. Take a note of that, Mr Halfhyde, if you please."

"That is noted, sir. But if I may make the point—or rather two points—are we not a somewhat large and visible task for a small purpose?"

"Our purpose is far from small, Mr Halfhyde," Watkiss said coldly. "This is a most serious matter, as I have been at some pains to indicate. Our size reflects the great concern of the rear-admiral and of Her Majesty's government. The Spaniards may well take the risk—for instance—of deploying their navy to prevent Colonel Stanley's escape." He waved a deprecating hand and went on slightingly, "The Spanish Fleet's a piddling enough affair, of course, but it carries guns, and we are here to oppose those guns if necessary. Nevertheless you have raised a vital point, my dear fellow. You must have a care. Whitehall has no wish—no wish at all—to provoke a state of war. If it comes it will be met—but woe betide the officer who brings it about by an act of omission or commission that could have been avoided. I think you will understand."

"Only too well, sir."

"Quite." Watkiss drummed his fingers. "I think you spoke of *two* points, Halfhyde, did you not?"

"Yes, sir. The second is this: if you are to return nightly, do you expect to meet favourable conditions of overcast upon each and every appearance?"

Captain Watkiss blew out his cheeks. "I shall leave that in God's hands, Mr Halfhyde. He is disposed to look favourably upon the British Fleet. You may all go back to your ships."

Halfhyde, sitting deplorably dressed in the stern-sheets of the sea-boat as later he was pulled by muffled oars from his ship towards the land, ground his teeth in sheer impotent fury. Once again he was to be used as, in a sense, a cat's-paw. When a mere lieutenant thrust his fingers into the fire and burned them, the burn was for himself alone; his seniors and betters

stood protected by another's pain. It was safer to sacrifice a lieutenant than to provoke a war, and that lieutenant's actions could
always be blamed for any subsequent mishaps. To some extent,
though a limited one, Captain Watkiss was at risk as well, or
might be; but he had rid himself of most of that risk the moment
Halfhyde had left his ship to act upon his own initiative, and
was thus no longer under direct command. Such were the ways
of authority; and they had to be accepted with as good a grace
as possible.

Still in darkness, the boat neared the shore; all was quiet
and peaceful, the whole coast apparently deserted. Silver sand
loomed as they approached, and soon the keel had touched
bottom. Jumping ashore, Halfhyde looked back, out to sea: he
found black shapes, nothing more than those deeper shadows,
indistinguishable as ships of war. He gave an ironic wave in the
general direction of the flotilla; if Colonel Stanley failed to turn
up, Captain Watkiss would soon be taking himself off to stand
into open water well clear of Spain's territorial limits. No doubt
he would steam around by day like a hen seeking a place to
lay her eggs, exchanging courteous signals with shipping bound
into Malaga or up to Barcelona, signals to indicate that, as an
important part of the combined Mediterranean and Atlantic
Fleets, he was on a harmless exercise . . .

Halfhyde nodded at the leading-seaman in charge of the sea-
boat. "All right, Parslow, back to the ship with you and no
noise."

"Aye, aye, sir. An' the best o' luck, sir."

"Thank you, Parslow." Halfhyde held out a hand. "The dark
will last a while yet. I may not be long." He felt the words to
be as empty as they sounded as he turned away and strode up

the sand towards tufty grass behind the shoreline. He had a strong sense of desertion and of utter aloneness, his only reassurance coming from the weight of the revolver with which he had equipped himself before leaving his ship. His orders were pitifully thin and in fact left him with all the initiative—that quality so dangerous to lieutenants! He might well find it hard to establish his bona fides in Colonel Stanley's mind. Though Stanley, Watkiss had told him before he left the leader, had been warned to expect him in his role as Able-Seaman Thompson, he carried no proof of his identity or standing; and a Queen's Messenger could be the target of many undesirables. Stanley would watch where he placed his trust, for a certainty . . .

Halfhyde paused briefly in his inland progress, and looked back towards the sea: the overcast was there yet, and the ships of the flotilla were safely concealed. Leading-Seaman Parslow was taking good charge of his boat's crew; nothing was visible, no spray as the oars took the water, no wake. It all increased Halfhyde's sense of desolation, and with a muttered oath he turned his back on the sea and faced inland resolutely. Around him there were high cliffs, though he himself had been landed where the cliffs were not. As he climbed rising ground behind the sandy beach he began to come round behind the cliffs and was soon striding at a good height above the shoreline; and it was not long before he had reached the pot-holed apology for a roadway that would take him into the village of Torremolinos some five miles east-north-east. He walked fast and unobserved, finding no sign of life, either animal or human.

It took him little more than an hour to reach Torremolinos. Captain Watkiss, as Halfhyde knew, had exaggerated but little: the place was tiny. The hour was not especially late; guitar music came from a doorway through which streamed yellow lamplight. There was a sound of laughter. Halfhyde approached the doorway and looked in. As he had thought, it was a bar, but one he had not known when last he had been in the province of Andalusia. Sooner or later he would have to make human contact, but first, perhaps, he should keep in the open and make himself obvious to Colonel Stanley who would scarcely be found in the bar.

He walked on. He was enfolded by the short village street, by the whitewashed hovels. A few men passed, staring at him curiously, suspicious of any stranger: word of his coming would spread quickly. There was a tingling in his shoulder-blades, brought about by his imagination: this was a fine setting for a knife in the back! Strangers might have *pesetas* for the picking, and justice was slow in Spain, a land of distances and poor communications and much sloth on the part of those in authority. Anger rose again in Halfhyde: if Stanley had not yet come through, a wait was going to be devilish tricky! If he lingered in Torremolinos he would soon stick out in the public view like the old sea forts in the Spithead approaches to Portsmouth dockyard.

At the end of the street he halted. There was silence; ahead lay the deserted countryside, the dusty track to Malaga. Behind him the village street was quiet, even the guitar and the laughter now stilled. He turned. He saw shadows distantly, shadows standing across the roadway, perhaps half a dozen of them. After a few moments he had the impression that the shadows were moving towards him. There was a strong desire to run; but flight, he knew, would not only be hopeless but would be much against the orders of Captain Watkiss. This had to be brazened out. Sliding his right hand around the butt of his revolver, Halfhyde advanced back along the way he had come, along the mean street between the hovels, down the centre towards the shadows' menace. He approached the bar, where light still streamed from the open doorway into the night's cool; now the shadows were close, had materialized into men—*hombres,* in blue working trousers and white shirts, with rope-soled sandals on their feet and wide-brimmed hats on their heads. Each man carried a short, thick club.

Halfhyde stopped; so did the men—there were in fact five of them. Halfhyde said evenly, "Are you here to rob, or to give succour to a shipwrecked sailor?"

There was a surprised response: *"Englesa!"*

"Englesa indeed, gentlemen, and one not worth robbing I assure you!" Halfhyde took a pace forward, still brazening the matter out. As he did so, another man came out of the bar, a short, swarthy man with a pencil-line moustache, a man with the look of authority about him and wearing a suit of clean white linen.

"Englesa?" this man asked.

"Si, señor."

The man spoke in Spanish, too fast for Halfhyde to follow him. But he appeared to be admonishing the five others, who reacted sheepishly and with respect. The men turned and made off, and the authoritative man bowed to Halfhyde, though not before Halfhyde had seen the enigmatic glitter in the dark eyes. "The apologies of Torremolinos," the Spaniard said in good English. "Visitors, guests, are not to be treated in such a way, and I, Señor Barroso, am much grieved."

Halfhyde made a dismissive gesture. "It is of no matter. All countries have their bandits and robbers, *señor*, as I know to my cost."

"You have travelled much, away from your own country?"

"I am a sailor, now without my ship, which has gone to the bottom, leaving only me so far as I know."

"So?" Barroso rubbed the palms of his hands together, and looked sympathetic. "A glass of brandy, my dear sir. It will warm you, and you shall tell me your story while you drink it. Come into the bar."

Turning, he led the way inside. The room, a small one, was crowded with men, young and old, and the atmosphere was thick with the fumes of tobacco and of wine and brandy. There were but two women, both young, dark-skinned and with the look of the gypsies of Andalusia, playing their flamenco music upon their guitars and flanked and guarded by what were obviously their own menfolk. As Halfhyde entered the music stopped, and there was a silence, while every eye seemed to search through his skin into his very soul.

His host called in Spanish to a man behind the rough bar. "Gonzalez, *Fundador* and glasses in my room."

He pushed through the throng of men with Halfhyde following closely. There was a stench of sweat and of drink-laden breath, and there was a curious underlying menace in the air. Once again, as he followed the man through a doorway beyond the bar, Halfhyde felt the warning prickling in his shoulder-blades. He cursed savagely beneath his breath; this was no place for any seaman, let alone a lieutenant of Her Majesty's Navy!

Chapter 3

"YOUR NAME, *señor?* Mine I have told you already."

"Indeed, you have. I am Albert Thompson, able-seaman."

"And shipwrecked on our local coasts."

"No. A long way off shore. An explosion in the boiler, and she went to the bottom."

"And so you swam, *señor.* And you are perhaps the sole survivor of the good ship *Ellabank,* bound home to the London River from far Madras with spices from the Orient to fill the warehouses below Tower Bridge!" Barroso laughed and rubbed his hands together. "You look surprised. Sit down, *Señor* Thompson, and I shall pour you some of our excellent brandy—the dark *Fundador* that is filled with the languorous sun of Spain."

Halfhyde sat on a cane-bottomed chair at a table that almost filled the small upstairs room. There was one tiny window, uncurtained, the table-lamp reflecting from its dark panes and nothing but the night itself visible beyond. As the Spaniard pushed across a glass of *Fundador,* Halfhyde asked, "How do you know so much about my ship, Señor Barroso?"

There was a chuckle and the eyes gleamed in the lamplight. "You do not think there has been time yet for word to filter through from the British base at Gibraltar—and you are right, of course—"

"I know nothing of Gibraltar."

"No?" The eyebrows went up. "I think perhaps you do. I must tell you—and this you should know already—you are not alone in this."

"In what?" Halfhyde tried to look blankly astonished. "You speak in riddles, Señor Barroso, and I am lost." He added: "I have swum a long way, and am tired. All I wish is bed."

Barroso shook his head and clicked his tongue sympathetically. "Bed you cannot yet have. I am sorry." He leaned forward, toadlike, his dark eyes staring into Halfhyde's with a compelling solemnity. "You must trust me."

"In what connection?"

"Your name is St Vincent Halfhyde, a lieutenant in the British Fleet."

Halfhyde shrugged. "Still you speak in riddles."

"I think not. You are not a cloak-and-dagger man, Lieutenant Halfhyde. I think no seaman is. It shows in your eyes that you know what I speak of." Barroso poured more brandy into Halfhyde's half-empty glass. "I am on your side, you understand."

"A Spaniard, on the British side?"

Barroso laughed, his eyes gleaming at what seemed to be an admission. "We Spanish are far from unfriendly towards your country, Lieutenant Halfhyde, and when we think a blunder has been made by the state we are willing to help." He leaned closer, dropping his voice as if instinctively. "My friend, I am from the British Embassy in Madrid, where I have an official standing. Three years ago I was the consul of my country in your port of Liverpool. I had been there for ten years and had grown to like your country and its people. When I returned to

Spain, I was asked by your Embassy to accept an appointment. I was delighted to do so." Barroso looked Halfhyde in the eye, directly. "Are you beginning to understand now?"

"Perhaps," Halfhyde answered offhandedly.

"I come with word of Colonel Stanley."

Halfhyde drew in a sharp breath through set teeth: Barroso knew it all, and it seemed that the time had come to cast a die for good or ill. Halfhyde said, "I see. And that word, Señor Barroso?"

"Stanley is not in Torremolinos, and he will not come. It is too dangerous for him to move from where he is. He is in Malaga."

"Indeed."

Barroso said, "You are to go to him. I shall take you, and we must not delay. That is why I said you could not have your bed yet, Lieutenant Halfhyde."

"And the nature of this danger?"

"The *politicos,* the government agents, are on his track. They do not know where he is precisely, only that he is in Malaga. If he shows himself, they will pounce."

"If he's to reach a boat, Señor Barroso, then sooner or later he'll have to show himself."

The Spaniard shook his head. "There are ways and means, but only once he is under your protection. We shall go into that later, when you are in contact with Colonel Stanley." Once again the glasses were refilled. "A last drink, Lieutenant Halfhyde, then we must be on our way to Malaga. I have horses stabled in the yard at the back of the inn, and the journey will be quickly accomplished."

"If I decide to trust myself to your hands. How do I know that you are speaking the truth, *señor?*"

"You do not, but you must take a risk. Without me, you will not find Colonel Stanley. Think, Lieutenant Halfhyde: were I acting for my government, I would need only to arrest you now!"

"A task you might find easier in Malaga with its good policing. I have experience of the country districts of Andalusia, Señor Barroso. They do not love the government and its agents, nor the police either. The rabble below in the bar might take matters and your person into their own hands, might they not?"

Barroso met his eye steadily and said, "Yes, all that is true. The decision is yours alone."

Halfhyde frowned, got to his feet and, bent almost double, paced the room so far as its size allowed, two steps one way, two the other. He knew without Barroso's confirmation that his summary of likelihoods had been accurate and he faced a quandary. Arrest and imprisonment might well await him in Malaga, unless he was remarkably quick off the mark when he saw trouble coming. There could have been a leak somewhere along the line as to Stanley's intentions and movements, and Barroso could have been despatched to effect a neat and bloodless apprehension of Stanley's support so that Stanley himself fell helpless into the net of the *politicos*. And his own orders from Captain Watkiss, of course, still stood: he had been bidden to await Stanley in Torremolinos. Watkiss abominated disobedience to orders; and Watkiss, ploughing the restless seas with his flotilla, anxious not to disturb the placid waters of diplomacy but keen as ever to inherit any glory that lay in the offing, would nightly but fruitlessly cruise off Point Calaburras awaiting Halfhyde's signal. Off Malaga, some ten to fifteen miles north of Calaburras, Watkiss would be conspicuous only by his absence and how he could be contacted was known currently to God alone. And if it was dangerous to move Stanley, then to attempt to move him as far as Torremolinos might prove fatal. Barroso had virtually said as much. Yet, despite all fancies, possibilities and dangers, the fact remained that Barroso was, one way or another, his only present link with Stanley; and the Spaniard's words had had a ring of sincerity . . .

Halfhyde halted and faced Barroso. "Very well, *señor,* I shall put my trust in you. We go to Malaga."

Downstairs and through the bar once again: the guitar-playing gypsies had departed, leaving the earnest drinkers to their brandy or their wine. There was some song, and many recumbent bodies lay on the dusty floor or slumped across the tables; a man could have become drunk from the fumes alone. In one corner sat a green-uniformed *guardia civil,* his flat-backed cap still upon his head and his rifle crooked in his elbow; he appeared to some degree intoxicated, but his eyes followed Halfhyde and Barroso to the door as they stepped over the inert customers.

Barroso led the way round the side of the building into the stable yard where the horses waited patiently at a hitching rail. Halfhyde swung himself into his saddle efficiently: the son of a farmer in the Yorkshire Dales, he was a fair horseman though he had no interest in horseflesh as such. When they rode back past the door of the bar the *guardia* was on his feet and staring out at them with his rifle held loosely across his body. When they reached the extremity of the village, Halfhyde turned and looked back: he could still see the outline of the policeman, standing four-square in the roadway. It was not reassuring; but Barroso seemed unworried.

They rode out into the night; there was, in fact, no pursuit and no sudden bullet from the *guardia*'s rifle, and Halfhyde relaxed though he cursed the difference between land and sea and spared a thought for soldiers in time of war: the officers and men of Her Majesty's Navy had the comfort of fighting at a distance, and from the bosom of close comradeship aboard with no infiltrating enemy to strike from the rear with bullet or bayonet. The sea was restless but clean and the winds that disturbed it blew straight from God, and to fight the elements was a noble thing. At this moment Halfhyde felt that he was engaged upon an ignoble task, one better left to the politicians and the diplomats and their seedy agents whose stock-in-trade was the subterfuge and the lie and the broken word. He and Barroso rode on, moving fast and in silence, a silence that was total but for the hoofbeats and the slow surging hiss of the Mediterranean close upon their right hand below the Malaga road. They saw no one; they passed by a handful of white-walled hovels, a few glassless holes in the walls showing lamplight. Ahead they saw the dotted lights of Malaga as they topped the cliffs, and the sense of a trap grew in Halfhyde's mind. But now he was committed: he had to trust the Spaniard and at the same time keep his senses alert.

They entered the town, riding—slower now so as not to appear too urgent—through sleazy outskirts and past the ends of dark alleys full of filth and potential danger, places where footpads and bandits lurked and scraggy, moth-eaten dogs foraged for scraps of food, places from which emanated foul smells of decay and dereliction.

"How far inside the city?" Halfhyde asked.

"Some way yet."

They rode on. They passed patrolling police—*guardias*—walking in pairs and armed, as the man in Torremolinos had been armed, with rifles and bayonets, their polished black boots biting into the dust as they moved, their faces showing as dim blurs beneath the hard black headgear. No attention was paid to the riders. As Halfhyde and Barroso came nearer the heart of the city, the buildings grew grander, the streets cleaner and in places paved with wooden blocks, and more people were to be seen. A few bars still stood open, even some shops. There was an absence of women except for one or two being handed into carriages by their male escorts: Spain, as Halfhyde knew, was a land of chivalry and of chaperons, of people more Victorian than Her Majesty herself. No woman of any pretension to birth would speak to a stranger nor would she ever be seen unescorted in public, and the rapiers of the gentlemen were ready upon the instant to defend her from the touch of the commonalty.

"Now," Barroso said, "we ride along the Guadal-Medina, the river of the city."

Halfhyde nodded, and followed the Spaniard along the bed of the river. A torrent in winter, the Guadal-Medina dried out completely in summer and was used as a high road. The two horsemen made down towards the harbour dominated by the 550-foot-high Gibralfaro Hill, a vast shadow in the night. On the fringe of the docks Barroso turned to the left, leaving the river bed for the higher surface of another maze of alleys more dangerous-looking than those they had passed earlier.

This time they plunged right in. Warehouses loomed along-side, great repositories of Malaga's seaborne commerce. The smells of wine and fruit, of flour and leather, fought those of refuse and urine—fought and largely lost. Halfhyde wrinkled his nose and brought out a handkerchief. As they came deeper into the maze of cross-alleys, as the state of the hovels grew more and more appalling, Halfhyde became more and more aware of the vulnerability of his back. It was an unnerving feeling; any of these hovels could spit out the man with the knife, the poverty-stricken gaining a little ready cash: men with no money did not ride horses. And afterwards, when the bodies were found if ever they were, the entire alley population would shake its collective head and swear it had seen nothing.

As Barroso made to turn again, this time left into a pit of total blackness, he brought up his horse and lifted a hand to Halfhyde, who also halted.

"What is it?"

"An old woman who wishes to speak." The Spaniard bent from his saddle and Halfhyde saw, at the horse's head, a bundle of darkness that had apparently emerged from the alley, a bundle in black clothing, with a black shawl showing snow-white hair at its fringe. There was some rapid talk in Spanish, talk that Halfhyde could not catch. Having had her say, the crone vanished again, back as it seemed into some obscure hole from whence she had materialized like a witch. Barroso said: "The old woman warns of persons watching the place where Colonel Stanley is hidden."

"What persons?"

"She knows not, but they are not in uniform."

"How far is the hiding place now?"

"Not far. At the bottom of this alley there is a left-hand turn. Twenty metres past the corner is the hiding place."

Halfhyde nodded. "And the old woman? She's known to you?"

"Yes. She is my intermediary for tonight's task."

"To be trusted?"

White teeth shone in a smile. "A little gold has ensured that, yes."

"What, then, do you advise, Señor—"

"Not my name—not here. There may be ears." Barroso had moved his horse closer. "I advise discretion."

"You mean retreat?"

"Until a more propitious time, perhaps—"

"That time won't come and you know it," Halfhyde said. "If Stanley's being watched now, he'll be watched until the moment of truth—the moment they move in to arrest him! It's now or never, isn't it?"

Barroso seemed suddenly undecided and ill-at-ease; he mopped at his forehead with a handkerchief, a white blur in the darkness. "I think we must be discreet as I have said. We must wait."

"Until it's too late? I have my orders. I think you know what they are?"

"Yes. You are ordered to avoid a diplomatic furore. I, also, must think of that."

Halfhyde asked coldly: "You are thinking of your own position?"

"As a member of staff at the British Embassy, yes. I must not be seen to be involved. And this is my country. It is not yours.

There is a difference, do you not see? You cannot be accused of being a traitor. My part is to remain under cover."

Halfhyde nodded reluctantly. "I understand that, of course. Under cover you shall remain, but you shall not let me down now. I am here and I shall stay."

"What do you intend to do?" There was much fear now in the Spaniard's voice.

"Wait, and I shall consider the matter."

"Quickly, then."

"Patience, patience!" Halfhyde frowned in thought. "I find it strange that your *politicos* should play cat-and-mouse with Colonel Stanley. If they know where he is, why not arrest him at once without a delay that may go against them?"

"They may wish to set a trap and catch more than Colonel Stanley."

"You?"

The voice quaked. "It is possible. They may suspect he has help."

"There I agree with you, *señor!* But I do not think they will expect me, nor will they wish to be burdened with me. They will wish no more than the British government for a diplomatic storm. It's scarcely usual for a Queen's Messenger to be interfered with and diplomatic immunity challenged even, let alone broken."

"So?"

"So I shall approach this hiding place, *señor,* if you will be so good as to give me precise directions and a full geographical description of the locality."

"If that is your decision."

"It is."

"Very well, then. And I? What do you wish of me?"

"Save your skin," Halfhyde said, "and I intend no disrespect. You have brought me here and that is all I can ask. It's up to me now to carry out my orders from my captain as best I can in the changed circumstances."

"Very well," Barroso said once again. He hesitated, searching Halfhyde's face. "I think I should know what your orders are in the event of Colonel Stanley not reaching Torremolinos tonight."

Halfhyde, anxious now to be away, nodded. "A fair thing to ask, *señor*. My captain will await me each night after dark, remaining until an hour before the dawn off the coast, in the lee of Point Calaburras. When I arrive, I am to light a flare. Then a boat will be sent to pick us up."

Barroso gave clear directions: Colonel Stanley would be found, alone, in the back room of the fourth hovel along the alley from the corner, on the left-hand side. Opposite would be other hovels and it was likely enough that it was in one of them that the unknown watchers were concealed. The alley was the last in the port area and beyond it were warehouses fronting a loading and unloading berth. There was access to the dwellings from both front and back. Away to the east was some waste ground, open and desolate, while to the west stood the main port installations and the open sea. The open sea was pulling strongly at Halfhyde as an eventual escape route; but as an alternative he prevailed upon Barroso to take the two horses to the waste ground and find a means of tethering them, after which the Spaniard would hasten out of the area on foot and make his way back to Madrid by whatever means was open to him;

he would, he said, make the journey by rail and upon arrival would make a full report to the British Ambassador.

Halfhyde walked fast along the pitch-dark alley, making for the turn at its end, keeping his eyes skinned and his hand ready on his revolver butt. His mind raced ahead of him: he had another theory about the watching men. Back in Torremolinos he had asked Barroso what the reason was for the Spanish desire to arrest Stanley; Barroso had said that he had not been entrusted with the background facts. Halfhyde had not wholly believed this and fancied that Barroso wished, not unnaturally, the fullest protection for his own position; but Halfhyde had been unable, in the circumstances, to press. It was, however, a considerable possibility that other parties could be involved; Halfhyde could make no guess at who or why, but it was worth bearing in mind that the watchers whom he was now approaching might not be agents of the Madrid government. If not, so much the better: to misuse Spanish officials would lead to much trouble, but the Spaniards might not be so concerned about the fate of nefarious persons. And after contact had been made with Stanley—what then?

Out by sea if such could be achieved, as no doubt it could? If a boat could be obtained, he could head south and fall in with Captain Watkiss, who might well be put out by finding Halfhyde's approach coming from a direction different from the ordered one, but who might forgive and forget in the heady excitement of success . . . Halfhyde grinned to himself as he made on through the dark night and its pervading stench: there was, at least, no doubt that Captain Watkiss would approve his present course of action. Watkiss, to give him his due, was no hanger-back. When action was in the offing, Captain Watkiss

was less inclined to turn and run than to thrust himself glori-
ously, vigorously and often foolishly into the very muzzles of
the guns; and Halfhyde could see him, were he present at this
moment, striding with much purpose along the alley, sword in
hand and gold rings of rank ready to shine out splendidly as
soon as they met light, red face truculently British and set firm
against the dagoes, ready to announce to all who stood and listened that he was the on-the-spot embodiment of Her Majesty
Queen Victoria, ruler of the seas and all lesser breeds of
mankind. And it was curious how often, how very often, such
bold and brazen tactics paid off! St Vincent Halfhyde, descendant of old Daniel Halfhyde, gunner's mate in the fighting
Temeraire under the glorious flag of Nelson, hoped devoutly
that the day would never come when things would be any different . . .

Approaching the end of the alley and the turn, Halfhyde
came down to earth. This filthy neighbourhood was not the
Spanish Main and he was bound upon no glittering enterprise
against a great Fleet. Instead of the roll of drums and the stri-
dent bugle calls and the immensity of the battle ensigns at the
mastheads as the embattled turrets opened in sound and flame
he must settle for the sordid, the mean and the sudden flash
in the dark . . .

Cautiously, moving slowly now, and then halting, he looked
along the side alley, counting to the fourth doorway on his left.
By now his vision was nicely night-accustomed and he was able
to see that all was quiet and no persons visible. No lamp glowed
along the whole narrow alley. A light wind was coming off the
sea now, a warm wind that blew dust and filth into his face,
bringing an increased variety of smells. Eschewing the alley in

which Stanley was said to be hiding, he moved ahead, along the main alley towards the warehouses and the berths. Over the tops of the warehouses he could see the masts of shipping waiting for daylight to bring the stevedores—sailing ships and steamships, large and small. It was likely enough that the British flag would be amongst them; but on the other hand the British flag would be well-watched by the men who were in pursuit of Colonel Stanley, and was probably best avoided.

Halfhyde reached the line of warehouses and looked along the backs of the hovels that on their other side faced Stanley's hiding place. Here, too, everything was quiet and peaceful and there were no lights showing. As on the road from Torremolinos the hovels had naked holes for windows, a line of them stretching along the backs towards the centre of the port. Halfhyde edged in towards them, walking now on stone that reached inwards from the jetty beyond the warehouses. Bending double and moving slowly and with infinite care to make no sound, he crept along, close to the back walls and below the holes, listening, pausing at each to catch the faintest breath or rattle of arms from men wearied by a long wait.

He heard nothing. The whole row seemed deserted in its dereliction. He went on past the fourth doorway, past Colonel Stanley's concealment across the alley, on to the tenth. He saw and heard nothing; the watchers could be in the hovels alongside Stanley, perhaps, but Halfhyde fancied that to be opposite would give them the better chance. At the eleventh doorway he turned back to draw the covert once again. As he came towards the fourth from the end, a sudden racket smote him: a terrible howling and screeching as of a man in the grip of torturers, and a cat shot out, spitting fiercely, from a broken door. Halfhyde

cursed viciously, and then another sound came: a furious bark-
ing that heralded an immense dog, appearing as if from nowhere
to pound after the vanishing cat. Halfhyde stood stock still as
a man came cautiously out from the next hovel's doorway, but
he was too late to avoid being seen as he dropped discreetly to
the ground. A hail came in Spanish, and not one man but two
ran like the wind towards him. He felt the painful thrust of
razor-sharp knives in his breast and side, and garlic-laden breath
fanned his face.

"On your feet," one of the men ordered. "Come with us, and
give no trouble, or you die."

Chapter 4

HALFHYDE was taken into the hovel, a smelly place and unlit; the knives pricked into his flesh. He stumbled over things—a table, a chair, heaps of refuse. He was pushed into a corner. The knives were withdrawn but his captors announced their close proximity by their atrocious breath.

"You are who?" one of them asked.

Halfhyde answered coolly: "I might well ask you the same question."

"But you have no knife, and now no gun." The revolver had been found and removed before Halfhyde was propelled into the building. "Why had you a gun?"

"To protect myself."

There was a laugh. "A dismal failure! You will tell me who you are. I think you are English. Is this so?"

"Yes." Halfhyde gave the cover story as propounded by Captain Watkiss aboard *Venomous*. "I walked into Malaga from the coast just to the south. I came to the docks, a natural enough thing for a seaman to do."

"And the revolver?"

"Stolen I admit. Not from anyone in Spain, though. Just before the ship went down, I took it from the master's cabin . . . just in case I should ever need it."

"And in the docks . . . what did you hope to do, to find?"

Halfhyde said, "A ship for England, a British ship."

"But to go to your consul is the proper proceeding, is it not, Señor Thompson?"

"Officialdom is tedious. I preferred to find a master willing to sign me on so I could work my passage, and the best approach to a master is the direct and personal one."

"You might not have been permitted to board. At the present time all British ships in the port have the *guardia* at their gangways, with orders to allow no one to board who is not specifically authorized to do so."

"Oh?" Halfhyde asked innocently. "Why's that?"

There was no immediate answer, though there was some whispering between the two men, so low that Halfhyde could pick up none of it. Then the knives pricked in again and the man who had spoken before said, "The reason is not important to you. You will explain why you were acting suspiciously near these dwellings."

"I was looking for shelter. The hovels looked deserted, derelict. I wanted somewhere to lie down and sleep."

"I think you will sleep soon," the invisible man said with a short laugh, "and for longer than you bargained for, my friend!"

"What do you mean by that?"

"The knife across the throat. We would rather be rid of you. And the water is handy to take your body, nicely weighted down with heavy stone."

"You'll not find me so easy to kill."

"Two to one, and the knives touching you already?"

"I've taken on worse odds in my time. But why the delay? Do you fear your fate too much, gentlemen, or is it the case that you may have a use for me, and are uttering threats to gain my agreement?"

There was another pause, and some more low, whispered discussion, which once again was mostly inaudible to Halfhyde. For his part, he was convinced that these men were neither *guardias* nor *politicos*; they had not the sound of officialdom, for one thing, but rather of amateurism—and more importantly Halfhyde fancied he had detected an accent behind the Spanish when he had been directly addressed. He was as yet unable to place it, but he was certain he was not dealing with genuine Spaniards. What he was able to hear of the whispered voices could have been Italian, or could have been Portuguese perhaps. His Russian and his smattering of Spanish apart, Halfhyde was not a linguist. But one thing was certain still: these men boded ill for Colonel Stanley in his hiding place across the alley.

The discussion ended; this time it was the other voice that spoke aloud. "Señor Thompson, if you will help us, we will spare your life."

"Tell me what you want."

"We wish to make someone show himself."

Halfhyde felt the increased beat of his pulse. "Go on."

"A man concealed opposite. You need to know nothing about this man, except that we wish him to come out into the open, and that if he does not, then your use to us will have vanished and you will die."

"How do I get him out?"

"You agree to help, Señor Thompson?"

Halfhyde laughed. "Not so fast, my friend! I'm fond of living, and what you want sounds easy enough. But afterwards—that's the point, isn't it? I'm not grass green, gentlemen: afterwards, I've an idea I'll know too much!"

"A chance you must take." There was a shrug in the air somewhere, night-concealed. "Whatever might or might not happen afterwards, it is certain you will die now if you do not do as we ask."

Halfhyde gave a scornful laugh. "Mere threats, such as you'll never carry out! Murder's murder, and not easy to conceal, harbour or no harbour handy."

"The carrying out is close," the voice said. Upon Halfhyde's body one of the knives moved and was laid against his throat. It nicked in and was drawn a little way and Halfhyde felt the warm run of his blood. "A quick decision, Señor Thompson, for the night will not last for ever and we have a need to be away before the dawn."

The ships of Halfhyde's flotilla had withdrawn on the order of Captain Watkiss some hours earlier after an abortive wait for Halfhyde's signal. The senior officer was in an uncertain mood, remaining upon his navigating bridge as the flotilla moved out into open water, the speed of the ships increasing as they cleared the land. Phosphorescent white spray went curling back from the bows and was flung over the turtle-decks that sloped towards the stems. Captain Watkiss paced back and forth, reviewing the situation in his mind. Something had gone wrong, or at least had not gone wholly to plan; and he was now faced with an indeterminate future, a future of steaming haphazardly about the seas hoping to be unremarked by any Spanish ships that appeared over the horizons with a nightly return to lie off the rendezvous and await Halfhyde's pleasure. Watkiss, an impatient man, was never at his best at times of waiting. Action was different; give him a point of aim for his guns and torpedo-tubes, and a dago flag flying from that point of aim, and he was happy. But now he was frustrated; and it was his first lieutenant's bad luck that he should choose this moment to nag.

"Captain, sir."

"What is it, Mr Beauchamp?"

"The ships' companies, sir."

Watkiss took a deep breath and sent it out again in a forbearing sigh. "What about them, Mr Beauchamp?"

"The question of what they should be told, sir."

"What they should be told," Captain Watkiss repeated sarcastically, facing his first lieutenant as short and square as a bulldog. "Are you suggesting a fairy story to lull them to sleep in their damn hammocks?"

"No, sir—"

"*Then what,* Mr Beauchamp, for God's sake *what?*"

"About the operation, sir. Our orders. Why we shall be steaming up and down, apparently uselessly and without purpose—"

"Mr Beauchamp, you will kindly hold your tongue! I of all people do not steam up and down uselessly and without purpose. I take that as an impertinence and you will repeat it at your peril. Damned rudeness!" Watkiss paused, face furious. "As for the ships' companies, they shall be told nothing—nothing at all, d'you hear me, Mr Beauchamp?"

"Yes, sir, but—"

"*Nothing,* Mr Beauchamp. The men are there to obey my orders, not to be cosseted by a damn nanny." Captain Watkiss turned away and strode to the fore rail of his bridge, where he stood tub-like, eyes ahead, telescope beneath his left arm. Beauchamp hovered politely. "They haven't the intelligence to understand in any case; that's fact—I said it."

"Er—"

"If you persist in arguing I shall consider it as mutiny, Mr Beauchamp, and you will be placed in arrest. Starboard five."

"I ask," Halfhyde said, "what I asked earlier; how do I entice this man out, and if I can do it, why can't you?"

"You are English, a voice the man will trust. And—"

"Can't you go in and take him?"

"The man is armed and may shoot."

"So I'm the cat's-paw."

"I regret, yes." The speaker paused. "What we want is this: you will go to the window—you see it?—and you will show yourself, and on each side of you there will be our knives. You will call out, not loudly—the distance is small as you will see. You will say, 'Come out, John Smith, I am your friend. Join me in this house.'"

"That's all I have to do?"

"Yes. And at once, please. You will say no more than I have told you. If you do, you die."

But not, Halfhyde decided, before John Smith was safely in their hands, which, providing he timed it right, could be a point worth remembering . . . He said, "Very well, I'm ready." He felt one of them move behind him and the knife pushed him ahead towards the window. As he reached it, both men moved in close on either hand. He felt the knives again, pricking gently in, ready on the instant to drive deep. He broke out into a light sweat; death was close, but not for the first time in his life. His anxieties were chiefly, in fact, for Colonel Stanley. His consolation was that it seemed scarcely likely that his present companions meant to kill the Queen's Messenger, at least not yet. And he would be in execution of his orders in placing himself at Stanley's hand; once the meeting had taken place, if not quite as Captain Watkiss had envisaged, then would be the time to take command of the situation.

"Now," the man on his right said.

Halfhyde took a deep breath and called out, not too loudly, "Come out, John Smith. I am your friend. Join me in this house."

His voice died away, seeming to leave echoes behind it. They waited; nothing happened. The men grew restive. One of them, after three or four long minutes, said, "Call out again, Señor Thompson. Say that you are British and from England."

Halfhyde called once more, adding the fresh information. Again there was no response, though there was a small sound from the other side of the alley, a sound that could have been a dislodged stone. On Halfhyde's left one of the men swore softly: Halfhyde had felt his reaction to the sound in the sudden jerk of the knife against his body. Fresh sweat broke: already there had been the warning that "John Smith's" failure to show would spell the end for him, and he had no doubts that these men meant all they had said. To escape would be a virtual impossibility: the knives were much too close. The wait continued. Halfhyde was not, as yet, told to renew his invitation, although the man on his right had started to speak when a sudden voice came harshly from the rear.

"The Englishman who wants me. Where is he?"

Alarmed oaths came from both Halfhyde's captors. As they swung round the knives ceased their pricking, but an arm went around Halfhyde's neck, holding him helpless. The unseen man spoke again: "I am armed and I can see you against the window. Don't move." There was a sound of progress across the small room, and as the newcomer reached the group a match flared and was held high. In its flickering light Halfhyde saw a lined face, a long face with a grey moustache hanging walrus-like over a firm mouth. The eyes were hard and haughty: "John Smith" might be an English tourist, but it was not easy to disguise a colonel of the Household Cavalry. "Which of you called me?"

Halfhyde said, "I, sir, under orders."

"Orders of—"

"These two persons, sir. Of no one else."

This was the best Halfhyde could do by way of warning; Stanley, however, appeared to have understood the implied message. Grey eyebrows rose, and he nodded. "Now, you two men. Who are you, and what do you want?" As he finished speaking the match went out; he seemed to be fumbling for another, but he had given the men their chance. They moved like lightning. Halfhyde was borne to the ground by the man holding his neck, while the other used his knife. There was a furious sound from Stanley as the blade ripped through his wrist; blood spurted over Halfhyde and the revolver fell to the ground. Halfhyde felt it against his foot, and kicked out viciously, but failed to prevent its seizure. Breathing hard, its finder came upright.

"Now, John Smith as you call yourself, the boot is on the other foot after all."

"You won't get away with this. Her Majesty—"

"Is in bed in Windsor Castle, a long way from Malaga. But tell me, John Smith, why you invoke Her Majesty Queen Victoria?"

The reply was arrogant, scornful. "Why, damn you, Her Majesty looks after all her subjects abroad. When I report this to the British Consul action will be swift, and—"

"But you will go nowhere near the British Consul, even if you could get away from us, because the British Consul's home and offices are being watched, as you must know." The voice had hardened. "We shall stop playing games. You are Colonel Stanley from Madrid, much wanted by the *politicos* on orders from the government of Spain. It is useless to deny this, for we know."

"And you?"

"For now, Colonel Stanley, we do not say. Strike a match, and I shall look at your wrist, and then we shall be on our way."

"To where?"

"You will find out. Now, the match."

The match was struck; Halfhyde's personal bodyguard, who was still holding him on the floor, brought a stub of candle from a pocket and handed it up. Lit, the candle was held, shaded from the window by the other man's coat, over Stanley's slashed wrist, which was dripping blood. "The blood is dark and comes without pulsation. The knife cut a vein but missed the artery, which is lucky. Your handkerchief, Colonel Stanley. The pressure of a bandage will suffice."

The wound was bound quickly. When the job was done the man said, "Now we leave, though not all of us. Señor Thompson,

I am sorry, but you would be an encumbrance and a danger to us, and you must die." He gestured to the other man. "The knife, and quickly."

Halfhyde, catching Stanley's eye and seeing his frown and his rapid glances at the two men, said, "I shall be equally an encumbrance dead, since my body is certain to be found eventually, even if thrown into the harbour."

"But too late, and the death of a deckhand from a merchant ship will be unremarkable and not worthy of a fuss, Señor—"

"Just a moment," Stanley said in a hard voice accustomed to instant obedience. "I'm interested in you, my good Thompson, and I'm not prepared to see you murdered."

"Sir, I—"

"I am about to give you an order which you will obey. Nothing will be lost, I assure you, and the time has come to cast aside all pretence. You are here to meet me—"

"I was told—"

"Yes, you were told. Now it is I who am telling you. You will inform these persons in full honesty who you are and where you are from."

It seemed madness to Halfhyde, but now he had no option but to obey. From his undignified position on the filthy floor, he said, "Very well, sir, since you give the order. I am Lieutenant St Vincent Halfhyde of the Royal Navy, commanding Her Majesty's ship *Vendetta* of the Fourth Torpedo-Boat Destroyer Flotilla."

"Precisely. Not a man to be murdered without the might of Great Britain to ask why, gentlemen. If I were you, I would most undoubtedly think again! If not, you will find yourselves in more trouble than you are already." Stanley, tall and disdainful, appeared almost to be in command of the situation despite the revolver held against him. He spoke again to Halfhyde. "Your senior officer, I understand, is Captain Watkiss?"

"Yes, sir."

"A gallant officer and a fine seaman."

"Indeed he is, sir."

"Never one to hold away from action."

"He is not, sir."

"But impetuous."

"Yes, sir."

"And that," Stanley said heavily, "is precisely where the danger now lies." He glanced again at the man with the gun. "Lead on, if that is still your wish."

Chapter 5

THE SOUNDS from outside went on and on: the creaking of ancient wheels, the crunch from the surface of what felt like a rough track, and now and again the cackle of hens from above. A country smell came through the air holes, a smell largely of manure, sharp and acrid from the hen-coops, and now and again of bonfires. Helpless, bound and gagged and lying side by side in a large wooden chest, Halfhyde and Stanley lurched towards an unknown destination. The timely intervention of the Queen's Messenger had undoubtedly saved Halfhyde's life, but in all conscience it had achieved little else. The reaction of the two men to Stanley's apparent use of Captain Watkiss as a threat had been sudden and summary: an arm had gone back around Halfhyde's throat and had almost strangled him; and at the same instant the revolver had been employed to strike Stanley down, senseless on the filthy floor of the hovel. While Halfhyde was held with his throat squeezed to within an inch of suffocation, the other man left the hovel, returning within five minutes to announce that the transport waited: through the pounding of blood in his ears Halfhyde had heard the approaching creak. The chest had been brought in with the assistance of a newcomer, a swarthy man in patched shirt and trousers and a straw hat. The two captives, Stanley being still unconscious, were bound and gagged, placed in the chest, and the lid had been shut firmly down and then secured with nails. It had been lifted and swayed out to the waiting cart, and slid onto the boards; then had come the chattering hens, and after this the journey had begun.

It was a nightmare journey of extreme discomfort as the rough farm vehicle, donkey-drawn, left the comparative flatness of the Malaga streets and struck out into the country districts beyond. Halfhyde lost all sense of time, though the air holes in the chest also admitted the daylight in due course, and then again the darkness: a long, long way. As dawn had showed for the first time through the small holes, Stanley had regained consciousness—at least, Halfhyde assumed this to be the case when his companion started a terrible groaning. Speech through the gags was not possible, and after a long while the groans ceased. Halfhyde feared that Stanley might well be dead; his body lay inert, not responding when Halfhyde nudged with a knee as far as his binding ropes permitted. The only life seemed to be in the swaying and bumping of the cart, and the appalling stench of chicken droppings, and the cackles, and the busily scratching feet, and occasionally a voice as their captors exchanged greetings with men and women in the villages through which they passed.

As with all things, an end to motion came at last: the cart, after seeming to climb for some way, staggered to a halt and voices were heard again. Commotion took place above, a noisy protest of hens as the coops were removed, and then the chest was lifted and drawn backwards from its conveyance, and more swaying took place, accompanied a minute later by the ring of boots on stone and an oath as a foot slipped. The chest banged against something hard, a painful experience for its occupants, and Halfhyde felt his body incline with the head down: they were descending a flight of steps.

It seemed a long way down, and it ended in a sudden thud on stone that was agony: Halfhyde had developed a blinding headache during the second day's progress. Pain was made worse by the extraction of the nails, carried out by a man who seemed to be in a bad temper, and impatient; when the lid of the chest came open, the swarthy man with the straw hat looked in. Halfhyde stared up into yellow lamplight that flickered eerily off dirty stone walls. Clearly, they had been brought to a cellar, and one that might be anywhere in Spain. Glancing sideways he saw life in the eyes of the Queen's Messenger: one had to be thankful for that at least. The straw-hatted man, with the assistance of the original two from the Malaga hovel, reached into the chest and lifted the occupants bodily out, and lay them on the cold stone floor. The ropes and gags were removed; Halfhyde and Stanley were too stiff to do more than blink in the lamplight. One of the men looked down, grinning. He said, "From here you cannot get away. Now we shall leave you. We shall return soon."

With the men, the lamp moved away, back up the steps, and as the flickers vanished Halfhyde heard the clang of a heavy door, a thud of doom, and then the turning of a key, and the drop of a beam into its sockets, and then a total silence took over, and a total darkness.

There was no quick return: Halfhyde occupied himself with rubbing life back firstly into his own limbs and then into those of Colonel Stanley, who had been badly shaken up by the blow from the revolver: he was not a young man. "I'm damned sorry, Halfhyde," he said. "I have been an incubus to you, and this is not seaman's work in any case."

"No, sir, it's not, I agree. But you are my duty, not my incubus."

Stanley managed a laugh. "Kind of you to say so. Now it's up to—" He broke off; sounds had come from above, the opening of the door, the tread of feet; the light from the lamp approached, throwing shadows on the walls. In that light Stanley's face was as pale as death, and there was a great lump on the side of his head. Down came the lamp, and the three men, two of them with guns, the third bearing food and an earthenware pitcher. The food and water were placed on the ground between Halfhyde and Stanley. There was fruit and blackish, dry-looking bread, and some nuts. The food-bearer said, "You must eat in darkness. If you are hungry, you will manage." The men went up the steps again with the lamp, and once again the doom-laden sound of the closing door smote down into the cellar.

Halfhyde gave a sardonic laugh. "If we are hungry! The quality looked poor certainly, but I shall fall to like a gannet."

Stanley said, "Eat it all, my dear fellow, I have no appetite, only thirst."

"Yet eat you shall, sir, as well as drink. You must keep your strength up."

"No, no—"

"I insist, sir. A sick incubus will be of no help to either of us. Allow me to crack you a nut, and urge it down with some fruit." Halfhyde cracked a nut between thumb and forefinger and passed it to the Queen's Messenger, who made no further protest as their hands met in the dark. The water seemed to help him, though Halfhyde feared for its effect upon both their stomachs: when in outlandish foreign parts it was as well to drink the bottled waters, such as that of Solares, or, if in France, Vichy; but beggars could not be choosers and their thirsts were intense.

"Now, sir," Halfhyde said when the food had been consumed and a little water retained in the pitcher against the future, "we have been given the opportunity, so let us take advantage of it."

"To do what?"

"Talk, sir. I need information—I was given as much as my captain had, but that was little enough. I must now be in possession of the facts."

"Walls have ears, Halfhyde."

"I doubt if dungeon walls have, sir. These are well below the ground, and must be thick. But I shall hear your whisper, if you prefer that." Halfhyde paused. "Have you any ideas as to where we may be?"

"Perhaps," Stanley answered. "I had the impression, when I was conscious, that the cart was climbing steadily, and turning often around sharp bends. I may be wrong—there are many cities of Spain that are high-set in the mountains, with climbing bends—but Granada seems the most likely of them all for various reasons."

"And those reasons, sir?"

"Largely a question of distance, and time. I am able to tell by the small growth of stubble on my cheeks that we have not been many days on the journey. We are possibly in Ronda, but I think not." Stanley paused. "I see I must take you into my confidence, Halfhyde."

"It will be respected, sir."

"I don't doubt it for a moment, and you are well entitled to know the facts. In all conscience they're simple enough, if atrocious and appalling." Stanley's voice dropped even lower, as if instinctively he was guarding vital matters. "It is inconceivable that such a diabolical thing be allowed to succeed, but we are up against much power." He paused. "I, personally, came by intelligence that a member of the Senate, the upper house of the *Cortes*, and one of Spain's greatest grandees—not an elected person, you understand—is planning a most wicked assassination, one that could not fail to involve a great war of spreading proportions. This person is the Duke of Villanueva de Cordoba. His victim . . ." His voice fell away as though he were unwilling even to speak the name in connection with an assassination. Then it came out starkly: "His intended victim is Her Majesty Queen Victoria."

The Queen's name had dropped into the pitch blackness like a bombshell: to attempt to assassinate the Queen of England must be a madman's dream, a thing surely impossible of execution! Yet it was true that Her Majesty, unlike many foreign monarchs, moved, when she moved at all, freely and without armed guards and detectives. Naturally, when upon her official functions and engagements she was accompanied by aides-de-camp and equerries and frequently by detachments of her Household Cavalry or Foot Guards; but there were the other occasions when she drove in her carriage from Windsor Castle or from her beloved Balmoral on Deeside with no more escort than would any well-heeled old woman taking the air upon four wheels. And attempts upon royal lives had been made before now: in March of 1882 a lunatic had jumped out from the crowd at the Queen's carriage upon a ceremonial occasion, but had been overpowered in time. Rudyard Kipling had written a poem of thanksgiving for her deliverance. And a bullet had shattered a window of the Prince of Wales's train—but that had been in a foreign land, which was a different kettle of fish. However, the act must be regarded as possible.

"Why, sir?" Halfhyde asked. "Is this grandee mad, or what?"

"Not mad. Obsessed, undoubtedly. A deep-seated bigotry that could be considered a family matter."

"Family?" Halfhyde repeated in some astonishment.

There was a low laugh from Stanley. "The Queen's related by marriage to virtually every royal house in Europe and half the aristocracy, is she not?"

"I know of no Spanish alliance via the marriage bed, sir."

"There is none," Stanley said. "That is, as yet."

"I beg your pardon, sir?"

"Like the Duke of Villanueva de Cordoba himself, you must project into the future, Halfhyde."

"I am no prophet, sir."

"Perhaps not. But very often Her Majesty is, at least to the extent that she does what she can to manipulate future events and project the future of Europe along the paths she wishes." Stanley paused. "As yet, as you have said, there is no Spanish alliance, but the Queen's said to desire one—this I have heard myself, indeed, and believe it to be both logical and likely. Royal marriages are often arranged whilst the protagonists are in their cradles. In this case they are out of their cradles but still in the schoolroom."

"And their names?"

Stanley said, "The Queen's youngest daughter, Her Royal Highness Princess Beatrice, is married to Prince Henry of Battenburg. She has a daughter, Victoria Eugenie of tender years. Our assassin believes, and he is not alone in this belief, that Her Majesty intends her granddaughter to marry the son of Maria Cristina, Regent of Spain—the boy who in due course will rule as Alfonso XIII."

"And?"

"And," Stanley said portentously, "Princess Victoria Eugenie is being brought up a strict and devout Protestant, whilst Alfonso is naturally to be a stalwart of Rome, as equally naturally is the Duke of Villanueva de Cordoba."

"So the grandmother is to be assassinated—"

"And the unholy marriage called off before the idea can take root. If the Queen of England dies at a Spaniard's hand, then there will never be any alliance between the royal houses."

Halfhyde laughed. "As to that, I agree! But the rest of it is lunacy. Do you know how the Duke means to proceed, sir, what his plan of murder is?"

"Yes. I know it very precisely."

"Then just one word of warning—"

"Exactly!" the Queen's Messenger broke in, his voice harsh. "A word of warning that only I can give. Or now you, if you can rejoin your ship while I die in this wretched dungeon!"

Halfhyde said, "I think we shall not be separated now, sir. The thugs upstairs will know you'll talk, and that I've become a danger as much as you. Who are these people who hold us?"

"Villanueva's own hired hands, I believe, but I can't be sure."

"And the official side, sir, the Spanish authorities? I understood my captain to say you were *persona non grata* with them
also?"

"True." Stanley sighed. "It's a long story—I'll summarize."
After a pause he went on, "The man Barroso—you have met
him. He is entirely to be trusted. He had heard rumours, whispers that Villanueva had been outspoken against the Queen. He
told me of this. He told me more: Villanueva had made arrangements for a clandestine meeting at his *hacienda* in the province
of Cordoba with some Italian nationals who were suspected by
the *politicos,* and he told me how, if I were willing to accept the
risk, I could overhear what took place. I went with Barroso to
the *hacienda.* He had been there often on official business, and
told me the geography of the house, and of a tunnel that led
from a disused stable building into the cellars. I was able to hear
every word of what was said by listening in a chimney . . . and
having heard, I left." Stanley paused again. "I rejoined Barroso
and we started on our journey back to Madrid, where I intended
to make my report to our Ambassador—"

"Barroso had not heard the conversation, I take it?"

"No, nor did I tell him what I had heard—perhaps I was
mistaken not to do so, since he can't pass on what he doesn't
know. Anyway, when we were some twenty miles from the
hacienda, two horsemen overtook us. It was night, and both
Barroso and I assumed them to be bandits. I was armed, and I
fired upon them, killing one of them. Before the other fled, I
had recognized him: Villanueva's personal secretary. The dead
man was another of the Duke's staff."

"The secretary recognized you, sir?"

"I believe so," Stanley answered. "Indeed, I now know so! I

sent Barroso on, and myself decided to avoid Madrid and the Embassy, and to make my way out of the country as fast as possible to warn Her Majesty. I instructed Barroso to make contact with the Governor of Gibraltar and ask for assistance, and later Barroso got in touch with me through intermediaries, and told me of the arrangements made."

"And Villanueva? You spoke of Italians, sir. Myself, I fancied I detected an un-Spanish accent from our friends . . . it could have been Italian or perhaps Portuguese. If we assume we're in the hands of Villanueva's hired assassins, it's an indication that he knows you overheard his plans."

"Which brings me no peace of mind," Stanley said harshly. "I am certain the threat to Her Majesty still stands. If we are in Villanueva's hands, that fact alone guarantees the threat's continuance."

"Unless he thinks you may have passed the information on, sir. However, I take your point." Halfhyde paused. "What do you imagine awaits us now?"

Stanley laughed without humour. "An unpleasant fate undoubtedly!"

"You depress me, sir," Halfhyde said lightly, and added, "May I ask about the diplomatic bag? Did you—"

"The diplomatic bag's safe in the Embassy. One does not conduct nefarious business in company with Her Majesty's diplomatic bag!"

Halfhyde grinned into the darkness. "Captain Watkiss will be disappointed. He was much excited by thoughts of rescuing the diplomatic bag. However, we should be thankful no secrets are at risk. And Her Majesty's person, sir? May I know the actual terms of the threat?"

"The Queen's to go north by train to Balmoral shortly—in ten days' time. When at Balmoral she likes to drive into the Grampians. It is wild country, very wild and desolate, very empty of humankind. From a hillside shots will come . . . there is nothing easier of success. One old woman in a carriage, with a coachman and postilion and perhaps a ghillie. Cruel and filthy murder . . . but Villanueva will not go before his God with blood upon his own hands. It is to be done by the hired Italians, with help from domestic traitors and assassins within Scotland. The plan is perfect."

"Perfection is seldom of this world, sir," Halfhyde said. "You and I shall be the flies in Villanueva's ointment, if God's on our side." Ever optimistic, Halfhyde projected his mind towards escape, and a fast ride to the coast to rejoin the flotilla, and then all speed to be made for the wireless station at Gibraltar. However, as the hours passed and they were left in the blank darkness, Halfhyde found little on which to base any real hope that he and Stanley could ever get away to freedom. If only the Queen's Messenger had passed on word of the planned assassination before going to ground . . . but Halfhyde could well appreciate the dilemma Stanley had found himself in. There he was, with a killing on his hands; at any moment the hue and cry would start, and it would start with the British Embassy. Protocol, of course, would have precluded any forcible entry by the Spanish authorities; but all persons approaching the building would have been stopped and questioned. Stanley might have reached the Embassy's shelter before the chase was up, and had he done so he would have been safe enough so long as he never again stepped out upon the street. But he had made the decision not to risk going near the Embassy; in Halfhyde's view that had been a wrong decision, but it had been made and had now to be lived with. The question remained: how to get free of their prison. Time was short; Her Majesty would leave for Balmoral in ten days' time and intended to spend six weeks on Deeside. From the moment of her arrival she must be considered to be at risk.

"It is diabolical, Mr Beauchamp." Captain Watkiss stood with his stomach caressing the forward guardrail of the leader's bridge and his telescope waving at his first lieutenant. His face was an angry red. "Diabolical and I won't damn well have it, d'you hear?"

"Yes, sir—"

"Then damn well *do* something about it, if you please, Mr Beauchamp! *All* the starboard side ladders are *my* ladders, clearly marked as such. Aren't they? What do they say, Mr Beauchamp?"

Beauchamp swallowed. "Captain only, sir."

"Captain only! Exactly! Yet a damn lower-deck rating, a common seaman—worse, a *boy* with bum fluff on his cheeks for a beard—sullies the rungs with his damn foot! Put him in my report, d'you hear me?"

"Yes, sir. With respect, sir—"

"Oh, balls and bang-me-arse, now what is it?"

"As you know, sir, we were exercising action stations—"

"That has nothing to do with it. My ladders are my ladders all the time; that's fact—I said it. Even more so in action. Is it not vital that the captain should have a clear path to his navigating bridge, Mr Beauchamp?"

"Indeed it is, sir." The first lieutenant, who was not without a certain dogged courage, cleared his throat and continued, "But the ship's company, sir, also—"

"Hold your tongue, Mr Beauchamp."

"I really must—"

"Another word and you can consider yourself in arrest."

"I—"

"Silence, and attend to your duties!" Suddenly losing interest in ladders, Captain Watkiss had lifted his telescope to his eye. He was staring at some smudges of smoke on the horizon to the north and was showing signs of much excitement. "I believe the Spanish Fleet may be bearing down upon us from Barcelona—the *Spanish Fleet*, Mr Beauchamp, and you stand there mouthing nothings at me! Kindly clear for action at once, and signal the rest of my flotilla accordingly."

Beauchamp's jaw hung in astonishment. "Clear for action, sir?"

"Yes, Mr Beauchamp, we have lost Halfhyde who may have made a dog's dinner of his orders. The ships may have hostile intent."

"But—"

"Hold your tongue, sir, and find out why *I* was the first person to see the damn Spaniards." Captain Watkiss maintained his forward-facing stance, telescope to his eye and face pugnacious. Imaginary gunfire flashed before him, the Dons went down below the waves as they had gone for Drake; he hummed a tune as the bosun's pipes shrilled for action and the ship's company doubled barefoot to their stations at the guns and torpedo-tubes, or at the roaring furnaces below in the boiler-rooms, doubled circumspectly up or down the port side ladders only lest something worse than the enemy should put them in the captain's report. It made for a slow response but it was disciplined and orderly. On the bridge Captain Watkiss made the disposition signal for the flotilla to continue in formation line ahead, maintaining course and speed to the north. The placid, deep-blue water of the Mediterranean swept past, thrown briefly into white-topped tumult as the flotilla's hulls sped through. Captain Watkiss called to his navigator.

"Mr Pomeroy, our position, if you please."

"Aye, aye, sir." Pomeroy checked his chart and reported, "Sixty-five miles eastward of Cape de Gata, sir."

Watkiss made a quick calculation. "Due south of Cartagena. I suppose the buggers may be out of the Balearics rather than Barcelona."

"Yes, sir."

"Where are our nearest main Fleet units?"

"I don't know, sir."

Watkiss turned. "You—don't—know! God give me strength! *Find out.* That is, make an assessment. You can do that at least, can't you?"

"I'm afraid I can't, sir. The combined fleets are on manoeuvres, sir, and they dispose themselves according to the circumstances as they find them, sir." Diversion came, heaven-sent. "Sir, the Spanish flagship is signalling."

"I can see that, thank you." Watkiss raised his telescope again. The oncoming warships were clearly visible now, under heavy smoke: four could be seen, in line abreast and disposed to starboard of the flag—four battleships, with a lamp flashing from the admiral's signal bridge. Watkiss turned impatiently upon his yeoman of signals. "What does he say, Yeoman?"

"He asks who you are, sir."

"I didn't ask for an interpretation, Yeoman, I asked *what he said*. Report the signal properly."

"Aye, aye sir. Signal reads, sir: *who are you?*"

"Just that?"

"Yessir."

"Well, no dago has any manners, I suppose," Watkiss said distantly, "but at least he speaks English . . . yes, Mr Pomeroy, what is it?"

Pomeroy, who had been leafing through a volume of ship identification, said, "The Spanish ships, sir. They're the *Alphonso XIII,* the *Infanta Maria Theresa,* the *Vizcaya* and the *Almirante Oquendo*. Battleships, sir—"

"Yes, yes, thank you—"

"Capable of fifteen knots, sir, and carrying two 14-inch and ten 4-inch guns and two torpedo-tubes—"

"Oh, hold your tongue, Mr Pomeroy, I am not afraid of dagoes. Yeoman, make: I am the *Fourth TBD Flotilla of the British Mediterranean Fleet.*"

"Aye, aye, sir."

"Who are you?"

The yeoman of signals paused, lifted a monkey's wrinkled face, browned by many years on flag decks around the world, from his signal pad. "Beg pardon, sir?"

Watkiss shifted angrily. "Add: *who are you?*"

"Oh—yessir, very good, sir."

The signal was made. The ships closed, Watkiss and the Spaniards maintaining their courses. The reply came back: *I am Vice-Admiral de Valdares commanding the First Battle Squadron of His Majesty the King of Spain.*

"I thought Mr Halfhyde said there was a regency," Watkiss remarked truculently, but reflected that no doubt a king was still a king even though he had to be acted for by his mother during his childhood, which vindicated what he had said to Halfhyde earlier. "They don't appear hostile at all events. Possibly Mr Halfhyde is still at large . . . now what's he making?"

The yeoman read off the further signal. *"If you go as you now go you will infringe the territorial waters of Spain."*

"Oh, damn the man!" Watkiss said angrily. "Tell him I'm well aware of my geography!" As the signal was made, Watkiss stared narrowly ahead; he was about to steam through the Spanish line, which was a rude thing to do and could be a matter for much offence, but it was too late to alter course without risk of collision, so he continued along his set path. "Mr Pomeroy, pipe."

"Aye, aye, sir." Pomeroy passed the order for the ceremonial salute. As the flotilla leader came abeam of the Spanish admiral, the bosun's pipes shrilled and along the decks all hands stood at attention as their captain saluted. The niceties were returned punctiliously by the Spanish flagship, but as he drew astern and brought his hand down from the salute, Captain Watkiss shook a fist in the air, briefly.

"We'll be marked now. That makes my task harder. Sooner or later some damn dago's going to want to know why I'm hanging about off his damn coast. Where's Mr Beauchamp?"

"Here, sir." The first lieutenant clattered up the ladder from the main deck. "Permission to secure from action stations, if you please, sir?"

"Yes, yes. Eyes skinned from now on, Mr Beauchamp, and resume cruising. Mr Pomeroy, bring the ship round one-eighty degrees to port. Yeoman, hoist the alter course signal. Mr Beauchamp, I'm heading back for yet another night of waiting upon Mr Halfhyde's blasted pleasure."

"Yes, sir. May I—"

"I'll be in my cabin if required, and until I am, use your initiative, Mr Beauchamp." Captain Watkiss swung round and went down the starboard ladder. His short, rotund body seemed almost to bounce from rung to rung, borne airily by confidence and a deep certainty that God was still on the side of the British Fleet. Yet doubts were creeping into his mind even so: three nights he had waited off Point Calaburras, three nights he had walked his bridge looking shorewards for the glimmer of light that would announce Halfhyde and Colonel Stanley, three nights he had crept outwards again empty-handed, putting distance between himself and the shore before the breaking dawn could reveal him. He could not expect his luck to last: he would creep in once too often and would be spotted, dark or no dark. Then matters would become extremely awkward and coals of fire would be heaped upon his head for shattering diplomacy. And what of Halfhyde, anyway? Where the devil had he got to, what sort of monkey's breakfast was he making? Captain Watkiss, calling for his servant to bring a clean white uniform, stood in vest and pants in his cabin pondering when the moment might come for him regretfully to abandon Halfhyde in the urgent interest of making a report to the rear-admiral in Gibraltar, who would be growing increasingly concerned at the lack of news.

Chapter 6

LATER, MORE FOOD AND WATER had come to Halfhyde and
Stanley. In the darkness, lit only at those times of the bringing
of food, they had lost count of hours. Their watches had been
removed and outside it could be daylight or dark. The men
who brought the food would answer no questions. Thoughts of
attack upon the food-bearers passed through Halfhyde's mind
but came to no fruition: the building above would be well
guarded and a fight below could end only one way. Alone again,
Stanley spoke: "I'm concerned about Captain Watkiss, Halfhyde.
In Malaga I referred to his impetuosity, whilst by no means disparaging his bravery."

"You know him well, sir?"

"Not well," Stanley answered with a laugh, "but well enough!
I've seen him in the hunting field. He rides a horse like a sack
of potatoes, but with courage and determination. He lacks
finesse . . . on many occasions he has bludgeoned off on his
own, and deflected the fox to its earth rather than a kill."

"And you fear something similar may happen now?"

"Yes, indeed I do. With all respect to him, I'd have preferred
a different officer in command."

"My captain's curious ways sometimes achieve success, sir,
if not quite in the way he expects. What do you fear he might
do now?"

"Under the circumstances, any naval officer, unless he has precise orders to the contrary, might land a search party. Would you not agree, Halfhyde?"

"I think I would, sir, but Captain Watkiss has always had a regard for diplomacy—until he loses his temper—in case the diplomats should turn upon him and bite."

Stanley laughed from the darkness. "Then let us hope he keeps his temper, for the combination of the killing of one of Villanueva's staff and an invasion by the British Fleet might prove too much for Whitehall to stomach, let alone the *Cortes!*"

"But only until Her Majesty dies, sir." Halfhyde reached out a hand and touched Stanley's shoulder. "A sound from the top of the steps. They're coming down again."

They were brought out from the cellar and put back into the chest and once again the lid was nailed down upon them. Once more, no questions had been answered; once more, with darkness beyond the air holes, they were on their travels into the unknown. After a while Halfhyde had the impression that this time they were descending from high ground. With the gags once again around their mouths, there was no communication: they jogged in extreme discomfort in the cart behind the patient donkey with their covering of hens a-cackle as before once the air holes lightened to the dawn. Halfhyde lay immobile and grim, both fear and anger surging over him like the storm-waves of the ocean. Like the earlier journey, this one began to seem interminable and Halfhyde felt that he could not last out much longer. The lack of air was stifling and enervating; he was bathed in his own sweat, smelled in his own nostrils like a whole battalion of infantry after a forced march on Indian service. Rest periods came when the motion stopped and then the hideous progress was resumed, shaking every bone in his body and bruising his flesh. Thought of any kind was impossible: all he could do was to sink into his own discomfort and pray for swift deliverance. Ultimately unconsciousness came as a merciful blessing: he knew nothing more until a long while later he was brought back again by the sound of water lapping against the sides of the chest, water that began to pour through the air holes and soak into his clothing.

A new fear gripped him: he and Stanley were to be drowned like helpless rats caught in a diabolical water-trap. There would be no hope; already the water-level was rising. They were somewhere out at sea and the chest, when filled, would take them to the bottom and they would not be seen again until the woodwork rotted and broke open and discharged their skeletons to the uncomprehending fishy eyes of the dwellers in the deep. Halfhyde checked his fancies: he was a seaman yet, and thought by instinct as a seaman; and his seaman's knowledge and experience told him one thing for certain, and that was, their water-borne coffin was not going down as fast as might have been expected. His lungs told him something else: air was trapped above the water, which was not rising far enough to fill the chest.

Curious! But fortunate too; luck could be with them yet. Their would-be murderers had miscalculated somewhat. The chest might float for quite a while, with its human freight alive in it—long enough, perhaps, to be sighted by a fishing boat? On the other hand the waters that lapped the coasts of Spain were wide, very wide. They could float for ever without being noticed, would die of starvation—or of the foul air breathed and exhaled a thousand times. Already that air's staleness was having its due effect: Halfhyde was drowsy, slipping back into unconsciousness. He didn't hear the approach of the boat, being pulled by muffled oars towards the shore, nor did he hear the excited voice as the sighting of the chest was reported, nor the thud from above his body as a grappling-iron bit into the wood and the chest was drawn towards the boat and then taken in tow as the boat continued towards the shore. He came back to awareness as the chest grounded, and, tilting, allowed some of the water to drain away through the air holes. Freshness came in, the stale air was displaced, and Halfhyde heard the voices outside.

"No one here, sir, by the looks of it."

"This was where the light showed." The voice was perplexed. "They would have stayed where they showed the light, I fancy!"

Halfhyde had recognized the voices: Leading-Seaman Parslow and Sub-Lieutenant Sawbridge. A miracle had been performed, and never mind that there must have been some connivance, as yet unexplained, on the part of their captors . . . Halfhyde brought up his knees and smote them hard against the lid above him. Outside, a voice checked what it had been saying, and there was a silence. Halfhyde banged again.

Captain Watkiss stood slumped against the forward guardrail of his bridge, shocked to the core. The Queen! Halfhyde's report, when he had boarded the leader after first seeing Stanley bedded down aboard *Vendetta,* had been the most appalling Watkiss had ever had the misfortune to receive. He had listened almost without hearing when Halfhyde had told him the sequence of events since he had first been put ashore, all the way through from his first meeting with Señor Barroso and his apprehension in the Malaga slum to his incarceration in the chest with Stanley and their sojourn in the cell, its whereabouts still not positively known. And the return aboard by floating chest, an unlikely and preposterous means of sea transport if ever there was one—Halfhyde had spoken of some sort of collaboration as having been fairly evident on the part of his captors since they had shown the light which the flotilla's lookouts had seen. Watkiss had been concerned to hear that Stanley was in too poor a shape to accompany Halfhyde aboard the leader; and he had expressed the hope that Prebble had enough savvy to treat him with proper respect. Prebble was from the lower deck, had come up through the hawse-pipe, while Stanley was a gentleman and from a good regiment, and was not just a damn lieutenant either . . . but Her Majesty! It scarcely bore thinking about! Watkiss's first reaction had been to imagine Halfhyde had taken leave of his senses; but slowly it penetrated, and Captain Watkiss passed the orders and the signals for all speed to be made into Gibraltar after a certain vital duty had first been performed: Watkiss had to have urgent words with Colonel Stanley in person, and if Stanley was too sick to attend aboard the leader, then Mahomet must go to the mountain.

Captain Watkiss's moon-filled monocle flashed in the gloom. "Her Majesty . . . dear God! I shall repair aboard *Vendetta* at once and so shall you. Mr Beauchamp?"

The first lieutenant saluted. "Sir?"

"My galley, Mr Beauchamp. Or rather, in the interests of speed, call away the sea-boat's crew and lowerers of the watch. Mr Pomeroy," he added to the officer of the watch, "stop engines."

"Stop engines, sir."

"And while I'm away ensure that my ship is ready to proceed to sea the moment I step back aboard, Mr Beauchamp." Captain Watkiss, jaw out-thrust in bulldog fashion, stood at his guardrail waiting for the sea-boat to be reported ready for his embarkation. He stared into the night, wordlessly but with his lips moving. Halfhyde watched the face of loyalty and of mounting anxiety. Captain Watkiss was possessed of a tremendous reverence for the Queen-Empress; and currently, because of his knowledge of infamy and base plot, had himself become, in his own eyes, a person of tremendous import, the one who held in the palm of his hand as it were the honour and well-being of the British Empire and the life of its sovereign. He alone, by making his report, could save her. Captain Watkiss, grave-faced, spoke at last. "The diplomatic bag, Mr Halfhyde. Is it safe?"

"There was none, sir."

"No diplomatic bag, Mr Halfhyde?"

"It existed, sir, but was not with Colonel Stanley. It is safe in the Embassy in Madrid."

"I see. Well, that's a relief at all events." Watkiss turned; Beauchamp was coming up the ladder. Within minutes Watkiss and Halfhyde were in the leader's sea-boat and being pulled over the placid waters to the *Vendetta*. Above them the great clusters of stars hung like lanterns to illuminate the whole sky; a scene of much beauty that had begun to reveal itself as some overcast had cleared away, but not one to commend itself currently to Captain Watkiss, who was staring heavenward in some concern.

"Too much damn visibility, Mr Halfhyde. We'll stand out like so many curates caught with their trousers down. I only hope

Colonel Stanley's fit enough to make short work of his report."

"Yes, sir."

They were pulled on, making good speed through the star-lit night. As they came alongside *Vendetta's* lowered quarterdeck ladder Captain Watkiss's bowman and sternsheetsman stood with poised boathooks, and down from the quarterdeck itself loomed the anxious face of Mr Prebble. Halfhyde's first lieutenant bent over the guardrail, sounding urgent as he called out: "Captain, sir!"

Halfhyde answered. "Yes, Mr Prebble, what is it?"

Prebble waved an arm towards the north-east. "Something moving, sir."

Both Watkiss and Halfhyde turned to look along the bearing indicated. Halfhyde said, "I see nothing."

"I am higher up than you, sir. I've just seen them, moving without lights."

"What are they, for God's sake, Mr Prebble?" Captain Watkiss demanded.

"I can't say yet, sir. Not large at all events. They could be fishing boats—"

"Or they could be advanced escorts for the damn Spanish Fleet, Mr Prebble! Coxswain, bear off immediately and return me to my ship. Mr Halfhyde, Colonel Stanley must wait—"

"And so for a moment shall you, sir—"

"Don't be impertinent, Mr Halfhyde. Coxswain—"

"Your pardon, sir, but I intend to rejoin my ship as you intend to rejoin yours." Halfhyde stood up in the stern-sheets, swaying the sea-boat dangerously and causing water to slop inboard upon Captain Watkiss. As the boat moved past the ladder, he made a flying leap and caught the rungs with hands and feet. Climbing up to his quarterdeck he looked back. Captain Watkiss, shaking his fist in impotent fury, was being borne away back to his command, his thick, white-clad back reflecting palely in the unwelcome starlight. Halfhyde, together with his first lieutenant, made his way at once to the bridge.

"Warn the engine-room," he said to the officer of the watch. "We shall be under way as soon as Captain Watkiss is aboard the leader."

"Aye, aye, sir."

"And Mr Prebble . . . Captain Watkiss is in a pugnacious mood. Close-up the guns' crews, if you please."

A signal had come by lamp from the leader, ordering the flotilla to follow Watkiss's movements as he crept out to sea, heading south-easterly to clear Point Calaburras and thence make all speed into Gibraltar—Spaniards permitting. On their ordered courses the British TBDs headed away from the shadows in the night, but those shadows, as Halfhyde observed from his bridge, altered to follow. There was a mounting tension throughout *Vendetta* as another signal came from Captain Watkiss ordering maximum revolutions. As the onward speed was built up the shadows remained: they had too much power to be fishing boats, and in any case so far as Halfhyde knew the Spanish fishermen relied still upon sail and oars rather than steam. It now seemed confirmed that those unidentified vessels were indeed small units of the Spanish Fleet; and within minutes, as the flotilla came clear of Point Calaburras, the matter stood revealed beyond all doubt: distantly ahead of them, right in their track, were heavy ships disposed in line abeam with thick clouds of smoke billowing from their funnels to dim the glory of the stars. The flotilla had been headed into them like so many sheep. Almost in the moment of their sighting, a signal lamp began flashing from one of the battleships. Halfhyde's yeoman of signals read the message and reported.

"Signal to the leader in English, sir: *heave-to immediately.*" The yeoman paused. "There's another coming through, sir, from the leader to all ships."

"Well?"

"Disregard the Spanish, maintain course and speed, sir."

"Thank you, Yeoman. Mr Prebble, warn the guns' crews that Captain Watkiss looks like risking action. And I think we'll go a stage further in anticipation."

"Sir?"

"Full action stations, Mr Prebble. And see well and truly to the efficiency of the damage control parties, if you please."

"Aye, aye, sir!" Calling for the bosun's mate, Prebble vanished down the ladder to the upper-deck. Within seconds the pipes were shrilling throughout the ship and men were running barefoot to their stations as the watch below were turned out from their hammocks. The flotilla rushed on under the full thrust of their pounding propellers, in line ahead behind Captain Watkiss, the sea curling back in bright green phosphorescence from the knifing bows and spray blowing back above the turtle-decked fo'c'sles to drop upon the bridge personnel.

Prebble came up to report. "Ship's company closed-up at action stations, sir."

"Thank you, Mr Prebble." Halfhyde, braced against the forward guardrail, had his telescope trained upon the Spanish line. "And Colonel Stanley—how is he?"

"Game, sir. He asked if he can be of assistance. I told him

this was not soldiers' work, sir, and that he would be better keeping a valuable person safe below."

Halfhyde nodded. "Quite right, though there'll be no safety anywhere if the Spanish guns open!"

"True enough, sir." Prebble paused. "There's something else, sir, if you have the time to listen."

"Go on, my dear Prebble."

"Aye, aye, sir. That chest, sir. I had it examined by the carpenter's mate while you were aboard the leader. There's something queer about it."

"And more precisely?"

"More precisely, sir, it's fitted with a sort of double bottom containing buoyancy tanks." Prebble paused. "Somebody in Spain, sir, went to a deal of trouble to make sure you and Colonel Stanley remained alive."

Halfhyde lowered his telescope and stared at Prebble. "You're right indeed. Remained alive, and were picked up by the flotilla." He had been much intrigued by the showing of the light from the shore. "Odd!"

"Yes, sir. It fails to make much sense."

Halfhyde put his glass back to his eye. "So, I think, does Captain Watkiss. The Spanish guns are swinging and depressing to bear upon him and us." He laid a hand on his first lieutenant's shoulder. "You've been a good shipmate, Prebble. If God is merciful, we shall meet again aloft!"

"No, Mr Beauchamp, and no again. If you are lily-livered, I am not; and that's fact—I said it." Captain Watkiss seethed. "I call it damned impertinence of any blasted foreigner!"

"But as a matter of simple prudence, sir—"

"Prudence my backside, Mr Beauchamp, I don't give a fish's tit for prudence. I am acting for Her Majesty's life and I intend taking Colonel Stanley into Gibraltar, and you may put *that* in your pipe and smoke it." Watkiss glared ahead at the formidable shapes of the battleships: he had identified them as being those that had faced him earlier and whose admiral had made the impertinent signal warning him out of Spanish territorial waters. As he watched, a gigantic flash of brilliant orange was seen upon the flagship's fo'c'sle as one of her turrets opened. Almost simultaneously a thunderous roar was heard and a projectile screamed overhead, fanning Captain Watkiss with the wind of its passage. Another explosion came from the starboard quarter and a great gout of sea spouted as the shell took the water.

"A warning shot, sir!" Beauchamp said in a high voice.

"God give me strength, I'm aware of that, you fool!" Watkiss bounced on the balls of his feet. "I'm taking not the slightest notice, but if the buggers fire again I'll damn well fire back! Warn the guns' crews, if you please, Mr Beauchamp."

"Sir, I advise—"

"I said, warn the guns' crews. Do you wish to be charged with mutiny, Mr Beauchamp?"

Beauchamp was sweating like a pig. He persisted. "I am no mutineer, sir, and no coward—"

"Oh?"

"—but it's my duty as your first lieutenant—"

"I have already told you what your duty is, Mr Beauchamp." Watkiss leaned over the forward guardrail. "If you won't do it, I will." He raised his voice. "You there—'A' Gun Captain. Stand by to open on the enemy. Mr Beauchamp, I—"

"You shall listen, sir!" Beauchamp sounded frenzied. "If you open, the whole flotilla will be blown out of the water, and so—"

"Mr Beauchamp, you're under arrest. Mr Pomeroy will—"

"—and so will Colonel Stanley, sir! Then who will warn Her Majesty, when all of us are dead or captured?"

Watkiss opened his mouth, his blood-inflamed neck bulging against the tunic collar of his white uniform. For a few moments, as the opposing ships converged, his mouth remained open; then slowly closed. "You have a point, Mr Beauchamp. You have indeed. Later you shall explain in writing why you failed to make it earlier, and thus imperilled my flotilla. Yeoman!"

"Yessir?"

"Make to the damn dago: *I intend heaving-to under duress but a full report will be made to Her Majesty's government accompanied by the strongest protest. Mr Pomeroy, engines full astern.*"

"Aye, aye, sir." Pomeroy passed the order. Bells rang and were repeated back from the engine-room. As the ship began to lose her way Watkiss's signal was made to the Spanish admiral and the ships astern were informed of the leader's intentions. Beauchamp once again approached his captain.

"If you please, sir, may I fall out the guns' crews?"

"Of course not!"

"But—"

"Hold your tongue, Mr Beauchamp." Up came Captain Watkiss's telescope again. "Now what's the fellow making? Yeoman!"

"Yessir. Admiral says, sir: *you are to report aboard the flagship.* He's sending a boat, sir."

Watkiss raised both fists in the air; the tattooed snake

squirmed into view. "Then he can damn well send it back again!
If he wishes to talk, he can come to me, not me to him. Tell
him so." A foot was lifted, and stamped hard upon the bridge
planking. "Blasted foreigners, who the devil do they think they
are, I'd like to know!"

Chapter 7

THE SPANISH ADMIRAL, de Valdares, was a polite and considerate officer: a message was flashed from his flagship to indicate that he would accede to the British captain's wishes. Watkiss preened. "It's the only way to treat dagoes, Mr Beauchamp. Don't ask 'em, tell' em."

"Yes, sir." Beauchamp was thinking his own thoughts: the Spaniard, having forced the flotilla to heave-to, was being magnanimous in victory, no more, no less.

"When he boards me, bring him to the bridge."

"Will you not meet him at the ladder, sir, yourself?"

"No."

"Aye, aye, sir." Beauchamp turned away to go aft, but was stopped by the captain.

"Remember what I've said before, Mr Beauchamp, when dealing with dagoes take care to stand with your back to a bulkhead."

"Yes, sir."

"And another thing. Not a word about Halfhyde or Colonel Stanley." Watkiss turned his back on his first lieutenant and stared ahead towards the massive Spanish battleships which, as had now been seen, had been joined by another ship since their last meeting at sea—a first-class cruiser. Already a boat was leaving the flagship and making towards the flotilla. Captain

Watkiss sniffed; very likely it would sink on the way, if he knew
Spaniards—look at what had happened to the Armada!

But it did not sink; the boat approached in a perfectly sea-
manlike manner and came alongside Watkiss's ladder smartly.
Watkiss moved to the starboard wing of his bridge and craned
his neck: from the boat three officers emerged and Watkiss
made the assumption that the admiral had brought his flag captain and flag lieutenant with him, an assumption that proved
correct when a few minutes later the three were ushered up the
bridge ladder by Beauchamp. Captain Watkiss sniffed again:
there was a smell like a lady's boudoir and it seemed to be coming from the flag lieutenant, who was waving a handkerchief in
the air like, in Watkiss's view, the nancy-boy he probably was.

Politely, the admiral bowed. "How do you do, Captain," he
said in excellent English.

"How d'you do. What's the meaning of this? How dare you
stop one of Her Majesty's ships of war upon the high seas?"

"Your pardon, Captain," de Valdares said gravely, "but here
the seas are not high—"

"Oh yes they are—"

"Exactly here, yes. But your ships came out of our territorial inshore waters, Captain. That is an infringement of our
right."

"I'm sorry," Watkiss snapped. "May I point out that I'm no
longer in your territorial waters, and you are now infringing *my*
right?"

The admiral shrugged and gestured with his hands in a
manner that, despite a firm and aristocratic face, Captain Watkiss
considered effeminate. "Certainly it is satisfactory that you have
left our coast, Captain, but I have the right and the duty to ask

what you were doing while there. You will tell me your reason, please."

"Oh, no, I shall not. Reason, fiddlesticks! I'm under no obligation to discuss the Royal Navy's business with you, my dear sir." Captain Watkiss flourished his telescope. "I suggest you return aboard your flagship and allow me free passage to Gibraltar before you find yourself in trouble."

De Valdares lifted a hand and pulled at his beard, studying Watkiss thoughtfully through narrowed, heavy-lidded eyes. He said peaceably, "I wish to cause no trouble for anyone, Captain, but my duty must be done. This I know you will understand."

"You're not the only one who has a duty to do," Watkiss said vigorously. "It might well be that mine is to arrest you in the Queen's name and land you on to British soil in Gibraltar!"

The admiral's eyes twinkled in the light from the low-slung stars, and he gestured towards his battlefleet and its powerful turrets. "I venture to suggest that you might find my arrest difficult, Captain—but do not let us disagree. Our countries are at peace, and there is much friendship between us, is this not so? Allow me to state my request in different words. Perhaps you will be able to tell me in general terms what brings a British flotilla into this sector of the Mediterranean?"

Watkiss nodded. "Well, I see no harm in that, though I fail to see why you need to ask. We're in the area of our base at Gibraltar, are we not? These waters are in frequent use by our warships, and merchant shipping as well. As for me, I'm on exercises, a part of the combined manoeuvres of the Mediterranean Fleet and the Channel Squadron out of our home ports. I really do not know what all this fuss is about!"

"Then perhaps I should tell you, Captain." De Valdares

caught the eye of his flag captain; all at once the atmosphere on the navigating bridge seemed to change, to become more formal and tense. The admiral's voice had hardened, was crisp as he went on, "Whilst returning from Ceuta to Barcelona I was overtaken by one of our frigates out of Cadiz with despatches. Does the name of Colonel Stanley convey anything to you, Captain?"

"It does not," Watkiss answered promptly. "Why should it?"

"This officer is wanted in connection with a death in the province of Cordoba. He was last reported as making his way to Malaga."

"Really. I quite fail to see the connection with me."

"You were inshore of Point Calaburras, Captain. That is not far from Malaga. Need I say more?"

"Yes!" Watkiss snapped. "A great deal more, all of which will be noted by my first lieutenant and my officer of the watch. Mr Beauchamp?"

"Sir?"

"A signal pad and a pencil. Take down all that is said for entry in the deck log. Mr Pomeroy?"

"Yes, sir?"

"Keep your ears open. You will be required as a witness before the Board of Admiralty and Parliament." Watkiss turned back to the Spanish officers. "Now, sir. Make your charges, and be prepared to substantiate them if you can! I should warn you that Her Majesty's government will react most strongly and with the utmost vigour if you have made any false assumptions."

Blandly, de Valdares smiled. "I shall make no charges until I am certain of my facts, Captain. I regret what I must do now, but again I quote my duty to the Queen Regent of Spain." He bowed, still polite. "I repeat my regrets, but I intend to place seamen and marines aboard your ships, to carry out a search of each one."

Watkiss exploded. "I'll be damned if you do! You'll do no such thing, d'you hear? Who do you think you are, pray?"

"I think I am the one holding the whip, Captain—"

"Whip indeed! I never heard such rubbish! Mr Beauchamp?"

"Sir?"

"Place these persons under arrest. An armed petty officer and six seamen, also armed. And take charge yourself."

Beauchamp dithered. "Are you sure that's wise, sir?"

"Oh, balls to wisdom! It's my order. See to it."

"A moment, Captain." The Spanish admiral stepped forward. "Hastiness is seldom wise." He gestured once again at his formidable squadron looming through the star-filled night. "I must ask you to make a signal to my flagship, as from myself, a few words only: *permission is granted.*"

Captain Watkiss stamped a foot. "Permission is *not* granted!"

"A pity," de Valdares said in a grave voice, "for I left certain orders behind me. If the signal is not made, my captains will open upon your flotilla and blow your ships out of the water."

There was a tense silence, while Captain Watkiss's face grew purple and his telescope trembled in his grip. The dago could very well be bluffing; his own gunfire would kill him as stone dead as everyone else. On the other hand his facial expression did not support the theory of bluff; and Watkiss knew that he himself, in common with every other commanding officer afloat, would equally chance his life in execution of what he considered to be his duty. Naturally, there would be an almighty fuss afterwards, but when it was established that Stanley had indeed been nefariously embarked from Spanish territory, snatched from justice, and that he, Watkiss, had indeed violated territorial waters with his flotilla, the British Admiralty might have not a leg to stand upon. As for present considerations, Halfhyde had Stanley aboard *Vendetta;* and Halfhyde, though a most tiresome officer to be sure, possessed initiative, imagination and a capacity to think ahead and assess situations before they developed. When a boat was seen approaching his ship, filled with armed dagoes, Halfhyde would react speedily. Perhaps Stanley could be nailed back into his seaborne chest and dangled below Halfhyde's stern until the danger was past . . . yes, it was wrong to be hasty! Captain Watkiss, wishing to God he could take the dago's neck in his hands and strangle it, hoisted his sagging stomach into his chest and snapped. "Mr Beauchamp!"

"Yes, sir?"

"Belay the last order, the one about arrest. I've decided to handle this differently. Yeoman!"

"Yessir?"

"Attend with your lamp upon the da—the admiral." Turning his back, Watkiss strode to the port wing of his bridge, vibrating with fury and shame.

"Boat approaching from the flag, sir."

"Thank you, Mr Prebble, I've already seen it."

"What do you think is going to happen, sir?"

Halfhyde laughed without humour. "You should use your head, Mr Prebble! I see the glint of bayonets. They mean to board and search." He waved an arm. "More boats. All ships are to be searched, that's my guess. The Spaniard has impressed the good Captain Watkiss with his strength!"

"What about Colonel Stanley, sir?"

"Exactly, Mr Prebble; the thought has not escaped me."

Halfhyde frowned; as if by telepathy, his thoughts ran along the lines of Watkiss's speculations. The chest might be a good hiding place, but on the other hand it might not. It would need to be secured, and an alert seaman detailed specifically to search might spot the securing rope. If it were allowed to wallow free, its movement would be obvious beneath the bright pattern of the stars. In any case, for all Halfhyde knew, the Spaniards, if they were on Stanley's trail as they clearly must be, might also be aware of the chest's existence; it would be safer, anyway, to assume they were. The chest was out; it would have to be destroyed. There was another alternative: Halfhyde could ring down to his engine-room for maximum revolutions and take Stanley out for Gibraltar before the Spaniards boarded; but, though he would have the heels of the slow-moving battleships, he had not the sea-room to get clear away before the big guns opened. Vengeance would be wreaked on all the ships of the flotilla and nothing achieved. That was not the way, either. Halfhyde reached a decision and swung round on his first lieutenant.

"Mr Prebble, axes and a razor."

"Beg pardon, sir?" Prebble gaped.

"When in Russian hands at Sevastopol, we dressed a British merchant officer as a naval rating and got away with it. We must do the same again, Mr Prebble, and time is short. Axes to smash up the chest and feed it into the boilers with the coal. A razor to remove Colonel Stanley's moustache. Have him dressed in stoker's rig and covered with coal-dust, and despatch him to the boiler-room. At the double, Mr Prebble—and pass the word to all hands that no mention is to be made of recent events or of Colonel Stanley's presence aboard."

Prebble slid down the ladder to the upper deck. Halfhyde watched the approach of the Spanish boat, the bayonets and rifles agleam between the oarsmen.

Aboard the leader, Captain Watkiss sulked and gloomed. De Valdares, remaining on the bridge with his two aides, tried to engage in conversation; he was, thought Captain Watkiss, attempting to draw him out and obtain some sort of admission so as to bring his prolonged search to a faster end. Watkiss, however, was too wily for such tricks to succeed. He remained aloof, nursing his indignities and thinking of the Queen. After a while, de Valdares gave up the attempt and conversed for a while with his own officers, speaking Spanish of which Watkiss had no knowledge. Watkiss considered this bad manners but was damned if he was going to show any reaction. He glared down from his bridge at his ship's company: by order of the search party's officer, the lower deck had been cleared and all hands mustered on the upper deck while the ship was undergoing search below. Each man had been closely inspected by the Spanish officer—in Watkiss's eyes a stupid waste of time, since Stanley was not aboard the ship! The search was thorough, plenty of time being taken over it. De Valdares was in no hurry, and seemed, Watkiss thought, most devilishly sure of his facts. When at last the search ended and a nil result was reported, the admiral appeared unworried: there were the other ships.

But upon the heels of the leader, the Spanish officers aboard those other ships reported in by lamp: all of them—and no sign of Colonel Stanley. Watkiss was delighted, if surprised; and blessed, in his heart, the name of Halfhyde, a first-class officer if ever there was one. He would be warmly commended in the official report of this high-handed business.

"So there you are, sir," Watkiss said triumphantly to the Spaniard. "There you are! Perhaps in future you'll trust the word of a British naval officer and not go to the lengths of this damn stupid fandango. If you'll be good enough to return to your flagship and allow me to proceed, I'll be much obliged."

Solemnly, de Valdares bowed. "Your pardon, Captain. I shall return to my ship with my flag captain and my flag lieutenant—"

"And good riddance!" Watkiss snapped, his face red and furious in the first glimmers of the dawn; he had not been able to contain his outburst, the indignity of the whole proceeding smiting him fully now it was all over. He shook his telescope in the admiral's face. "Good riddance, I say! The air will be the fresher when your damn popinjay takes his scents and powders and pomades away from my nostrils! What a Navy!"

The admiral lost some of his politeness, speaking coldly. "I think you are ahead of yourself, Captain. I go, as does my staff. My search party, however, remains."

"The devil it does, sir! The devil it does! You must be mad as a hatter in any case, to wish them handed over as—as *pirates,* to the Fleet in Gibraltar!"

"Not Gibraltar. Barcelona, and no British Fleet. I am not satisfied that Colonel Stanley is not aboard one of your ships, Captain. Each will be under command of the armed search

party and its officer, and you shall accompany me to Barcelona
for further investigation."

Captain Watkiss's jaw fell open. He was about to call for his
first lieutenant when four of the Spanish seamen were seen
mounting the ladder to the bridge with Beauchamp under guard
in their midst. The rifles and bayonets of the leading file were
pointing menacingly at himself.

Chapter 8

ABOARD *Vendetta,* aboard each of the torpedo-boat destroyers of Captain Watkiss's command, similar events had taken place. The boarding parties of seamen and marines had been strong both in numbers and weapons; each ship had been provided with sufficient Spanish personnel for armed guards to be placed in all strategic positions: bridge, guns and tubes, boiler-rooms, engine spaces and along the mess decks. All the ship's small-arms, the rifles from the racks and the officers' revolvers, had been impounded. Halfhyde stared down grimly from his bridge as the Spaniards took over. He, like the other commanding officers, was being left to sail his ship, but he knew that one step out of line would bring down the thunderous voice of the guns that now steamed in company towards Barcelona. And the closer, smaller weapons also: behind him on his bridge Halfhyde was only too well aware of the Spanish seamen with their rifles and bayonets, somewhat smelly men and none too clean but with dangerous faces and watchful eyes. Already Halfhyde had used various subterfuges to assure himself that those currently on guard had precious little English, which was as he had hoped since it was urgent that he have some words as privately as possible with his first lieutenant.

"A certain person, Mr Prebble. How is he?"

"Weary, sir, and with bloody hands."

"Yet he is to continue to stoke. It can't be avoided, though you can try to have a word with the stoker petty officer of his watch, Mr Prebble, and see if an easier task can't be devised."

"Aye, aye, sir." Prebble rubbed at tired eyes and stared into the breaking dawn. "Something like 36 hours' steaming into Barcelona, sir, at the Spaniards' speed . . . and then what happens?"

Halfhyde shrugged. "A more thorough search, and made by the *politicos* rather than ham-handed seamen and marines!"

"And the certain person, sir?"

"Won't have a cat in hell's chance. I don't believe he will mind that so long as his message reaches London, but at this moment, Prebble, I see no chance of that at all. All the knowledge is here with him, upon the open sea—with you, me and Captain Watkiss!"

"But the man you met, sir, or rather, who met you—"

"Yes. No names, if you please, our bridge has ears today and Spanish names might register. That person, I understand, had not been told the facts, any more than has the Embassy." Halfhyde paced the bridge with his first lieutenant, frowning, scanning the empty seas as if for inspiration: if only a battle squadron of the British Mediterranean Fleet would appear over the horizon! A mere seventy miles south-west of their current position lay the fortress and garrison of Gibraltar . . . so near and yet so far. There was no knowing where the combined fleets might be exercising, but it was hoping for too much that they would appear so conveniently just when needed. And if the flotilla allowed itself to be taken into Barcelona, and Stanley was discovered—as for a certainty he would be once the *politicos* got to work—a diplomatic furore was the least that might be expected, the very thing that Captain Watkiss was under orders to avoid. And the fate of Watkiss—and of himself as cat's-paw and illegal, if very temporary, immigrant into Spain for nefarious purposes—would also be a subject for debate once they entered Barcelona. The proceedings might be very long drawn out, much too long drawn out for the Queen's safety. It might be possible for a message to be got through to the Embassy in Madrid, but it might not. It was perfectly possible, indeed likely, that the British ships' companies would be held *incommunicado* . . .

But the Spanish authorities: there had been no suggestion from Stanley that the threat to the Queen's life had been government policy, and indeed such would be totally unthinkable. So why not simply inform the Naval Command at Barcelona and nip the Duke of Villanueva de Cordoba's scheme in the bud? Why not, indeed, simply inform Admiral de Valdares forthwith?

Halfhyde paced on. It was too easy: there had to be a snag. If that was what Stanley wanted, then he would have made it clear. The reason for not doing so was perhaps clear also: Spain was Spain, a land of intrigue and no man knew for certain who could be trusted. If the wrong receptacle was chosen for the information, that would be that. Nothing would be passed on and the Queen of England would die in the wild hills around Balmoral. Halfhyde had a moment of fear when he fancied that Captain Watkiss might decide to pass the information to de Valdares as a result of cogitations similar to his own; but this was short-lived. Captain Watkiss had obviously and properly denied all knowledge of Colonel Stanley; his bounce, his bombastic nature, his pomposity would not permit retreat. It was true that Watkiss was subject to sudden changes of mind as different whims floated into his head; there was as ever that element of the chameleon in Captain Watkiss . . . while occasionally a proper prudence penetrated the self-importance far enough to rectify a wrong decision and avert disaster—but the abounding pride that had sustained him through a long career and a number of near catastrophes would never allow him to walk back flat upon a statement that he had uttered as fact. He would leave it in Halfhyde's hands as long as possible.

Ahead on the port bow Cape Sacratif came up as the morning wore on; beyond lay Cape de Gata around which the flotilla and its escort would turn to the north-east for Cartagena and Barcelona. Tired by now, Halfhyde left the ship to his officer of the watch and went below, as did Prebble, to snatch a meal and some sleep with armed guards on the cabin doors. Once in the comfort of his bunk Halfhyde twisted and turned, his mind still active and visiting him with nightmares in which loomed, horribly, the Spanish Inquisition of old, the agency of the Holy Office of Rome which in the name of the Virgin Mary had perpetrated terrible tortures upon those accused of heresy: presumably it would not be heresy to kill the Protestant Queen of England! Halfhyde awoke after only a brief sleep. He dashed water on his face from the copper can in his wash stand, and felt more refreshed though none of his anxieties had left him. There were so many inconsistencies, so much left unexplained: it was urgent that, before entering Barcelona, he should have words with Stanley.

Sitting on his bunk, he put his head in his hands. Words between a commanding officer and a coal-black stoker would appear odd to the Spaniards, and could do nothing but focus attention upon that stoker. There would be no point in assisting the *politicos* in their eventual task.

Halfhyde pondered: a subterfuge was needed, and quickly. A foolproof subterfuge that would be above suspicion. Officers in command of Her Majesty's ships of war came into frequent contact with lower-deck seaman ratings in the course of their duties, though more usually via the agency of a petty officer or leading-seaman; but with stokers, never—except in one particular. Smiling to himself as the idea took hold, Halfhyde left his cabin and proceeded to the bridge, followed by the armed Spaniard on guard. From the bridge he sent word for the first lieutenant.

It was efficiently and expeditiously done: the stoker petty officer of Stanley's watch, after a brief and discreet word with the first lieutenant, spoke out of the corner of his mouth at the black-faced, sweating former Colonel of the Blues, instructing him in the formalities of captain's defaulters, and passing certain orders from Halfhyde. Thereafter, watched by a Spanish marine, the stoker PO began hazing Colonel Stanley, calling him everything that long service in the boiler-rooms of the Fleet had taught him. Very realistically, when the petty officer proffered his face, Stanley smote him on the jaw and threatened him with his shovel. Ten minutes later, under escort and with the torpedo-coxswain—the man who in torpedo-boat destroyers acted as master-at-arms, head of the ship's police—bringing up the rear, Stanley was upon the bridge and facing Halfhyde.

"Off cap," the torpedo-coxswain ordered. Stanley removed a filthy cap from his head, using the thumb and forefinger of his left hand and bringing the cap smartly down to his left side. "Stoker First-Class Smith, John, official number 121357, sir. Did act in a manner prejudicial to good order and naval discipline in that he struck Stoker Petty Officer Timmins, his superior officer, sir."

Halfhyde, standing with his hands behind his back, nodded judicially. "What have you to say in answer to the charge, Smith?"

"Nothing, sir." Stanley, as a regimental officer, was familiar enough with the responses to be expected at the defaulters' table; also, he was being nicely obsequious.

"Nothing. I see. Then I shall have some questions to ask you. Do you understand?"

Stanley nodded. "Yes."

"Yes, *sir*," the torpedo-coxswain said from beside the captain.

"Yes, sir."

"Then listen carefully." Halfhyde cleared his throat. "Buoyancy tanks. You follow?"

Stanley looked puzzled. "No, sir, I don't."

"Unsinkable objects, Smith."

"Ah, yes. I've wondered about that too, sir. I've come to no conclusions."

"But one conclusion is this: death was not on the cards. You would agree?"

"Yes, sir."

"Why? That is what bothers me. And another thing: a certain person . . . I told him of the plan for rejoining. No one else knew. Ergo, he must have been in touch with those other persons. It was at his own request that I told him, perhaps foolishly. Is he really to be trusted?"

"So far as I'm aware, yes, certainly."

Halfhyde nodded. "This I must know. Be careful when you answer. The high authorities not ours, but others. You follow me?"

"I think I do, sir."

"Then can they be told the facts?"

Stanley looked him in the eye. "It might be unwise, sir. In the Mediterranean lands, more perhaps than elsewhere, people are not always as they seem. The vital thing is to get me home."

"Or to Gibraltar."

"No, sir. Home."

Halfhyde kept his face expressionless. "I see. Can you, very carefully, elaborate on that?"

"It would be a risk to say more."

"Oh, I think not."

"I don't agree, sir. I haven't necessarily only our armed friend in mind." Fractionally, he inclined his head towards the Spanish seaman . . .

Halfhyde's eyebrows went up. "You mean my ship's company? Perhaps I take your point, but am surprised nevertheless."

"The risk is there. The very highest is at stake, as you know, sir."

"Yes." Halfhyde rocked on his heels, thoughtfully. In all conscience he had got no further, was no wiser. Stanley, meanwhile, was showing some natural strain; a cool breeze was blowing across the bridge, yet he was sweating profusely and there was a shake in his fingers as he stood at attention. Halfhyde said abruptly, "Very well, the matter must rest for now." He met the torpedo-coxswain's enquiring look and was about to utter some official sentence upon the alleged defaulter when the seaman lookout at the starboard after end of the navigating bridge raised his voice and reported in high excitement.

"Captain, sir, smoke on the horizon, bearing one-three-five!"

Halfhyde swung round. He saw four heavy trails of smoke; he lifted his telescope, but found the ships were still hull down. There was an excited shout from the Spanish seamen, one of them calling to the deck below. The officer of the boarding-party came up the bridge ladder, taking the steps two at a time.

"*Capitan*—"

"All correct, Lieutenant." Halfhyde grinned. "But for how much longer? What do you wager we're being chased by a British battle squadron?"

"You are too confident," the Spaniard answered. "We, also, have ships at sea."

Halfhyde gave an ironic bow. "Your pardon. I assumed your entire navy was here with us already. May I offer you the courtesy of my telescope, to set your mind either at rest or staggering under a sense of defeat?"

The smoke had been reported aboard *Venomous* as well. Captain Watkiss, making an early assumption in his own favour, was cock-a-hoop. "I knew the Fleet wouldn't leave me in these buggers' hands, Mr Beauchamp! I knew it!"

"But our situation's not known to the Fleet, sir—"

"Oh, hold your tongue, Mr Beauchamp, and don't pick holes in everything I say." Watkiss turned impatiently and strutted across his bridge to the Spanish officer in whose control he would not for much longer be. "You there, that Spaniard." He waved his telescope towards the smoke and the funnels that by now stood clearly up from the horizon. "Nemesis, my dear sir! Out there! Approaching fast. *Now* what will your blasted admiral have to say, I wonder! Him," he added witheringly, "and his powdered popinjay! By God, they're both due to have their balls fried for breakfast I shouldn't wonder!"

He applied his telescope to his eye, and stared out across the bright blue of the sea. The ships, whoever they were, were closing fast; upperworks appeared, painted a light yellow, and masts stood visible from time to time through the heavy black smoke that was blowing ahead of the hulls on the prevailing breeze. Watkiss stared hard and excitement rose along with thoughts of glory and revenge: he saw flags, ensigns. There was white, there was red, there was blue he fancied. The leading ship became more visible: it wore more white and more red. Watkiss swelled with pride and joy. In the upper corner nearest the mast stood proof positive: the single ball of a British vice-admiral, also red. Captain Watkiss lowered his telescope, closed it with a snap, and waved it above his head. Then he removed his cap and waved that with the other hand.

"It's a battle squadron of the Mediterranean Fleet! Four battleships, first-class battleships, no less! With a vice-admiral in command—you can tell that," he added pompously to the Spanish officer, "by his flag." At once he regretted having been so forthcoming. British rear-admirals wore two red balls upon their flags, vice-admirals one; full admirals had no balls at all. The Spaniard's face wore a smile; in the dago Navy, as Watkiss was aware, the reverse was the case: the higher the rank, the more the balls. The Spaniard's mouth opened—to offer insult to Her Majesty's Fleet, Watkiss was certain; fortunately a light from the Spanish flagship enabled Watkiss to deflect the man's sardonic amusement.

"Your flagship's signalling," Watkiss said loudly. "What's the message? One of apology, as I trust." He waited while the

Spanish signalman read the winking lamp and reported to his officer. "Well, what does your admiral say?"

"He says we are handily off Cartagena, *Capitan*."

"Yes, yes, yes. But—"

"It is there we shall go instead of Barcelona. I am ordered to alter your course. We shall reach safety before the British come, and they will not follow into Cartagena."

For once Watkiss was speechless: the disappointment was cruel. He put his cap back upon his head and watched helplessly as the Spanish battleships and their attendant cruiser, moving in as a closer escort than hitherto, swung on their new courses to shepherd the flotilla into the great fortress and arsenal of Cartagena.

Halfhyde's dismay was as great as that of Captain Watkiss as the flagship's signal was read off and reported. Cartagena loomed close, much too close. They would all be inside the port within the next hour, just out of reach of the British ships; and as it was they were inside the territorial limits of Spanish waters.

"They'll turn away," Halfhyde said to Prebble in disgust. "There'll be some messages exchanged, then they'll turn away."

"They have no alternative, sir, have they?"

"Once they would have done. Lord Nelson would have followed in!"

"We were at war with Spain then."

"You're quite right, Mr Prebble, of course." Halfhyde paced his bridge, his face hard and his mouth set. "Well, let us look on the bright side: at least our whereabouts will be reported to Gibraltar now, and then to the Admiralty in London, and that's something."

"And the likely response, sir?"

Halfhyde grimaced. "Diplomatic exchanges, polite at first and growing more pointed as time passes. To be frank, it's not much of a gain after all. Time is the very thing . . ." He halted his restless pacing and stared towards the British ships with narrowed eyes. He looked across at his yeoman of signals, at the sun-browned, wrinkled face and the bright eyes that could read the fastest signal that any man could send. The yeoman could send as fast as he read; for that matter, so could Halfhyde—almost. Precious moments would be wasted if he were to use the yeoman as an intermediary. Halfhyde walked across, casually, towards the signalling projector on the starboard side of the bridge. Reaching it, he moved swiftly. He swung the big lamp to bear upon the British flagship and started calling her up; but he had no chance. The Spanish seamen on bridge guard reacted instantaneously: one of them, covered by his companion who held Prebble and the officer of the watch back at bayonet point, reached Halfhyde before he had done more than send the short-long-short-long flashes of the two A's that formed the general call-sign. A rifle-butt crashed down numbingly on the hand that worked the transmitting lever; then the weapon was reversed and the bayonet pressed into Halfhyde's chest. The man spoke rapidly in Spanish; though his words conveyed nothing, his meaning could scarcely be misunderstood. Halfhyde glared frostily; he would clearly have no chance now to use the lamp. There was perhaps another way . . . Disregarding the armed seaman so far as was possible when assailed by garlic, Halfhyde called to his officer of the watch. "Mr Sawbridge, take her out."

"Sir?" Sawbridge turned, looking puzzled.

"Out of the line, Mr Sawbridge, and full speed for the Fleet. Quiet orders to the engine-room down the voice-pipe, no telegraphs. Before these onion-eaters realize what's happening, we should be clear. Away you go!"

"Aye, aye, sir." Sawbridge looked quickly all around, fixing in his mind the relative positions of the Spanish battleships. As last in the line of torpedo-boat destroyers there was no need to worry about the rest of the flotilla's whereabouts: *Vendetta* could slip clear with ease so far as they were concerned. Sawbridge passed the word to the quartermaster at the wheel. "We're moving out to join the Fleet. Pass to the engine-room by voice-pipe, maximum revolutions."

"Maximum revolutions, sir—"

"Wheel hard a-port."

"Wheel hard a-port, sir!"

Halfhyde called out, "Mr Prebble, mark your man. When I move, you move. Get his rifle, then guard the bridge ladders. Understood?"

"Understood, sir."

As the vessel began to heel and an immense vibration started in her plates in response to the increasing thunder of the screws, Halfhyde moved his body back a little way and brought his knee up hard into the Spaniard's groin. There was a howl of pain and Halfhyde seized the rifle-butt just behind the bayonet, wrenching it from the man's grip as he doubled up. Leaping over the writhing body, Halfhyde went to Prebble's assistance against the second Spaniard, who was quickly brought to book. By now the ship was heeling fast as she came tight round to starboard with the wheel to port, and her guardrails were awash with foaming water, every part of her seeming to vibrate like something alive as the engines worked up to maximum power. Consternation had broken out along the upper deck and the Spanish officer in charge was dashing for the bridge ladder. From the foot of it he came face to face with the rifle in Prebble's hands.

"No farther," Prebble said in a tight voice, "or I shall shoot."

"You are in Spanish water. You will be executed."

"But too late to save you." Prebble looked along the back-sight of the rifle, his fingers clearly itching to squeeze the trigger. There was a great exultancy in his face, a plain determination to back his words with action. "Get off the ladder, my friend, and stay off. And remember this: if the British ships hear gun-fire, they will be justified in opening on your flagship, and your admiral will find himself outgunned by better ships than his!"

His dark eyes flashing, the Spaniard moved away, seeming irresolute now. As the decks heeled farther over, he lurched back and grabbed for support at the ladder's guardrails but made no move to climb up again. At the binnacle now, Halfhyde had taken over the conning of his ship out of the line, and was aiming her course to move through the gap between the Spanish flagship and the *Infanta Maria Theresa,* now distant only some four or five cables'-lengths. The Spanish seemed to have been caught off their guard: the great guns were still trained to the fore-and-aft line and elevated to their proper angles for cruising, and there was as yet no movement of them to bear on the racing *Vendetta.* Halfhyde made reference to this.

"Prudence, perhaps, Mr Sawbridge!"

"Yes, sir. To open would be—"

"An outright act of war, Mr Sawbridge." Halfhyde spoke with evident relish. "If only they would, then the spirit of Nelson might enter Captain Watkiss's soul and—" He broke off. "Mr Sawbridge, tell the engine-room I want all they can give me. Look ahead there!"

Sawbridge looked and caught his breath sharply: right ahead of them the flagship and the *Infanta Maria Theresa* were closing in towards each other, presenting what was becoming a solid wall of steel to the onrush of the torpedo-boat destroyer. Sawbridge followed Halfhyde's eye to port and starboard. The *Vizcaya* and the *Almirante Oquendo* had manoeuvred ahead of the other two ships, steaming close down the flanks in such a fashion that *Vendetta* was left with virtually no sea-room to either side; at the same time the first-class cruiser was being handled like a sheepdog, ready to dart in and block any escape. Sawbridge glanced at his captain's set face: Halfhyde, eyes narrowed, was staring ahead with a muscle twitching rapidly at one corner of his mouth as he steadied the hurtling vessel on course for the closing gap between the immense battleship hulls.

Chapter 9

"MR BEAUCHAMP!"

"Sir?" Beauchamp, undignified at the sharp end of a Spanish bayonet, responded in a shaking voice.

Watkiss said angrily, "For God's sake control yourself, Mr Beauchamp, don't act like a wilting lily in front of dagoes. What do you suppose Mr Halfhyde is doing? Has he gone mad?"

"I—I can't say, sir. But it seems likely he intends to join our battle squadron—"

"Yes, yes, yes." Captain Watkiss, rebounding like a bias-based toy gnome, had regained much of his pomposity: he was, as ever, a resilient officer. "What I mean to say is this: he's had *no damn orders* from me to do so! Has he, Mr Beauchamp?"

"No, sir—"

"Then it's flagrant disobedience!" Watkiss flourished his telescope, an act that caused his personal guard to press with his bayonet. Watkiss yelped. *"Don't do that!* By God, when the tables are turned upon you, your guts shall be my garters. Disobedience, Mr Beauchamp! And damn stupidity!"

"But . . . why stupid, sir?"

"Oh, don't ask ridiculous questions! Can't you see, Mr Beauchamp, it's an indication—" Watkiss broke off, coughed in some embarrassment, heaved at the toggle of his monocle and placed the glass in his eye. He had cut short, in the very nick of time, an indiscretion about the whereabouts of Colonel Stanley. "If you can't think of anything better to say, Mr Beauchamp, don't say anything at all."

"No, sir."

"Mr Halfhyde will feel the weight of my displeasure in due course. I detest disobedience—*detest it.*"

"In my opinion, sir, Halfhyde has shown some initiative—"

"Which is more than you show, Mr Beauchamp," Captain Watkiss said promptly, "and now you may hold your tongue, your opinion was not asked for, and don't be impertinent to your superior officer who knows best; that's fact—I said it." Having turned away from his view of his junior ship in order to harangue his first lieutenant, Watkiss now turned back to look once more at disobedience. As he did so, he gave a gasp and his face mottled. "Good God above, Mr Beauchamp, he's hazarding his damn ship now!"

Sweat poured down Halfhyde's face; by his side Sawbridge stared in disbelief. The yeoman of signals, a man of few teeth, sucked and champed nut-cracker jaws, and held fast to the guardrail behind his body. Halfhyde stood like a statue, a statue that gave almost second-by-second helm orders, small alterations of direction, to the quartermaster. Halfhyde was still aiming his knifing, hurtling bows for the gap between the battleships as the other two vessels, firmly in position to cut him off from any move to port or starboard, maintained their courses. The whole manoeuvre was taking place within little more time than half a minute from the start; there was in fact nothing left to do but continue on course. Time had run out for any massive turn away to safety; the helm simply would not answer fast enough now. Even so, events seemed to happen in something like slow motion: Halfhyde was aware of the tremendous loom of steel as he raced into the gap, the great rams on either side giving the appearance of enclosing mountains, of a dash into the confines of an Afghan pass. Faces looked down in utter disbelief, faces that flashed past far above: the battleships' compass platforms and flag decks and control tops reared like the peaks of Himalaya as Halfhyde, rock steady behind the binnacle, took his ship through, sliding with inches to spare past the anti-torpedo bulges that ran like steel whales along the side plating. Exultancy swept the bridge: they were going to get away with it . . . with everything against them, they were going to win through! Sawbridge had already removed his cap for a joyful wave of triumph when the ship lurched like a shot deer. Everywhere men went flying on their faces and from aft came a shriek of scraped steel, and the way came off fast though the hull still had movement enough to drag her free of whatever had nipped her stern.

Halfhyde swore viciously, his face contorted with fury, with a cruel disappointment, with concern for his ship and her company. Swinging round he bent over the guardrail and stared towards the stern. He called, "Mr Prebble?"

"Yes, sir." Prebble answered from the upper deck; he had taken a tumble down the ladder and was badly bruised and shaken. Picking himself up, he faced the drawn revolver of the Spanish officer.

"Are you all right, Mr Prebble?"

"I think so, sir—"

"Good. I fancy we were nipped by the bulges. The damage shouldn't be great, but the initiative's gone." Halfhyde turned to look ahead: beyond the gap, the Spanish cruiser stood fair to race in. As the *Vendetta* limped into open water, the cruiser swung to shepherd her back into the captive line. "So near and yet so far, Mr Prebble. Our battle squadron is too far off. We must follow into Cartagena. Carpenter's mates to sound round below and report. And I'll want word of the ship's company. Mr Sawbridge, starboard ten."

"Starboard ten, sir."

"And revolutions for the speed of the flotilla, as before." Halfhyde watched the ship's head on the standard compass. "Midships . . . steady. Steer to take station astern of the flotilla, Mr Sawbridge. Yeoman, make to the leader: *I am rejoining your command.*"

"Aye, aye, sir."

"Fellow's a bloody fool," Captain Watkiss said briefly. "*Anyone's* a bloody fool, to act without orders! Nevertheless, it was a brave attempt, I'll not deny him that, though there's going to be all manner of trouble when we've entered Cartagena. What's his damage report, Mr Beauchamp?"

"Stern plating badly dented, sir, but screws and rudder serviceable."

"He's seaworthy, is he?"

"Yes, sir."

"Let us be thankful for small mercies. Ship's company?"

"Twenty-three men bruised, sir, in varying degrees of severity.

Four with broken legs or arms. Five stokers burned but none seriously." Beauchamp paused. "Three able-seamen lost overboard, sir."

Watkiss dropped his monocle and looked grave. "Lost? Not recovered?"

"I'm afraid not, sir. They were crushed as the ship continued through. It seems it was unavoidable, sir."

"Yes, yes. Except by not having been so damn stupid in the first place, of course. But I'm deeply grieved, and I know Halfhyde will be also. A sad business—brave fellows all. Dear me. Their families will be told they may be proud, they died for the Queen. It'll be a consolation, Mr Beauchamp." Watkiss braced his shoulders, putting a genuine regret behind him: no captain welcomed the loss of men and Watkiss, tantrum-prone disciplinarian though he was, had always nursed a basically deep pride in, and regard for, his common seamen. "Now, Mr Beauchamp, we must consider the imminence of what lies ahead."

"Yes, sir."

"We must take matters as they come and remain calm in adversity. We shall be under much stress when the damn *politicos* board, but first things first, Mr Beauchamp."

"I beg your pardon, sir?"

"First, there will be an admiral in Cartagena—Spanish it's true, but still an admiral, am I not right?"

"Yes, indeed, sir—"

"He will have a flag. It must be saluted with proper punctiliousness. See to that, if you please, Mr Beauchamp."

Beauchamp looked surprised. "You intend paying full courtesies, sir?"

"Oh, don't be so stupid, Mr Beauchamp, of course I do," Watkiss said in a forbearing tone. "Why ask?"

"Because, sir, you insisted on *not* paying such respects to Admiral de Valdares—"

"Oh no I didn't. I expressly ordered Mr Pomeroy to pipe, and Mr Pomeroy piped."

"Yes, sir. I was referring to when the admiral boarded. You refused to meet him as he came aboard, sir."

"That's quite different, Mr Beauchamp, quite different, and if you cannot perceive that a captain does not leave his bridge when encountering foreign warships at sea, then you will never be fit for a command of your own. I shall make a note of that, Mr Beauchamp, to jog my memory when considering my report upon you at the end of the commission."

Captain Watkiss turned away and made for the ladder with the clear intention of descending it. He was baulked by the Spaniard with the bayoneted rifle; this person grinned at him insultingly, showing blackened teeth and emitting the customary garlic smell. Captain Watkiss glared through his monocle but decided not to bandy words with the lower deck when they held the upper hand. "Damn dagoes!" he said huffily and bounced his way to the forward guardrail instead, as though such had been his true intention all along. In the starboard wing Beauchamp watched him, recognizing the signs: Captain Watkiss was standing with his thighs pressed tight together. He had a need to visit the heads to relieve himself, one fairly cast-iron excuse for a captain to leave his bridge whatever the circumstances short of action . . . Beauchamp's spirits, low already at the thought of capture, which would be unpleasant even in the piping times of peace, sank still further. It was impossible to please his captain; and Beauchamp had been a senior lieutenant for long enough. More than anything in the world, he desired to adorn his cap-peak with the golden oak leaves that denoted a commander in the Royal Navy.

"Heroics, Mr Prebble. Beware of them, as I should have been. I killed three men."

Prebble shook his head. "That's not true, sir. You did your duty as you saw it."

"There I agree: as I saw it! I was wrong, and I have only myself to blame. What's worse, I failed. I've not helped the Queen's safety, Prebble. I may have damaged her interests."

"No, sir—"

"Yes, sir!" Halfhyde brought a fist down hard into his palm. "Think: I make a dash for it, the only ship of the flotilla that does. That will concentrate the Spanish mind for the search. Stanley will be found."

"Perhaps, sir. That was always likely—you said as much yourself—once we enter a Spanish port. I can't see that you've made anything worse." Prebble looked at Halfhyde with concern showing in his round, unsophisticated face. Prebble had come to admire as well as like his captain; he was the fairest officer Prebble had ever encountered in his long journey from boy seaman, up through the various lower-deck stages to the ward-room via the transitional rank of mate; as a seaman Halfhyde was in his view unsurpassed; as a commanding officer not only Prebble but every man and boy of his ship's company would follow him to the death. "Don't take it too hard, sir. The Queen's service never was an easy option and we all of us knew that when we joined. I—"

"Thank you, Mr Prebble, we shall say no more about it for now. There will be letters to write soon, and only I can write them, however poor a hand I am at it. Until then we have other matters to attend to."

"Yes, sir."

"We are not far from the entry now. Fall in for entering harbour, Mr Prebble, if you please, and see it smartly done."

Prebble saluted. "Aye, aye, sir." He turned away, lifting a hand for the bosun's mate of the watch. The pipe sounded round the ship: "Special sea dutymen to your stations . . . cable and side party muster on the fo'c'sle. Divisions fall in for entering harbour, all men not in the rig of the day clear the upper deck!" It would indeed be smartly done; under escort or not, a captive vessel or not, *Vendetta* was still one of Her Majesty's ships of war, and as such would show any foreigner how to conduct affairs in the proper service manner. Soon men were doubling from the hatches and along the decks to fall in under their officers and petty officers, wearing clean white uniforms and blue jean collars whose three white bordering lines stood in commemoration of Lord Nelson's three great victories of Copenhagen, the Nile and Trafalgar. The torpedo-boat flotilla, with the ships of de Valdares placed between them and the still distant units of the Mediterranean Fleet, moved into the lee of Cape Tinoso under a brilliant sun shining down upon bright-blue water. The voice of the yeoman of signals broke a brooding silence on *Vendetta's* bridge.

"Speed signal, sir: *reduce to four knots,* sir."

"From the Spaniard?"

"No, sir." There was a chuckle in the yeoman's voice now. "From Captain Watkiss, sir." He paused. "The Spanish flag's signalling now, sir. Four knots!"

"Thank you, Yeoman." Halfhyde passed the order to his officer of the watch, smiling inwardly. Captain Watkiss would be congratulating himself most mightily on his pre-emption of the order! Halfhyde watched closely as Sawbridge conned the ship in behind the rest of the flotilla. As they closed towards the great fortress of Cartagena the waters narrowed; they were now shut into the land mass of Spain, into a dry, brown land of sherry and castanets, flamenco and chaperons, overworked donkeys and mules with long ears a-poke through their incongruous straw hats, a land of hot passion and aristocracy and peasantry, of cruelty and of long memory, a land that once, and not so very long ago, had been one of Britain's bitterest enemies until fought to a standstill by Wellington and Nelson. An unpropitious land for a Queen's ship to enter in such circumstances: Captain Watkiss, Halfhyde knew, would now be a most agitated officer, however pompously he might strut his bridge and anticipate signals.

They moved on into the confines of the harbour, into the very heart of Spain's naval power. Halfhyde looked about him, frowning. There was something curious in the air, something that seemed not quite right, something vaguely out of place and yet at the same time familiar and to that extent perfectly proper. It took him a while to pin down, but then it came to him: the whole concourse of warships, the escort and the escorted, was in fact being led in not by Admiral de Valdares but by Captain

Watkiss who, importantly strutting his bridge and disregarding his captors, had somehow contrived to manoeuvre the Spanish flagship out of the way so that he could shoulder through the entrance and bravely flaunt the White Ensign before the flag of Spain . . .

In obedience to signals from the port command the ships had proceeded to their berths, the British flotilla being ordered to lie alongside a quay below the fortress, still in their order of steaming. The Spanish warships went past them, slowly, ponderously, in the care of steam tugs; as Admiral de Valdares passed, pipes sounded from each of the British ships, and each commanding officer saluted from his bridge. The salutes were returned by the brassy sound of the flagship's bugles, the notes echoing off the fortress walls and the arsenal buildings. As the battleships and the cruiser moved away in line ahead, Halfhyde heard the sound of many marching feet coming along the quay.

"Soldiers, Mr Prebble," he said, looking down. A body of troops of something like half company strength was approaching; they were halted in the centre of the line of torpedo-boat destroyers, and broken up into smaller detachments that were then marched under sergeants, one to each ship. Already Halfhyde had ordered a gangway to be rigged from his damaged quarterdeck to the quay: as soon as this was in position, up marched the detachment detailed for the *Vendetta,* without so much as a by-your-leave.

Halfhyde glared. "Mr Prebble, go and ask their business, if you please—even though we know very well what it is! The sergeant is to report to the bridge."

"Aye, aye, sir." Prebble went down the ladder and returned within a few minutes, accompanied by a sweating NCO with lank, greasy black hair beneath an infantry helmet.

Halfhyde looked the man up and down. "Have you any English?" he asked.

The swarthy face widened in a grin. "Enough, *Capitan*."

"Then tell me the purpose of your visit."

"As relief, *Capitan*, for the naval seamen."

"Your orders?"

The sergeant shrugged and picked at his teeth. "To guard. Two men, armed, on the quay. Two men, armed, on the deck. Day and night, *Capitan*. Also two men, armed, at the engine. Two men, armed, at the steerplace, which is here. No person will be permitted to set foot on the shore except by permission—"

"Of you?"

"Yes, *Capitan*, of me. This will be given for the one purpose only, of visiting your chief *capitan* in the leading ship, when wanted."

"Generous!"

The sergeant grinned again. "Your chief *capitan* is to remain in command. With this we do not interfere, it is not our business. Only that you do not leave, not go to sea, you understand, *Capitan*?"

Halfhyde nodded. "I understand, Sergeant. Is there anything else?"

"For now, *Capitan*, nothing. Except that the confiscated rifles and revolvers will now be taken from your ship. They will be given back one day." The soldier paused. "I am ordered to say this: all British will be respected. Our countries are good friends, not at war."

"Quite—I agree. Is there to be restriction on the movements of myself or my ship's company?"

"Only for the shore, *Capitan*. Aboard the ship, no."

"I see. Then make your dispositions, Sergeant. If I'm wanted I shall be in my cabin aft. Mr Prebble, a word, if you please."

Halfhyde went down the bridge ladder, followed by his first lieutenant, his mind probing busily into the implications of all the Spaniard had said. In his cabin he gestured Prebble to a chair, remaining standing himself and looking out of the port with an absorbed expression. There was a knock at his door and his servant entered, and stood looking expectant.

"Ah, Bodger."

"Yessir."

Halfhyde lifted an eyebrow, reached out and lifted a corner of the white cloth draped over the arm of Able-Seaman Bodger. "Dirty, Bodger. I go further: filthy!"

"Very sorry I'm sure, sir—"

"Change it, Bodger. We may be in Spanish hands, but we shall not let our standards drop, shall we, Bodger?"

"Oh no, sir—"

"And bring gin for the first lieutenant. For me, whisky."

"Aye, aye, sir." Bodger's portly, comfortable figure moved backwards through the doorway as though leaving the presence of royalty. Halfhyde sat on his bunk and stared thoughtfully at the first lieutenant.

"Well, Prebble, what do you make of it?"

"Make of what, precisely, sir? I don't like capture—"

"I was not referring to that, my dear Prebble. What bothers me is this: there's been no mention of a search."

Prebble fingered his jaw and frowned. "They have no need to mention it, have they? When the time comes, they'll simply go ahead and do it."

"Perhaps—we shall see. But I don't like it. In their minds by now we must surely be what in fact we are: the ship that has Stanley aboard. Yet they talk only of guards and confinement to the ship, and I find that strange."

"Early days, sir! Why, we've only just secured alongside."

Halfhyde sighed. "Well, you may be right. Perhaps my sense of the dramatic has made me see visions . . . things that don't exist. Imagination is not always a friend, Prebble."

"Can you be more precise?" Prebble asked.

"Yes. I see chicanery in high places, and—" Halfhyde broke off as Bodger came back with gin and whisky, followed closely by the leading-signalman, cap under arm and signal clip-board in hand. "Thank you, Bodger. You have a signal for me, Umpleby?"

"Yes, sir." Leading-Signalman Umpleby handed his board across.

Halfhyde, having read the brief message, glanced up at his first lieutenant. "Drink up, Mr Prebble, duty calls me in the person of our leader." He passed the signal to Prebble; it read: *you are to repair aboard immediately.* "The style of Captain Watkiss changes little," Halfhyde observed. "And, as ever, immediately must be taken to mean five minutes ago. There'll be news awaiting me, I shouldn't wonder, from the port authorities."

At the shore end of the gangway a soldier was detached to accompany Halfhyde along the quay to the flotilla leader. The man's heavily booted feet clumped, and his rifle and bayonet rattled: the sounds of escort irritated Halfhyde, as did the blown dust of the port. Everything was dusty, including the soldier's uniform and equipment; dust descended into Halfhyde's lungs with every breath, and the smell of Spain filled his nostrils. Goats roamed the quays and the narrow passages between the dockyard buildings, depositing excreta and urine in the wake of a juvenile goatherd wielding a stick behind encrusted rumps as the beasts searched for fodder and munched at all manner of unlikely refuse. No doubt they were there to provide fresh milk for the seamen of the Spanish Fleet. It was a far cry from the cleanliness and order of the Royal Naval dockyards at Portsmouth, Chatham and Devonport: even the barrack hulks, though decrepit enough and airless below-decks, were better than this. Halfhyde reached the side of the leader and proceeded up the gangway, his guard remaining behind to chat with his comrades on watch and emit a stream of tobacco-stained saliva on to the quay. At the head of the gangway the officer of the day, in company with Beauchamp, stood at the salute. The bosun's pipes shrilled in recognition of an officer commanding a seagoing ship.

"Captain Watkiss demands my presence," Halfhyde said as he stepped on to the quarterdeck. "Is this a case of all commanding officers, Mr Beauchamp?"

Beauchamp shook his head. "No. Just you."

"I see. And the mood, or need I not ask?"

"Touchy . . . very touchy."

"Well, that's to be expected in the circumstances." Halfhyde followed Beauchamp down to Captain Watkiss's cabin, an apartment far larger than those of the other commanding officers, its size being due partly to Watkiss having, upon his appointment, taken in the cabin next door by process of the removal of a bulkhead. Watkiss, seated at a large roll-top desk, was clad in a curious uniform of his own devising, one that Halfhyde recognized from their late sojourn in Russian waters: a white number ten tunic in conjunction with a pair of white shorts, so long in fact that, dangling from the stomach's immensity like a kilt, they reached a little way below the knees. Halfhyde made the assumption that in sporting this strange rig Captain Watkiss intended disrespect towards the Spanish authorities.

Watkiss looked round at Halfhyde's approach. "Ah, Halfhyde. All right, Mr Beauchamp, that's all, thank you." He remained silent, staring rudely, as Beauchamp took his departure, then he placed his monocle in his eye and surveyed Halfhyde. "Now, my good sir. I hope you're satisfied with your blundering about between two heavy Spanish ships, without orders to do so— mark that: *without orders to do so*. You have lost three men dead—I'll say no more. I pay you the compliment of knowing well that you are blaming yourself, and that you hate losing your men as much as I."

"Thank you, sir. For my part, I offer no excuses. I acted on impulse, and I failed. I'm sorry, sir."

Watkiss nodded. The monocle dropped back to the end of its toggle. "Then we understand each other, Mr Halfhyde. You will not have heard the end of it, but now we must pass to other matters."

"Colonel Stanley, sir?"

"Yes. Sit down."

Halfhyde sat on a settee below a couple of scuttles, the thick glass of which was in each case closed against the inrush of the dust; Watkiss swivelled to face him, thrusting into his gaze an area of knobbly knee between the bottoms of the long shorts and the tops of long white stockings. "Stanley hasn't been interfered with yet, I trust?"

"No, sir. He is tired, no doubt, of a stoker's life, and he is black as coal, but—"

"A stoker's life, Mr Halfhyde?" Watkiss's eyebrows went up. "What's this I hear?"

Halfhyde explained. "It was the only course—"

"*Stoker!*" Captain Watkiss interrupted disparagingly. "A Colonel of the Blues! I don't like it, Mr Halfhyde, I don't like it at all. One of the best county families, don't you know!"

"But a *safe* member of such, sir—so far at any rate. It was unavoidable."

"Yes, well." Watkiss breathed hard down his nose, still put out. "Oh, very well, Mr Halfhyde, very well! But how the devil are we to get him to Gibraltar, I'd like to know!"

"A problem, sir, but I've never yet met a problem that wasn't accompanied by its solution, if only one could see it."

Watkiss shifted irritably. "Words, words! It's action I want, not words. I thought of the Embassy, of course, but those buggers won't allow access."

"Incommunicado? As I thought."

"Very clever of you," Watkiss said sneeringly. He polished his monocle with the corner of a handkerchief. "Have you no other thoughts to offer, Mr Halfhyde?"

"I have one, sir." Halfhyde proceeded to formulate the theory he had started to discuss with Prebble. "There has been no insistence upon a search, sir, that is, of *my* ship—"

"Nor of mine. Nor, so far as I'm aware, of the rest of the

flotilla—but that will come, Halfhyde, that will come."

"I suggest that it may not, sir."

"May not? My dear fellow, that was the whole point of bring-ing us into Cartagena, wasn't it?"

"Ostensibly, sir. But I have managed to speak circumspectly to Colonel Stanley . . . Stoker First-Class Smith, who struck the petty officer of the boiler-room watch." Halfhyde explained the circumstances briefly. "Colonel Stanley conveyed that not all persons were to be trusted. At that moment he was referring to my ship's company, those who were on the bridge and could overhear. But I believe his words are capable of a wider appli-cation, sir. My own mind had run along similar lines earlier—that is, I had thought more people than the Duke of Villanueva de Cordoba could well be involved."

"Against Her Majesty?"

"Yes, sir."

"Spaniards?"

"Highly placed Spaniards, sir. I would by no means impugn the Spanish government as such, but Villanueva is not the only fanatic, I'll be bound."

Watkiss pursed his lips. "Well, I dare say you're right. Yes. But what, precisely, are you suggesting?"

"That there will be no search, sir—"

"Oh, rubbish! What other excuse can they offer for their damn highseas piracy, I'd like to know!"

"Plenty can be trumped up, sir. False accusations, inexact statements—"

"Don't be mealy-mouthed, Mr Halfhyde, I dislike it. Spaniards, like all dagoes, are bloody liars. What?"

"If you wish, sir. I suggest there will be no search because certain persons don't particularly want Colonel Stanley *per se*. Indeed, from the diplomatic point of view, which is said to be important, it would suit them better perhaps if he were not found. Once found, he would have to be removed and would become the centre of an international furore."

Watkiss stared uncomprehendingly. "You mean, just leave him?"

"Exactly, sir. So long as he remains in Cartagena, the threat to the Queen exists."

There was a startled silence, broken by Captain Watkiss. "Good God, Mr Halfhyde, are you serious?"

"Perfectly serious, sir. While we and Colonel Stanley are held helpless here, the Queen will die. When she is dead, some formula will be found to release us with profuse apologies. The Spanish will not be seen to be involved. The Queen's death will have come at the hands of Italians, who will have been got out from Scotland by sea . . . and will no doubt be taken to some South American state, well lined with Spanish gold."

"But Italy—will Italy not become involved, even if Spain is not?"

Halfhyde nodded. "Undoubtedly private Italian citizens will, but what skin is that off the nose of Spain, sir?"

"Yes. Yes, I see that." Watkiss looked sage for a moment, then grew excited. His face darkened and he shook a fist in the air. "By God, Halfhyde, what devious buggers these dagoes are to be sure! It's damn clever, just to hold us here, willy-nilly! Well, they'll never get me to play that game!"

"But what will you do, sir? We must think practically now— that is, if my ideas are right. You are allowed no communication with the Embassy, or the British Consul I take it. And the port is heavily guarded. The flotilla wouldn't have a cat in hell's chance of getting clear away to sea."

"I don't know so much about that, Halfhyde, we're not lily-livered, are we?" Watkiss waved a hand in the direction of the open sea. "Out there lies a British battle squadron, and—"

"We can't be sure of that, sir."

"*I* can," Watkiss said promptly. "Why, no British admiral would slink away and leave any of Her Majesty's ships at peril—that's unthinkable!"

"Diplomacy is diplomacy, sir. I understood you to make the very point earlier, that the rear-admiral in Gibraltar has under-lined the need for full diplomatic handling of the whole situation?"

"Yes, yes, yes! Oh, balls to the diplomats, Halfhyde, why can't the world be run by seamen? Are you saying the battle-ships won't lie off, just in case some damn diplomat is given the vapours?"

"More or less, sir—"

"But at the very least they'll make a report in Gibraltar, won't they?"

"Certainly—we can be sure of that—"

"Then the fur will fly! Our release will be demanded!"

"But will not be granted, sir."

"Oh, God!" As if in supplication, Captain Watkiss raised two pudgy fists and flourished them towards the deckhead above. "All this rubbish . . . it's no more than your own stupid sup-position, isn't it? Where's the supporting evidence, may I ask?"

"Hard to come by, sir. It's circumstantial . . . but it points in the direction I've outlined. That signal by lamp from the shore . . . the fitted chest, that floated us safely and with intent towards the flotilla. Someone, sir, had no wish to apprehend Colonel Stanley—only to inhibit him, perhaps." Halfhyde paused, then added sombrely, "There's another thing, sir— Colonel Stanley was emphatic on one point that struck me as curious: he does not wish to be taken to Gibraltar."

"Well, of course not, since the Queen's to die in Scotland!"

"You miss my point, sir. There's a wireless station in Gibraltar, and his warning can be passed by cable to Whitehall—"

"Oh, yes. Yes, of course. That was the original object—I agree." Watkiss looked for a moment pathetic. "I have so many worries, don't you know. Command of a flotilla brings its cares, I am responsible for everything, the mind becomes burdened. The ward-room cheese has become uneatable because the damn steward forgot to place it in a cool stowage. One thing after another! But I take your point." The pathetic aspect was overcome by a surge of belligerency. "Why, then, does he not want to be put in communication with the Court, Halfhyde?"

"I don't know, sir."

"Find out, then."

"Yes, sir."

"A matter of priority, Mr Halfhyde, a matter of priority." Watkiss frowned. "Is there something fishy, is that what you're saying now, something fishy about Stanley?"

"I don't say that, sir—"

"And you'd better not!" Watkiss said energetically. "It would be damn impertinence! Why, the feller's a former Colonel of the Horse Guards; he can't be fishy! Man's a *gentleman!* He rides to hounds—you don't do that if you're fishy!" He simmered, gradually calming down. He frowned. "Avoiding a wireless station . . . h'm. That *is* what you're saying, isn't it, Mr Halfhyde?"

"I don't know, sir. But there are some curious aspects. I'll carry out your orders and investigate—"

"Yes, do. Report as soon as possible. You'll not find me wanting if there's fishiness. Her Majesty's safety is my first consideration. I am part of her Fleet, Mr Halfhyde, part of her succour and salvation." Captain Watkiss stood up in his extraordinary shorts; a draught along the alleyway, ruffling the curtains across the cabin door, also ruffled the shorts so that they flapped briefly like an ensign around a flagstaff: for a rotund officer, Watkiss had remarkably thin legs, like knitting-needles thrust into a pumpkin. Borne as it were along the wings of the draught came Mr Beauchamp with tidings.

"Captain, sir—"

"Oh dear, yes, what is it, Mr Beauchamp? Not the cheese again, I hope. Must I be bothered with every damn detail?"

"No, sir, not the cheese, sir. A message for Mr Halfhyde from his first lieutenant, sir, brought by a—"

"Oh, get on with it, Mr Beauchamp, for heaven's sake get on with it!"

"Yes, sir. A stoker has died aboard *Vendetta,* sir, and Mr Halfhyde's presence is required immediately."

Chapter 10

ON HIS WAY BELOW Halfhyde spoke into Prebble's ear. "Stanley?"

"No, sir."

Halfhyde let out a long sound of relief. "Thank God for that! The whole thing quickly, if you please, Mr Prebble."

"Yes, sir. Leading-Stoker Peters, sir. Natural causes, not that I'm a doctor. He's not young, sir, and was overcome by the heat in the boiler-room, that's my diagnosis."

Halfhyde nodded, bending his tall frame beneath the deck-head as he entered the stokers' mess. The dead man had been brought up from below when he had collapsed, and laid on a table in his broadside mess. Halfhyde, his cap removed as he had entered, looked down sadly on the body. It was grey-haired, the face seamed with lines and puckers, the flesh now pallid, the mouth hanging open slackly as though in a last effort to draw breath. In the absence of a doctor in the flotilla, Prebble had acted, but had in fact been unable to do anything. The man, he said, had been dead on his arrival in the boiler-room: there had been no pulse, no flutter from an overworked heart, no breathing. Halfhyde, his face grim, felt in his pocket for his knife: with the opened blade he made a small cut in a vein. There was no movement of blood. He straightened. "Dead undoubtedly. We're not having much luck, Mr Prebble."

"No, sir. On the other hand, sir, it's an ill wind as they say."

Halfhyde looked sharply at his first lieutenant. "I don't follow you." Frowning, he stared down once again at the silent body on the table. "Or do I?" He swung round on the torpedo-coxswain who had accompanied him below with Prebble. "Have the poor fellow taken to the beefscreen, Cox'n," he ordered. "It's the coolest place we have. I shall report to Captain Watkiss and see what arrangements can be made for a funeral. Mr Prebble, a word with you in my cabin."

They left the mess, coming back on to the upper deck to go aft to Halfhyde's cabin. On the quay and at the head of the brow to the shore the Spanish sentries lounged, their rifles slung from their shoulders. Farther along the quay two policemen, armed members of the *Guardia Civil,* walked a slow patrol, chatting as they moved along. The day was hot; the body could not be kept long. In his cabin Halfhyde, curtly dismissing the attentive Bodger who had emerged from his pantry, motioned Prebble to a chair.

"Well, Prebble. I fancy you have the stratagem this time, not I. When you sent your report to me aboard *Venomous,* you could have given the dead man's name to set my mind easy about Stanley—but you did not! There's a connection, isn't there?"

Prebble nodded. "I thought it best no one should know."

"In case I accepted your stratagem, which is to announce the death of Colonel Stanley rather than of poor Peters?"

"Yes, sir."

Halfhyde shook his head. "I think not, my dear Prebble, I think not! To do that would be to admit that we had Stanley aboard all along."

"Which the Spaniards would seem to know in any case," Prebble said.

"Yes. But an official admission would be too much for Captain Watkiss to stomach, I fancy. For one thing, his unblemished reputation for truthfulness apart, he has still to consider the diplomatic aspect, and the diplomats will wish for no admissions."

"Even if the Queen were to die, sir?"

Halfhyde paused, looking hard at Prebble. After a moment he nodded. "Go on, Prebble. You have something to say, I think. Say it."

"Yes, sir. For a start, sir, I dispute your reasoning. The Queen's the nub of this whole business, and her safety's paramount, as Captain Watkiss would be the first to agree. If the diplomats object to an admission, then I say let them object, they're of no real consequence—"

"Other than to the career of the good Captain Watkiss, Prebble."

"Perhaps, sir, but Captain Watkiss has connections, as you know. One sister married to the First Sea Lord, another to the Permanent Secretary to the Treasury. He has good guns to bring to bear against fractious diplomats—"

"Not good enough, Prebble. But go on."

"There's another point, sir. Captain Watkiss responds in different ways according to how he's approached. You'd agree to that?"

Halfhyde grinned. "Indeed I would, Prebble. I take your point. In some ways he's a very malleable man, at least until obstinacy intervenes—and his very obstinacy can often be provoked and guided in the proper direction!"

"That's what I meant, sir—"

"Then let us know the plan, Prebble."

"Yes, sir." Prebble paused. "We announce Colonel Stanley's death, sir, via Captain Watkiss, and we ask permission for burial. With Colonel Stanley dead—"

"Which they'll not believe, Prebble. They're not fools. It's too obvious. However, you may finish."

"Thank you, sir. We ask permission for burial, but not in Spain. A sea burial. Not from one of the flotilla, of course— they wouldn't allow that, I realize. But from a cutter, sir, under oars—and with sail ready."

"And under close escort from the Spaniards too! Then, I suppose, we sail to Gibraltar, moving faster than the ships that will at once steam out from Cartagena?" Halfhyde laughed. "A well-meant suggestion, Prebble, but too full of holes for me."

"I disagree, sir. There will be British battleships outside, off Cape Tinoso."

"Watkiss made the point too, Prebble. But at best it's problematical."

"Worth the chance, sir. If they're not there, there's nothing lost."

"And if they are there, the Spaniards won't allow us out, not even in a pulling cutter—having once admitted we have Stanley aboard, even though he's said to be dead . . ." Halfhyde paused, eyeing Prebble thoughtfully. "It occurs to me there might be another approach to this! Why use Stanley? Why try to be too clever?"

"Sir?"

Halfhyde said, "We have no need in the world to break diplomacy, to mention Stanley at all, Prebble. He's superfluous, don't you see? The facts are there plain for all to look at, the Spaniards included, are they not? Consider: a man lies dead, and must be buried. That's all. The truth always lends conviction, Prebble—and it's true I'd like to see any of my ship's company committed to the sea rather than buried in this filthy dust of Spain!"

Prebble looked anticipatory. "Yes, sir, indeed. You'll ask permission, then?"

Halfhyde said, "I'll speak to Captain Watkiss first, and Colonel Stanley. Then we shall see."

It was a curious conference, conducted more or less clandestinely: it was vital that no suspicions be aroused. Captain Watkiss, contacted by messenger, strutted along the quay with his first lieutenant, ostensibly to inspect his flotilla; this took time, for Watkiss considered it necessary to visit all ships in the interest of authenticity, and *Vendetta*, as junior ship, must needs be last. Halfhyde waited in growing impatience: Captain Watkiss was, it seemed, making a genuine inspection and would no doubt be sliding a white-gloved hand along the concealed tops of steam pipes and whatnot in a search for dust that should not be there. Watkiss, however, at length arrived and came importantly up the gangway to the wail of the bosun's pipes.

"Mr Halfhyde, it is not the proper service manner to send messengers to a post captain. You either come yourself, or send your first lieutenant, or make a damn signal, which is different."

"I'm sorry, sir."

"Yes. Well. Oh, in the circumstances . . ." Watkiss cast a disparaging look aft towards the damaged stern plating. "That stern! A dockyard job, of course. I'll take the opportunity of looking at it."

"Yes, sir." Halfhyde coughed. "Also the damage below, I think."

"Below?" Watkiss stared, and screwed his monocle into his eye. "You never said—"

"Your pardon, sir. A regrettable omission. I apologize."

"So I should damn well think! An incomplete report—scandalous! I would have expected better of you, Mr Halfhyde."

"Yes, sir. May I suggest we go below first? There's a very nasty fracture and a bend that may let water."

"Are you in danger of sinking, Mr Halfhyde?"

"Not imminently, sir. If you'll please follow me below?" Halfhyde turned away without more ado, catching Prebble's eye. Prebble moved in behind Captain Watkiss and, whilst shepherding him down the ladder from the main deck, gestured to the officer of the day to engage the Spanish guards in conversation. The order had been passed in advance to the ship's company that the party was to be left alone once they were below. Down the ladder they went; through hatches and along alleyways until they reached the aftermost part of the ship below the waterline. A stoker stood there, black as to face, neck and hands, and dressed in boiler-room gear. No one else was present. Watkiss stared.

"I see bent plates, Mr Halfhyde, but no damage leading to the possibility of *sinking!*"

"No, sir. Merely a decoy, to steer you towards privacy—"

"That man." Captain Watkiss pointed at the stoker. "Cap on back to front! Never seen such slackness. Take his name, Mr Halfhyde!"

"I know his name already, sir. It's Colonel Stanley."

"*What!*"

"Your voice, sir—keep it down, if you please."

"Good gracious me! Stanley! Well, you did say he'd been employed below, of course. Yes." Watkiss turned to face Halfhyde. "Now what's all this about?"

"A plan, sir, proposed by Mr Prebble. You know, of course, that one of my stokers has died—"

"Yes, yes." Watkiss surveyed Stanley through his monocle. "My dear Stanley, I'm so glad it wasn't you. What a terrible time you've had!"

"Indeed, but I'm grateful to you, Watkiss—"

"I beg your pardon?" The monocle dropped in sheer surprise: men dressed as stokers did not address Watkiss as Watkiss. Then he recollected himself, replaced the monocle, and cleared his throat. He extended a hand, which Stanley took. "I shall be doing my best to get you out, you may rely upon that. Now, Mr Halfhyde, what is this plan, pray?"

Halfhyde explained; as the explanation developed Captain Watkiss grew more and more restless. There was a gleam in his eye and a pugnacious thrust to his jaw. "Oh, capital! Capital! A brilliant scheme, Mr Prebble, and I congratulate you!"

"There is a snag, sir," Halfhyde said warningly.

"What snag, Mr Halfhyde?"

"We don't know whether or not our battleships are lying off, sir."

"Oh, nonsense, of course we do—that is, we *assume* it. Have you no faith in your own Service, Mr Halfhyde? Of course they'll be there. The snags I see are different: will the Spaniards permit it, and that will be known as soon as we ask their permission. Another is, will a cutter be able to reach the battleships in time? Will it be able to evade the Spanish escort?"

"We can but try, sir."

"*We*, Mr Halfhyde?"

"I must go myself, sir. You and I and Prebble are the only ones apart from Colonel Stanley who know the facts for onward transmission. It is obvious you can't go yourself—"

"There's Prebble," Watkiss said. Then he paused, looking Halfhyde's first lieutenant up and down with an air of disparagement: Prebble, ex-lower deck, was not a gentleman, and this was a task for gentlemen. "Perhaps not, however. Perhaps not."

"I prefer to go myself in any case, sir. I was involved from the start. I should like to finish it."

"And accept the greater risk—well said, Mr Halfhyde, spoken as befits a commanding officer!" Watkiss prodded Halfhyde with his telescope. "A brave officer indeed—but you must not lose sight of the risk to myself as well. Why, if this plan should succeed, I shall be left in the line of the dagoes' fire, shall I not?"

"Only metaphorically, sir."

"Yes, yes, but kindly do not underestimate what you're asking of me and my ships' companies, Mr Halfhyde—not that I or they will be found unequal to the occasion, naturally." The monocle, which had dropped from Watkiss's eye, was replaced. "And you, my dear Stanley? What's your view?"

"It's worth the attempt, I think, Watkiss. Anything's worthwhile in this situation. There's just one thing, and if you decide to go ahead I must insist upon it, I'm afraid."

"Anything you say, my dear fellow." Reaching for Stanley's

shoulder, Watkiss laid a hand gingerly on coal-dust. "I'm here to help, you know."

Stanley nodded. He said, "I must go in the boat with Halfhyde."

Watkiss looked interrogatively at Halfhyde, who had drawn in his breath sharply. "Well?"

"I don't advise it at all, sir," Halfhyde answered. "It's far too great a risk. We shall have no better than a fifty-fifty chance, and if we fail, Colonel Stanley will be removed ashore with the rest of us and the information will never reach England."

"Oh, stuff-and-nonsense! Those buggers can't keep us here indefinitely!"

"Not indefinitely, sir. But for long enough—until it's too late. We have little more than a week in hand now."

"H'm." Watkiss frowned. "Yes, yes. I see what you mean. Yes. A point, is it not, Stanley?"

"I thought I had made myself clear, Watkiss." Stanley said coolly. "If this expedition is put in hand, then I go too. Whether or not it is done at all is up to you and Halfhyde." He laughed, but there was an edge to his voice as he went on: "Must we talk in terms of failure, gentlemen? In my experience as a regimental officer, failure was never so much as considered. Do you *expect* to fail?"

"It's not customary in Her Majesty's Navy," Watkiss snapped, much put out, "but a wise officer considers it in his calculations. I tend to agree with Halfhyde: I think you should remain aboard, and see what happens."

"Then the attempt will not be made at all." Stanley was cool and emphatic, his attitude contrasting so strongly with his stoker's rig as to make Halfhyde fear Watkiss might at any moment charge him with insubordination. "This is my business, and while I'll be grateful for any help, it must and will remain mine in basis. It is for me, and me alone, to pass my information to the proper quarter." He paused. "You'll recall that I brought no diplomatic bag with me. My information is in my head alone, and it must remain there. I'm sorry to be uncooperative to that extent, but as Her Majesty's Messenger my tongue is tied."

"You mean you have further information, my dear fellow?"

"Yes."

Watkiss screwed his monocle more firmly into place. "I am, I think, to be trusted?"

Stanley made an impatient gesture. "Of course! That's not in dispute, Watkiss. I, however, have my orders, and—"

"Yes, yes. Yes, indeed—I shall certainly not pry. Well, Mr Halfhyde, I think I have no option but to agree. You will take Colonel Stanley."

"You are making a mistake, sir, if I may say so—"

"You may not say so, Mr Halfhyde, you are impertinent and I dislike impertinence, dislike it intensely." Captain Watkiss once again shook Stanley warmly by the hand and wished him good luck; then he turned on his heel and strutted back along the alleyway, his hands clasping his telescope behind his thick rump.

To Halfhyde's surprise, Watkiss's request was granted by the Spanish authorities without any delay; Halfhyde suspected that de Valdares might well have put in a word. De Valdares was a gentleman and a seaman, and would understand seamen's ways.

Besides, their countries were officially friendly and the Spanish might have decided to go out of their way to make some sort of amends to a man who had died whilst in their, strictly illegal, constraint. Along with a saturnine person of self-importance who was fairly obviously a government agent, a decrepit man with thin white hair and a dirty skin came aboard, announcing himself to be a doctor of medicine; this man viewed the body and satisfied himself as to the fact of death. He issued a certificate; the *politico* carried out a close scrutiny of the body and stipulated that, when sewn by British naval custom into its hammock, with fire-bars at the feet to ensure a clean and swift descent, it should have its face left uncovered. Halfhyde protested, but to no avail: there was evidently to be no loophole for a substitution. The *politico* would personally view the body again as it went over the side for the sea burial, which was to take place that same afternoon outside the port. *Vendetta's* cutter was approved for use by a Spanish naval officer who boarded shortly after the doctor had finished his business; and an escort of two armed steam tugs would be provided with marksmen in the bows. A firing-party would not be permitted to accompany the cortège, but, if the British captain wished, the men aboard the steam tugs would fire a volley over the corpse as it took the water. Frostily Halfhyde refused: no one but British seamen, he said, would be permitted to take an actual part in the ceremonies.

"We may as well not bother now," he said privately to Prebble. "We can't expect to have the heels of steam tugs!"

"It's a blow, sir, I don't deny, but it's too late to walk back on it now."

"True." Halfhyde, frowning, paced his quarterdeck. "Well,

we may be lucky, much as I doubt it. If the battleships are there, and close us when they see the White Ensign . . . there may just be time."

"They could support us with small-arms fire, I suppose. At least to hold off an easy pursuit . . . seeing as the Spanish have acted improperly in the first place."

Halfhyde nodded. "If I knew the vice-admiral personally, Prebble, I could say more certainly. Some would take a chance, others would play safe. We must hope and pray, that's all. It's in the lap of the gods, for good or ill." Suddenly, Halfhyde gave a shiver, an involuntary movement that he could not control. "I fear ill, Prebble."

"That's not like you, sir."

"No." Halfhyde forced a laugh. "Then I shall direct my glass to the side of the good! I'm going to my cabin, Prebble. Be so kind as to send Colonel Stanley to me." He turned away and strode towards the hatchway leading down to the cabin alley-way. In his cabin he awaited Stanley, now under orders to transform himself into an upper-deck rating, a member of the seaman branch: Stanley had said he was handy in a boat; though unaccustomed to naval procedures, he would at all events not appear a greenhorn. After a couple of minutes the former Colonel of the Blues appeared, attired in clean white uniform with three good conduct stripes upon his left upper arm and his cap held smartly down his left side as he faced Halfhyde. Halfhyde bade him enter, and then shut the door behind him.

"It promises to be a tricky business, sir," Halfhyde said. He told Stanley of the steam tugs. "The committal will, of course, be completed before I make any attempt at escape. I regret the need to use a sea burial as a subterfuge, but the cause is just.

The moment the body is safely in the water I shall make towards our battleships—if they're there. If not—" He shrugged. "We return, in the acceptance of defeat, no better off, and no worse, than when we set out."

"I understand that," Stanley said. "How do you propose to make way—by sail, or oars?"

"Oars in the first place, sir. If the wind is fair, the mast will be stepped and sail sent aloft while we are under way." He added, "We shall have a chance, but a slim one. The steam tugs will, I expect and hope, have their engines stopped during the committal of the body to the deep. Strong arms can get a cutter under way faster than a steam vessel's engine can overcome its inertia, and we shall make fair speed across the territorial limit."

"And the guns, Halfhyde?"

"I doubt if they will open into international waters in the presence of a battle squadron of the Mediterranean Fleet, sir. I also doubt if they will in any case shoot to kill, but only to recapture." His tone became solemn, full of warning. "I have to say—to repeat—that the chance is a slim one. If you are taken by the Spaniards, what happens to Her Majesty?"

Stanley's face was bleak. "I must then leave her in Captain Watkiss's hands and yours. But accompany you I must."

At six bells in the afternoon watch the cutter left *Vendetta*'s quarter-boom and was pulled alongside the lowered accommodation-ladder for the embarkation of the body and its bearer-party. When the *politico* had made his identification of the yellowish, immobile face it was decently covered with the folds of the White Ensign, symbol of Britain's maritime might, and the hammock-sewn corpse was brought on deck and carried down the ladder to be grappled in by the hands of the cutter's crew and laid, head to bow, along the thwarts between the stalwart seamen who would pull it out to sea on its last journey. Behind the corpse came Halfhyde, wearing his sword, his head bowed and a prayer-book in his hand. As he stepped aboard his glance rested for a moment on Colonel Stanley, now seated with his oar held up-and-down between his knees, blade uppermost in the proper manner of a boat's crew waiting for the order to pull away.

Sitting in the stern-sheets, Halfhyde glanced up at Prebble, with the officer of the day and a full gangway staff, standing at the salute on the quarterdeck. He nodded at the boat's coxswain.

"All right, Parslow."

"Aye, aye, sir." Leading-Seaman Parslow raised his voice. "Bear off for'ard, bear off aft." Bowman and sternsheetsman both thrust out with their boathooks and the cutter moved out into the stream. Parslow gave his next order, and down came the oars, dropping into the rowlocks and feathering the water with the flats of the blades. "Hold water starboard, up hard port." Then, as the cutter swung round and found its outward course, "Give way together!"

They went at a respectful funeral pace for the entrance, past the curious crowds of dockyard workers on the quays, past Spanish warships. The word had spread and there was deep reverence for death. Salutes came from the ships, to be punc-tiliously returned by Halfhyde; the dockyard sounds—the ham-mers and the furnaces, the steam engines and the riveters—were for a space in a kind of suspension. From towards the harbour entrance the two steam tugs appeared, dispersing the silence with their busy engines and billowing out their thick black smoke to lay it across the port waters like a shroud dropping from the sky. The cutter moved towards them; the crew pulled easily still, conserving their energies for the dash to freedom afterwards. They had been told the present objective, but Halfhyde, who normally believed in taking his ship's company into his full confidence, had not on this occasion been able to go further; but no matter. The men had full trust in their captain and would do all that was required without question. As the steam tugs took up their stations and headed out in company for the entrance Halfhyde, looking away to starboard towards Cape Tinoso, found his heart leaping into his mouth: distantly, he could see the masts and fighting-tops of heavy ships.

Watkiss had been right: the Mediterranean Fleet had indeed left its battle squadron guarding yet.

Chapter 11

THEY EMERGED from the port's constriction into wider waters, the cutter with its sad cargo and the tugs with their billowing funnels and their great side-paddles churning the blue water into sand-coloured turbulence. Outside there was a little wind, no more than a puff as the sun lowered towards the west, but Halfhyde was relieved to find it. Gently it ruffled the deep sea beyond the territorial limits of the power of Spain; it might be enough to carry him into free waters ahead of the tugs and the rifles, far enough at least to reach the spread umbrella of the British Fleet.

With the boat's compass Halfhyde checked his bearings: he was approaching the position authorized by the port authority for the committal, a point far enough off shore for the purpose but well inwards of the territorial limit. "Nearly there, Parslow," he said, "but we'll continue past and see what happens."

"Aye, aye, sir." Parslow went on calling the stroke, still taking it easy. Set fore and aft atop the thwarts the single mast lay alongside the shrouded corpse, ready to be brought out and stepped in its shoe; the mainsail lay untrapped in the bows. It would not take long to shake out and set, though it might prove just a shade too long . . . Parslow, a hand shading his eyes from the glare off the water, said suddenly, "The battle squadron, sir! It's under way, sir, and moving in!"

"Thank you, Parslow, I've seen for myself. They'll come no closer than the international limit, but every fathom of distance gained is to the good."

"Will they have got the word, sir, do you suppose?"

"No, but every glass aboard those ships will be trained on us, Parslow, and the White Ensign has a habit of standing out." The move to sea continued: the water slid past, spray flew from the blades as they dipped and rose again. After a while there was a hoarse, metallic-sounding shout through a megaphone from one of the steam tugs, and Halfhyde said calmly, "They're calling us. We've gone a shade too far, I fancy, Parslow!"

"Belay pulling, sir?"

"One moment. I am an ageing man, if not so much as you! I have heard nothing."

Parslow grinned, showing a few stumps of teeth. "As for me, sir, I'm deaf as a gun-barrel."

"Good!" The cutter moved onward. The shouts and yells increased, and Halfhyde, fearing rifle fire, sighed and said, "All right, far enough, we mustn't provoke them too much just yet." As Parslow gave the order to lay on the oars, and then to bring them inboard, Halfhyde took up his own megaphone and called to the tug: "I'm sorry, I went past the point. Now I am heaving-to and will start the committal. Do you understand?"

From the tug's bridge a hand waved in acknowledgement. Halfhyde called to his bowman, who bent and began pulling out a plank laid beneath the thwarts. When clear this plank was sent amidships and balanced across the gunwhale; then the corpse was with some difficulty and much sweat manoeuvred on to the plank, the end of which was held securely inboard by two seamen who at the same time laid hold of the inboard end of the White Ensign. Gently the cutter rocked to the movement; the light breeze was blowing still, and giving some welcome coolness.

Halfhyde, standing in the stern-sheets, began the simple service, speaking in a strong voice and with sincerity as the boat's crew sat with bowed and capless heads. "Man that is born of woman hath but a short time to live, and is full of misery. He cometh up, and is cut down, like a flower . . ." He read on, his voice going out across the waters. When the prayer was ended, the Navy's time-honoured hymn was sung in voices that were not untuneful and held no self-consciousness, even though those same voices were more accustomed to the earthy badinage of the mess decks of the Fleet: "Eternal Father, strong to save, Whose arm hath bound the restless wave . . ." the hymn was sung to its tremendous conclusion, and then Halfhyde, coming to the committal itself, nodded at the seamen holding the plank's inboard end. Bracing themselves, they lifted it a fraction so that it tilted towards the water.

"Forasmuch as it hath pleased Almighty God of his great mercy to take unto Himself the soul of our dear brother here departed: we therefore commit his body to the deep . . ."

Another nod, watched for anxiously by the two members of the bearer-party: the end of the plank went up farther and, with the White Ensign gripped firmly inboard, the body of Leading-Stoker Peters slid into the enfolding waters. It was visible for a few moments as a rolling cigar of white canvas hammock, like some enormous perique of tobacco, then the fire-bars at the feet began to exert their pull and the body with its sad, exposed face slid beneath the surface and was gone. Halfhyde said a final prayer; and then, his heart beating fast though outwardly he was calm, allowed a few moments of reverence and silence to pass. This done, without moving from his bowed stance in the stern-sheets, he passed his orders.

"Get that plank stowed. Parslow, get us under way. Bates and Colonel Stanley, step the mast and send up sail. Smack it about now, we have not a second to lose!"

The drill was perfect: scarcely half a second seemed to pass before the oars were taking the water, the blades biting deep and pulling well and with every ounce of beef and muscle behind them. The cutter shot ahead for the limit of Spanish jurisdiction, making a straight cleave through the blue sea and heading direct for the flagship of the vice-admiral commanding the battle squadron. The British ships had continued to move in, but now there was a curfuffle below their counters as the screws thrashed astern to bring them up short of the line: the vice-admiral was not risking any infringement of sovereign rights. By Halfhyde's reckoning they had some two miles of sea to cover and the chance was as slim as ever, though he had been right enough about the comparative slowness of the steam tugs to get way upon them: they had, in the event, been left standing, with enormous gouts of smoke coming from their funnels like the foul breath of an angry Lucifer.

As the boat's crew pulled away from them with long but wonderfully fast strokes, Bates and Stanley withdrew the mast from the thwarts and set its heel into the shoe protruding from the bottom boards. Stanley set about securing the guys while the more nimble Bates brought out the sail. Halfhyde, looking back, gave a shout of joy. "We look like doing it! They have trouble back there!" He removed his cap and waved it astern towards the tugs, a wave of sheer exultancy. Steam was a two-edged sword: steam could lead to mechanical breakdown, to overheated bearings, to all manner of misfortunes—especially when engineers and their messy machines were being harried to greater effort! From one of the tugs there was coming a tremendous plume of white steam accompanied by a great blasting noise. The second tug, although beginning now to move, was somewhat farther off, and every second brought the speeding cutter closer to the British shield beyond. Firing had started, and there were small pinpricks in the water as the bullets, falling short or wide or over, spent themselves uselessly. Disregarding bullets, Halfhyde waved once more and called over his shoulder: "We're all but there! Pull with a will, my lads, and make sure of it!"

Then disaster came: there was a shout from for'ard and Halfhyde turned. He turned in time to see arms and legs flying as a man went overboard, and he heard the renewed shout: "It's Colonel Stanley, sir!"

Halfhyde swore roundly. "The devil it is!" He looked astern; Stanley was already well aft, coming to the surface but wallowing inert with his head down: by the look of it he had hurt himself as he went over, had very likely knocked himself out. Halfhyde looked all round: the tugs were still well astern, the British warships were still too far ahead and in any case could still be presumed to be unwilling to enter Spanish waters. Halfhyde broke out in a sweat of fury and frustration, but made up his mind to it. "Bring her round, Parslow. Back for Colonel Stanley. We have no damn option now!"

It was a return in ignominy to face much trouble, with Stanley, conscious now but of formidable face, saturated upon a thwart.

His manner was as forbidding as his face; he refused to answer Halfhyde's questions, snapping out that he was not to be interrogated like a criminal or a prisoner-of-war. The steam tugs kept close astern; mechanical defects had apparently yielded to human ingenuity, and the tug that had been lame now swam with its sister, emitting noises that could have been taken for those of triumph. Halfhyde was in a foul mood: his luck had been cruel, even wicked. As they re-entered the port, there was a stir of interest, but interest of a less reverent kind than on their outward journey: the tugs had signalled ahead. Halfhyde wondered wretchedly what would now face his ship and Colonel Stanley: the Spaniards could not help but react badly to an escape bid and the British word would no longer be trusted in the circles of authority.

Moving in, Halfhyde came within visual range of the rest of the flotilla. Lifting his telescope he trained it on the leader's bridge and saw what he had expected to see: at the guardrail stood Captain Watkiss, staring back at him from beneath the gold-encrusted rim of his cap-peak. If Captain Watkiss knew the facts already, he would be a-boil; and in any case he would know them before long, and Halfhyde could not escape the scalding that would be the result of the boiling process. Watkiss, however, he had survived before and would survive again. But what of Her Majesty, a little closer now to her journey to Balmoral—and the assassin's hand?

It was a return to a kind of arrest: as he set foot upon his quarterdeck Halfhyde was informed by Prebble that already the port authority had reacted: no one was to leave the ship in future.

"And Colonel Stanley?"

"No word yet, sir. They won't know about him, will they, sir?"

"No, but they're clearly going to suspect he was in the cutter. Trouble is on the way, Mr Prebble. The first thing to do, and to be done double quick, is to return Stanley to the boiler-room whether he is fit or not, and substitute another seaman rating to complete the cutter's crew. See to it, if you please, Mr Prebble."

"Aye, aye, sir."

Halfhyde went below to his cabin, eyed with curiosity by the Spanish guards at the head of the brow on the other side of the ship. His mood was foul still, and bitter, and was made no softer when a couple of minutes later Prebble came down to report a sight of Captain Watkiss coming along the quay.

Halfhyde gave a sour smile. "For what purpose we may well guess! And made the angrier for being denied his usual signal for me to repair aboard immediately!"

"Yes, sir." Prebble coughed. "He has an angry look, as a matter of fact—"

"The obvious, my dear Prebble, calls for no report from you. I'll come up. Captain Watkiss shall be properly received and his heart may be touched thereby—though I doubt it." With Prebble at his heels, Halfhyde climbed the ladder back to the quarter-deck, arriving at the head of the gangway just as Captain Watkiss reached its foot and was intercepted by the sentry and a stream of Spanish. Captain Watkiss looked up at the deck, impatiently.

"I don't understand this man, Mr Halfhyde."

"I think he's stopping your progress aboard, sir."

"Damned impertinence!" Captain Watkiss thrust out with his telescope and pushed the sentry inexorably backwards. "You shall *not* stop a post captain in Her Majesty's Fleet boarding a

vessel under his command." The Spaniard seemed utterly astonished and uncertain; Captain Watkiss turned his back upon him
and bounced up the gangway. The Spaniard on guard duty at
the inboard end was as flabbergasted as his comrade on the
jetty, and stood helpless before the angry eyes and red face of
the senior officer. As the shrilling of the bosun's calls stopped
and the arms came down from the salute, Watkiss said, "Now,
Mr Halfhyde, a word in your ear below."

"By all means, sir."

"That is impertinent, Mr Halfhyde, as you well know. It sug-
gests agreement. I do not seek agreement, I give orders, and
orders are obeyed."

Halfhyde glared, made no answer, but turned towards the
hatchway. Upon arrival in his cabin, Watkiss seated himself
without invitation, placing his gold-oak-leaved cap on a shelf
where it caught the last rays of the late afternoon sun streaming through the port. "You have made a monkey's breakfast,
Mr Halfhyde, as I suspected you might."

"I'm sorry, sir. I cannot be expected to control Colonel
Stanley's lack of sea legs."

"While aboard your ship or its boats, he is under your command, one of your ship's company in effect. As the officer commanding, all hands are your responsibility. In any case, why did
you not proceed to sea and join the Fleet?"

"Because I could not leave a man to drown, sir."

Watkiss snapped, "He wouldn't have drowned."

"With respect, sir, I was there and you were not. He had hit
his head, and had gone into the water unconscious. My duty
was to pick him up."

"Your duty was, and is, to Her Majesty, Mr Halfhyde—"

"And the best way to perform it is to ensure the safety of Colonel Stanley—"

"Don't damn well argue with me, Mr Halfhyde, I am your superior officer. I shall tell you what your duty is, and you shall perform it. That's fact—I said it. Your duty was to make contact with British ships and speed the word to London, and you have not done it—"

"No, sir, I have not done it, but I submit that I have rescued Colonel Stanley—"

"You—"

"Who is a former Colonel of the Blues—"

"I—"

"A good regiment. A gentleman. Rides to hounds. A Queen's Messenger. Do you not see, sir?"

"See what?"

"I have saved your bacon, sir. Colonel Stanley's various attributes just itemized could not be allowed to sink. Or if they had, then so, I think, would you."

"Oh." Captain Watkiss's monocle dropped from his eye. "Why me?"

Halfhyde made a sweeping gesture and gave a mocking half bow towards his superior officer. "Your responsibility, sir. You command the flotilla, we are all your minions, are we not?"

"Yes," Watkiss answered absently. He frowned. "You have a point, I'll agree. We've saved poor Stanley—kept him out of dago hands, what's more! We were ordered to do that, were we not?"

"Exactly, sir. But for how much longer will Colonel Stanley remain free of Spanish investigation? I think, sir, we have now to consider the future rather than the past."

"Well, of course, we have indeed—which is why I object to your habit of harking back on water that's gone under the bridge, Mr Halfhyde, in an attempt to justify your actions or lack of them. You've done nothing but waste time—" He broke off: Prebble was in the doorway, looking anxious. "What is it, Mr Prebble, can't you see I'm busy?"

"If you'll excuse me, sir, *my* first lieutenant," Halfhyde said coldly. "Yes, Mr Prebble?"

"I'm sorry, sir, to interrupt. Able-Seaman Morgan has a report to make to you, sir."

"Morgan . . . bowman of the cutter, Mr Prebble?"

"Yes, sir. He says the matter's most urgent and that Captain Watkiss should hear it as well as you."

"Very well, Mr Prebble, and the report?"

"I have brought Morgan with me, sir. I think you should hear it from him." Prebble stepped aside and held the curtain back. Able-Seaman Morgan appeared, looking deferential, his cap at his side. Beneath a thick black beard, his lips seemed to tremble slightly, and there was a wary look in his eyes: Halfhyde read the signs. Morgan was about to enter dangerous waters, and had screwed up his courage to face them doggedly.

"Well, Morgan, what is it?"

"Beg pardon, sir." Morgan stopped there, sweating.

"You have come to say something, Morgan. Say it. You'll not be eaten for supper!"

Morgan smiled and swallowed. "No, sir. I know that, sir. But it sounds daft, sir. It don't sound right, not to me even, and it won't to you, sir."

"I shall be the judge of that."

"Yes, sir." Morgan licked his lips, lifted his right hand to deal with an itch at the end of his nose. "It's the gentleman . . ." He glanced quickly at Watkiss, then away again. "Stoker First-Class Smith, sir."

"Go on."

"When 'e went in the drink like, sir. I reckon 'e went in deliberate, sir." There was a startled silence. Morgan went on, "I said it sounds daft, sir, but it's what I saw, sir, honest, strike me dead if it ain't, sir."

Chapter 12

MORGAN WAS SCARED but adamant: Colonel Stanley had gone over the side, clumsily enough to hit his head on the gunwhale as he went, but with full deliberation and a positive intent. Questions, angry ones from Captain Watkiss who plainly disbelieved, failed to shake Able-Seaman Morgan. Halfhyde looked at Prebble in bafflement and in growing concern: what could possibly have been Stanley's motive? Scarcely suicide; had he not hit his head, he would have been safe enough—he was a swimmer or he would hardly have gained any proficiency at boat-handling. It was true that very many naval ratings, the older ones especially, refused to learn to swim in case, being cast adrift in the sea from a foundering ship, their proficiency should prolong the agony of dying. But that would not apply to an amateur yachtsman . . .

Halfhyde nodded at Morgan. "Very well, Morgan, thank you. That's all for now. You've done right, have no fears about that."

"Thank you, sir." Clumsily Morgan turned about and put his cap back on his head. As the man departed, Halfhyde blew out a long breath.

"What do you make of it, Mr Prebble?" he asked.

"He was stating the truth as he saw it, that's beyond doubt in my view, sir."

"Mine too—"

"As he saw it!" Watkiss pounced. "A likely story, Mr Halfhyde, a likely story! Man must be mad! Morgan—he's *Welsh!* Taffy was a Welshman, Taffy was a thief! My God. Damn liar too, I say!"

"No, sir. Morgan's a steady hand, one of my best seamen, honest as the day, and intelligent. Besides, he was scared of what he had to report. Frightened men don't come to the cuddy with lies, sir, when they have no need to open their mouths at all."

"Really! In that case, Mr Halfhyde, you must have a damn sight more experience of command than I, a damn sight." Captain Watkiss brought a large maroon handkerchief from the pocket of his immense shorts, and mopped at his face. "If he's right, what's the reason? Hey?"

"Colonel Stanley has refused to answer my questions, so that's hard to say, sir."

"Yes, it is, isn't it?" Watkiss said with triumph. Then he frowned. "This morning, Halfhyde, you impugned Colonel Stanley's behaviour, or seemed to. When you said he didn't want to be put in touch with London via Gibraltar. No doubt you remember?"

"Yes, sir."

"I told you to find out. Have you?"

Halfhyde said, forbearingly, "There has been no time, sir. We've all had a busy day."

"So the answer's no, and you would have done better to say so than to make excuses. I dislike excuses, dislike them intensely." Watkiss put his handkerchief away again. "You suggested there was something fishy, then we were interrupted by a man dying, were we not?"

Halfhyde said, "It's a way of putting it, I suppose, sir."

"What's that?"

"Never mind, sir. The important consideration is—"

"The important consideration, Mr Halfhyde, is the Queen."

"I agree, sir, but we have not yet arrived at the Queen. In between, there is Colonel Stanley. And, most importantly, we have to consider what we should do in the light of Morgan's report—about Stanley."

"What d'you mean?"

Halfhyde moved irritably. "What I say, sir. Should we face him with it, or should we keep our own counsel?"

"To keep our own counsel would be to insult him, Mr Halfhyde, to find him guilty without trial, without allowing him even to speak in his own defence."

"Then you're accepting, are you not, that there is something to answer for?"

"No, I'm not, Mr Halfhyde, kindly do not put words into my mouth." There was a pause, and a shrewd look. "Can you suggest precisely what this 'something' might be?"

"I can't, sir, at this moment." Halfhyde caught Prebble's eye and gave an almost imperceptible wink: Watkiss was, not for the first time, tending towards agreement without wishing to be seen to do so. "But I think we should consider what *might* be in his mind."

Watkiss said promptly, "I can tell you that: merely a desire, a proper desire, to retain the fullest secrecy!"

"By jumping into the sea, and presumably into Spanish hands, sir?"

"Don't be silly."

"I beg your pardon, sir." Halfhyde bowed again, ironically. "If I may, I shall advance my own theory."

"Well?"

"The reason lies, or may lie, in the result of his going overboard, sir."

Watkiss snapped, "Plain English, if you please, Mr Halfhyde, I dislike riddles, dislike them intensely."

"Yes, sir. What was the result? The result was this: we were prevented from making contact with the British Fleet." Halfhyde once again winked fractionally at Prebble. "And that's fact, sir!"

Captain Watkiss, flying into a temper, had bounded to his feet with the hot announcement that he refused to listen to sedition, slander and impertinence, and would return at once to his own ship rather than have his ears sullied. He strutted along the alleyway, stomach hoisted, shorts flapping, telescope a-cockbill, leaving in his turbulent wake angry remarks about good regiments, gentry, the hunting-field and who the devil did Mr Halfhyde think he was. Seen over the side with proper ceremony, he was halted by the Spanish sentry and made to suffer the indignity of proceeding back to his ship under armed escort like a criminal. Halfhyde sparing a deal of sympathy for Beauchamp who was clearly going to be dog's-body for the rest of the day, watched his senior officer's angry progress for a moment then beckoned Prebble to the other side of the quarterdeck and spoke in a low voice.

"Captain Watkiss is of little help, Mr Prebble, so we must act on our own now."

"In what way, sir?"

"First, Morgan is to be told to keep his mouth shut—I've no doubt he will in any case, but it's to be impressed upon him that Colonel Stanley is not to suspect we have any reservations about him."

"Have we, sir—reservations?"

"I don't know yet," Halfhyde answered, frowning. "Or should I say . . . yes, I have reservations, but as yet nothing more than that. Walk with me, Prebble, but keep quiet. I have some hard thinking to do, and difficult decisions to reach before the Spaniards react to what happened this afternoon." He walked on, his mind busy on all the possible implications. Again he pondered on the light shown from the shore in the lee of Point Calaburras . . . on the questioning of himself by the man Barroso . . . of the buoyancy tanks fitted into the chest. Also of the easy way in which he had made his contact with Barroso in Torremolinos; and of Stanley's apparent determination not to make use of the wireless station in Gibraltar, something that seemed totally unexplained by Stanley's words about secrecy and his inability to trust anyone but himself with his knowledge until he reached London in person. What appeared to emerge was the strong probability, as Halfhyde had reflected before, that other eminent personages besides the Duke of Villanueva de Cordoba were involved in the assassination plot, and that, ludicrously, the persons who had seized Stanley and himself in Malaga, and taken them in the chest to the dungeon, *wanted* Stanley to return to British hands rather than fall into the hands of Spain.

"It makes no sense," he said aloud.

"What does not, sir?"

"Never mind, Prebble. Let me think on. I'll try not to do it aloud." He returned to his brown study: today, if Morgan was right—and Halfhyde felt convinced by the man's patent honesty—

then Stanley had deliberately prevented not only himself but Halfhyde also from being picked up by the Mediterranean Fleet units. Why? What was Stanley's game? Could there be some self-seeking, something to be gained personally by Stanley, some megalomaniac's wish to retain all the kudos for himself alone, the sole saviour of his monarch's life, the saviour thereby of a widespread Empire's integrity? The resultant honours, certainly, would be great indeed: riches, fame, adulation, a duke-dom—all were possible! But if so, where did those Spaniards fit, the apparently friendly ones who wished to get Stanley out of Spain? And how, for God's sake, did Stanley expect to get out of Spain now unless it was by way of the British ships outside the port?

Watkiss himself had used the word: fishy. True, he had used it only to reject it in connection with Stanley, but the word stuck in Halfhyde's throat, a veritable fish-bone. He paced on alongside the silent Prebble, coming to no conclusions other than the one that seemed inevitable: soon, the port authorities would come aboard, stiff with important brass and accompanied by the *politicos,* to search again for Stanley with carbines and revolvers and heavy hands—and likely enough to arrest Halfhyde himself and send him along with Stanley to some stinking inland gaol. The prospect was appalling, both for his own person and for its implications for the Queen's safety. Halfhyde broke out in a sweat; such had at all costs to be prevented. At all costs—and the costs he had in mind now would be high, very high.

He ceased his perambulation and spoke in little more than a whisper. "Mr Prebble."

"Sir?"

"If any Spaniards board—I should say *when* they do—they are to remain aboard. Do I make myself clear?"

"I'm not sure, sir." Prebble sounded puzzled.

"Think, Mr Prebble! How are such Spaniards to be prevented from setting foot ashore again, and how are they to be prevented from removing from my ship any person for whom I'm responsible?"

Light dawned and Prebble's face cleared. "I see, sir. You intend them to be overpowered—to be attacked and taken prisoner?"

"Exactly so, Mr Prebble."

"An uphill task, sir."

"An understatement, Mr Prebble, but it can be accomplished and it shall be. You shall detail assault parties—I think you know the general drill—and in the meantime we shall pray that the Spaniards don't come too soon—too far, that is, before full dark, though I fear we'll scarcely be so lucky!"

"No, sir." Prebble paused. "And then?"

"Then, Mr Prebble, at full dark or soon after, I shall take my ship to sea for Gibraltar, and to the devil with the Spaniards. Colonel Stanley will be aboard. For now there are to be no overt preparations but you'll see to it that we're ready for sea in all respects by sunset."

"Yes, sir. And Colonel Stanley, sir. Do I take it you'll not want him to be told your orders in the meantime?"

"Yes, you may certainly take it as you say, and also see to it that he is allowed no communication with the guards." Halfhyde looked curiously at his first lieutenant. "There is a look of disapproval in your face, Prebble. Do you disagree with my reservations about Colonel Stanley?"

Prebble appeared embarrassed. "Well, I don't rightly know,

sir, and that's the truth. There've been funny goings on, of course. I think I'm . . . unsatisfied about him, I'd not put it more than that, perhaps. And I expect I'm wrong," he added, "to doubt him at all."

"Why so?"

"Why, sir, because gentlemen of Colonel Stanley's sort, they behave properly."

"As gentlemen?" There was a sardonic look in Halfhyde's eye. "Is that what you mean to say?"

"Well, sir, yes it is—"

Halfhyde gave a brief and scornful laugh. "Don't you believe it, Prebble—that is, not as an infallible proposition! Like my own ancestor, old Daniel Halfhyde, gunner's mate under Lord Nelson, you started as a seaman boy. You've come a long way, but by God you have a lot to learn! There are black-hearted gentry as there are black-hearted common people, Prebble, and you should not be dazzled by the brilliant glitter of their backgrounds and upbringing. It's been said, and truly said, that there's none so villainous as the gentleman who's turned from honesty. A gentleman, at least, does not do things by halves."

"Then Colonel Stanley—"

"I don't know any more than you do, Prebble, and I make no accusations in precise terms. But I say this: if Stanley turns out to have been less than honest with us or with Captain Watkiss, it'll have nothing to do with whether or not he's a member of the gentry and late of a fine regiment."

"But," Prebble persisted, "you do believe, in fact, that he *has* been less than honest?"

Halfhyde frowned. "Yes, Prebble, I do. And I am determined

to remove him from Spain and see the result of his landing at Gibraltar."

"Aye, aye, sir. And Captain Watkiss?"

"Captain Watkiss must wave us goodbye and then make his explanations to the Spanish authorities as best he can devise. Myself, I shall in effect only be carrying out my orders from the rear-admiral commanding the Particular Service Squadron."

Below-decks, out of sight from the sentries at the gangway and on the quay, Prebble gave his orders to the torpedo-coxswain, the torpedo-gunner's mate and the gunner's mate, the senior petty officers of the seaman branch; and also to the engineer in charge of the ship's engine-room and its complement. Since arrival the ship had remained at two hours' notice for steam, no order having yet been given by the Spanish to draw fires. The engineer guaranteed to bring his boilers to immediate notice without any sudden or undue signs that would be remarked by the port authorities. Parties of seamen were detailed to hold themselves in alert but unobtrusive readiness in the various sections of the ship, mustering for attack on any Spanish boarding party when given the signal to do so by the leading hands, who would be in charge. Such attacks were to take place strictly below-decks, when the Spaniards would be carrying out the anticipated search of all compartments. When the word should come from Prebble via the petty officers that the ship was about to get under way, the other parties as detailed would rush and disarm the deck sentries and bring them below at speed; and at the same time six seamen under the gunner's mate would move down the gangway and take the quayside guard, bringing the men back aboard to sail with the ship. It was unlikely that in the darkness the taking of the jetty guard, or their subsequent absence, would be seen by the guards on the other ships of the flotilla along the quay; there was enough distance between the ships to ensure reasonable seclusion. Until the Spaniards' weapons had been seized, the ship's company must needs go into action without arms: this had to be accepted, and in any case it was obvious that shots would have brought the whole weight of the local garrison down upon the ship. There would be other weapons, makeshift ones, that would have to be concealed about the person or placed in handy positions without arousing any suspicions from the Spanish guards already aboard: pieces of timber, iron bars from the engine-room, lengths of lead-weighted rope, marlinespikes, and heavy pulley-blocks would be used to their fullest potential. Prebble spoke warningly about the overriding need to lull the Spanish guards: the ratings were not to look too eager, too anticipatory. And he added, his face formal and his tone unwelcoming of questions, that Stoker First-Class John Smith, if not currently on watch below, was to be put on watch and was to remain there without being allowed communication with the guards. If he protested, as no doubt he would, he was to be told it was the captain's order that in his own interest he should be kept as anonymous as possible.

In Halfhyde's cabin half an hour later Prebble reported, "All orders passed, sir, for the moment."

"Thank you, Prebble. And—the ship's company? They're in good heart?"

"Aye, sir. The torpedo-cox'n says they'll be right behind you, sir, and they'll make it a success."

Halfhyde nodded briskly. "Good men and true! If it fails, it'll not be their fault, of that I'm sure at all events. I—" He broke off, suddenly, and crossed to the port. When he turned back his face was tense. "I heard movement . . . troops, Prebble, with sinister men in plain clothes." He brought out his watch and looked at it. "Three bells in the first dog watch, a little after. We have three hours to full dark—a longish time to fill, but not so long as I had feared earlier. Pass the word to stand by, Mr Prebble—and good luck to us all!"

The small cabin was crowded; military officers and *politicos,* the former a-glitter in dusty, faded uniforms, left little room for Halfhyde. Arms were being waved, voices were high. There was an overpowering smell of sweat and not a little garlic. Armed soldiers filled the alleyway outside the cuddy.

A thin man with a cadaver's face prodded Halfhyde's chest. "You will answer, Captain. Where is the man Stanley?"

"I've told you, and I am sick of telling you: I've never heard of him."

"He is aboard your ship!"

Halfhyde shrugged. "Find him then."

"He will be found. There will be a search."

"Good! Then perhaps you'll go away. Admiral de Valdares searched, and found no Stanley."

"I am not Admiral de Valdares—"

"Quite. De Valdares is a gentleman."

The thin man fumed and gesticulated. "You are being so foolish, Captain. You are harbouring a dangerous man, a man who has committed the atrocious crime of murder—of a citizen of Spain, in Spain! If you do not assist the law, then you shall be yourself arrested. Already you have tried to escape, to reach the British ships."

"A natural act, and one expected of any British officer finding himself restrained illegally. Am I and my ship not already in arrest, *señor?*"

"*Si, si!* But more specifically I refer to your own removal ashore to the fortress. This will follow your continued obstruction of justice. In the fortress of Cartagena, life is not pleasant."

"No doubt, but it will not be I who shall sample its horrors." Halfhyde laughed. "Already our ships have been in Cartagena for almost twelve hours, and it is longer since Admiral de Valdares was seen by the British battleships to force my flotilla to enter. It can't be long now before the battleships seek orders—if they have not already done so. One of them will be despatched to Gibraltar, and in all conscience, *señor,* Gibraltar's only a stone's-throw from here! Do you really think the British Admiralty will leave us here to rot at your pleasure?"

"If I were you, Captain, I would not be relying on an entry by your Mediterranean Fleet. Such would be an act of war, would it not?"

"Perhaps. And your act in taking us? What is that, may I ask, if it is not hostile?"

"An act to further the ends of justice, as I have said. You harbour a murderer, and you must give him up."

Halfhyde pulled at his jaw, looking thoughtful. "If I had such a person aboard, and I gave him up, what then?"

"You and all the British ships would be allowed to leave, Captain."

"We would, would we?" Halfhyde asked sardonically. "Tell

me, just as a matter of interest, has my senior officer been told of this?"

"The Captain Watkiss?"

"Yes, the Captain Watkiss."

The Spaniard nodded. "He has been told, but his answer was rude." He paused, eyeing Halfhyde craftily. "Since you have no Stanley, the matter is, what you would say, academic. So I wonder why you ask, Captain?"

"Mere inquisitiveness. The reactions of the Captain Watkiss are always strong, as perhaps you have found out for yourself!"

The dark eyes glittered. "The Captain Watkiss is a strutting dolt who believes himself to be God. I think he forgets he is in Spain."

"I don't think he forgets it at all," Halfhyde said with a grin. For a certainty Watkiss would not have believed in the honesty of the Spanish offer of release any more than he himself did. "But enough of the Captain Watkiss. Let us return to Stanley. I say again, I've no knowledge of him, but my interest is much aroused by all this fuss. Can you be more precise about his crime, and why he committed murder—that is, if he did?"

"It is not your concern," the thin man said offhandedly. "It is a matter for Spain."

"And England doesn't come into it at all?"

"No, no, no! The concern of you and your country is none but to return this man to our justice!" The Spaniard was grow-ing angrier, and could perhaps be provoked into an indiscre-tion in time. Halfhyde continued his questioning, using every possible twist and turn to keep the conversation going: time was passing nicely towards the cloak of night. Once the dark began to come, it would descend swiftly: here as in Gibraltar, the twilight was short. Halfhyde prodded and probed, inflaming the Spaniard's temper more and more, turning all the counter-questions adroitly until the man could stand it no longer.

"I talk no more." The dark eyes were smouldering. "Time is wasting. A search will be made at once."

Halfhyde gave a slight bow. "My ship is at your service. My first lieutenant will accompany you, *señor,* and will give you every assistance."

"Thank you." The agent and his expensive-looking military retinue left the cuddy. With them went the armed men from the alleyway, except for the two who were left to guard Halfhyde. They lounged back against the bulkhead outside his cabin with their rifles held loosely across their bodies.

The search was a lengthy one: Prebble was seeing to that. In accordance with orders already issued, everything that was lockable was locked; even the watertight doors between sections were clipped down hard. Each time a locked compartment was encountered, the rating despatched to find the key seemed to lose himself. Spanish tempers grew more frayed. Prebble was full of apologies and soundly berated the dilatoriness of the key-fetchers. In the coal-black boiler-rooms, lit by the red glow of the furnaces, chunks of coal did curious and unstokerlike things when the search party appeared, and shovels and coal-dust impinged against military splendour until the troglodytes on watch were, by Spanish order, removed from the boiler-room and paraded with their off-watch mates in their mess deck. The plain-clothes man prowled the ranks, studying faces critically and presumably comparing them mentally with Stanley's dossier.

He came to the supposed Stoker First-Class John Smith. He frowned: his nose, or at any rate his photograph-fed eyes, were now picking up the scent, as Prebble saw. Prebble took a deep breath, glanced out of a port, saw the fading light. It was still too early yet for a move to sea, and more waiting, very tense waiting, would be called for, but clearly Stanley was now within an ace of being taken into military custody. Prebble raised a hand high above his head, brought it smartly down to scratch his nose. At the entry to the stokers' mess the seaman boy acting as first lieutenant's messenger vanished from sight, quietly and without attracting attention. He made his way at the double to the airlock into the engine-room, stood for a moment at the top grating, and lifted a hand. Below on the starting-platform the engine-room artificer on watch reached out for the telegraph to the bridge, and brought the handle down smartly in a short movement. On the bridge, the repeater bell sounded briefly. The signalman on watch at once lifted the cover of the captain's voice-pipe.

"Captain, sir. Executive, sir."

"Thank you," Halfhyde said evenly from below. "Warn the gangway to stand by." He left the voice-pipe cover open and went to his door, stared coolly at the Spanish soldiers. "Your commanding officer calls. The voice-pipe in my cabin." Neither of the men seemed to have any English, and Halfhyde indulged in pantomime; one of the soldiers ticked over and went into the cuddy. Smiling pleasantly, Halfhyde turned to face the other man, who was standing close in the alleyway's confined space. Still smiling, he brought his knee up hard into the groin: as upon the bridge earlier, his aim was true and his knee hard. Giving a gasp of agony, the man doubled up and Halfhyde wrenched his rifle away in time to thrust the bayonet towards the first man, who had turned sharply from the silent voice-pipe.

"Out," Halfhyde said, gesturing with the rifle. The man came out, his face tense. "Your rifle. On the deck."

There was a stream of Spanish. Halfhyde reached out and touched the rifle, then pointed to the deck. Taking the hint, the man dropped his rifle with a clatter. Halfhyde waited till the other man had clambered to his feet again, then kicked the spare rifle away behind him and herded the two soldiers along to the after end of the passage where they fetched up against a blank steel bulkhead. Within the next half-minute the gangway had responded to the message from the bridge: a party of seamen in white-duck working rig came at the double into the alleyway from the other end, armed with marlinespikes.

The leading-seaman in charge asked, "You all right, sir?"

"All right indeed, Wicks." Halfhyde passed over the rifle he was holding, and indicated the one on the deck. "Arm two of your men and leave them here with two others. They're to get our Spanish friends gagged and securely bound, and keep them under guard in my cabin."

"Aye, aye, sir."

"You come with me, Wicks, with the rest of your party, when you've detailed sentries. Make sure the marlinespikes are hidden."

Wicks gave his orders, then followed Halfhyde to the quarterdeck, where all was peace among British and Spanish. Sawbridge, officer of the day, was at the head of the gangway with his quartermaster, bosun's mate and side-boy. The armed guards lounged nearby, no more cognizant of what was going on than were their comrades on the quay.

"Nicely done, Mr Sawbridge," Halfhyde said. "I have guests in my cabin . . . taking their ease, if you follow me."

"Yes, sir."

"Is there word of Mr Prebble?"

"There's fighting in the stokers' mess deck, sir, but Mr Prebble needs no extra assistance." Sawbridge grinned. "The seamen's mess decks were full of men with time on their hands, and—"

"Quite, Mr Sawbridge. Send your side-boy, if you please, to the vicinity of Mr Prebble. When he can get a word in, I'd like a party of men to be detached to take over the engine-room and boiler-room. Wicks?"

Wicks saluted. "Sir?"

"To the navigating bridge, Wicks, with the rest of your hands. Regain me the control of my ship."

Wicks saluted again, grinning hugely. "Aye, aye, sir!"

As the leading-seaman went off, Halfhyde turned to the officer of the day. "Two more groups—our friends on deck here and on the jetty. They shall wait a while. Their premature disappearance might be somewhat obvious to the inquisitive, I fear."

"Aye, aye, sir. And then, sir?"

"Then the fresh sea breezes will call, Mr Sawbridge. Be ready to answer them."

"All ready now, sir."

"Good!" Halfhyde nodded and walked, slow and cool, to the other side of the quarterdeck, for all the world like any captain in any peaceful situation taking a sniff of the night air before going below to his dinner, relaxed and unworried. He looked out along the harbour towards the entry. From where he was

he would not be able to see any lights from the British battleships: they might be there yet, or they might not. The vice-
admiral might well have made the decision to sail all his ships
for Gibraltar, there to request wirelessed orders from the Lords
of the Admiralty: few modern flag officers would risk fractur-
ing the peace on their own initiative.

Halfhyde gave a sigh; the advent of wireless stations in handy
parts of the world—which would no doubt, one day, be a fea-
ture of shipboard life as well—were a mixed blessing, for they
detracted from a commanding officer's and an admiral's freedom,
sapping his initiative and his will to make on-the-spot decisions
for good or ill. For good or ill: Halfhyde pondered the words
in his mind as he studied the harbour. Tonight would go either
well or badly, and which way it went would be up to him, as
would the repercussions to his ship's company. The possibility
of many dead had to be accepted in the name of the Queen's
life: the solitary old lady in Windsor Castle, preoccupied with
her sad thoughts of Prince Albert, was as hard a taskmistress as
ever, but Halfhyde knew full well that not a man among his
company would grudge his life in her interests, for she repre-
sented Britain and the Empire and the security of home.

   Halfhyde turned as he heard footsteps ashore, approaching
his ship rapidly. He walked across to the other side of his quarterdeck. Along the quay came the unwelcome sight of Captain
Watkiss.

Chapter 13

TELESCOPE IN HAND, Captain Watkiss mounted the gangway: behind him on the jetty, the Spanish guards shrugged helplessly and grimaced. The British . . . they were unpredictable and did not know when all the cards were stacked against them. In victory self-effacing, in defeat they bounced and strutted like the Captain Watkiss . . .

"My ship is under search, sir," Halfhyde said.

"Yes, Mr Halfhyde, I'm aware of that." The monocle glittered in the gangway light. "Is all well?"

"Well enough, I fancy, sir."

"I've come to lend you my support."

Halfhyde stared. "That's much appreciated, sir, and I thank you, but it'll not be necessary."

"Not be necessary, stuff-and-nonsense! What d'you mean, it'll not be necessary? Look!" Watkiss tapped himself on the shoulder, by some manual dexterity, with his telescope. "Four stripes, Mr Halfhyde, a post captain. I carry weight."

"I fear not at this moment, sir, in the eyes of the Spaniards—"

"Oh, to hell with the damn dagoes," Watkiss said impatiently and in a loud voice. "So long as I'm aboard, Mr Halfhyde, you should have little trouble. They respect rank, you know, and of course in their country older persons, those on the verge of middle years, are much honoured as—as—"

"Sages?" Halfhyde enquired.

"Yes. So I shall be here when you need me." Watkiss stared, eyes wide. "Well? Shall we not go to your quarters, Mr Halfhyde, it's only polite, is it not?"

"My quarters are not free, sir."

"Not free, what d'you mean, not free? Have the damn dagoes had the damn effrontery—"

"In a sense, sir," Halfhyde gave a warning cough. "I suggest we go to the seaward side of the quarterdeck, sir."

"Oh, God damn—"

"If you please, sir!" Halfhyde turned away from his senior officer and strode purposefully and grimly back to the other side. Watkiss came after him, angrily. "If you'll be so good as to shout in a low voice, sir—"

"Don't be impertinent, Mr Halfhyde, or I shall have you before a court martial."

"Very well, sir. But matters are at a touchy stage, and already the Captain Watkiss has been mentioned—"

"*The* Captain Watkiss, did you say?"

"That was how they referred to you, sir."

"Did they—did they?" Watkiss was obviously flattered. "*The* Captain Watkiss! I rather like that—*the* Captain Watkiss. Yes, indeed I do like it—and as a matter of fact, Mr Halfhyde, it supports what I said just now: I carry weight. That's fact—I said it. Now then, your cabin. Be so good as to explain."

"The Spaniards are in there, sir, against their will."

"Against their will?"

"Bound and gagged and under armed sentries—"

"What the devil have you been up to, Mr Halfhyde?"

Halfhyde turned as a rating approached. "I'm sorry, sir, there's not the time to explain fully. Yes, Bennett?"

"Leading-Seaman Wicks, sir, reports bridge under control, sir."

"Thank you, Bennett. Further orders will be passed at any minute now." Returning the man's salute, Halfhyde bent to speak into the ear of Captain Watkiss. "I suggest you make your way ashore, sir, or you will be shanghaied. I am taking my ship to sea. We have now reached full dark and I must not delay."

Watkiss stared disbelievingly. "What did you say?"

"I think you heard, sir. I must use every endeavour now to get Colonel Stanley to Gibraltar or the Queen is lost. Therefore I am proceeding out of the port, and shall if necessary use my main armament to ensure my passage—"

"By God, Mr Halfhyde, you'll be blown to smithereens!"

"A risk I must take, sir. Will you go ashore, or must I have you dumped?"

"Dumped?" In the glow coming across from the gangway light Watkiss's face resembled a blood-red sun. "Damn you to hell, Mr Halfhyde, you are being high-handed and impertinent. Dumped my backside, I shall come with you."

"In my ship, sir, under my command?"

"Yes—no! Under *my* command, of course, as senior officer of the flotilla, damn you to hell." Suddenly a disconcerted look came into Watkiss's eye and he scratched at his chin. "On the other hand—upon reflection—it wouldn't do, I'm sorry to say."

"Indeed, sir?"

"Well, don't you see, if I go with you, it leaves poor Beauchamp as senior officer to deal with the Spanish." Watkiss breathed out hard through his nose. "Feller's an ass!"

"It's not for me to comment, sir." Halfhyde produced his watch. "With respect, sir, you have two minutes either to go or stay."

"Hold your tongue, Mr Halfhyde, you've been insubordinate enough already and that shall be reflected in the report I shall write upon you eventually." Suddenly, the gangway light was extinguished. "God, what's that for?"

"You shall see, sir." Shadowy figures had appeared now through the after screen: the deck guards were at once engaged and taken utterly by surprise. Down the gangway went the gunner's mate with his six determined seamen. There were muffled cries and blows, and the party returned aboard, its number increased by two recumbent Spaniards.

"God bless my soul!" Watkiss said, staring.

Halfhyde loomed over him. "Your decision, sir, if you please."

"Yes, yes." With dignity Captain Watkiss said, "I have decided to go ashore. I can be of more use to you there. You are doing a brave thing, Mr Halfhyde, and I wish you well. If only I could come! I—"

"Shall we go to the gangway, sir, before I have it brought inboard?"

"Oh yes, certainly." They approached the gangway. Seamen were standing by to lift it aboard. Watkiss took Halfhyde's hand and shook it warmly. "A brave man, and a brave ship's company. All my men are sound—the example set is clearly good. May God be with you. Carry in your mind's eye," he added sententiously, "a picture of Her Majesty the Queen. She will sustain you, Mr Halfhyde." He rose and fell on the balls of his feet. "As for me . . . Mr Halfhyde, I fancy your movement may be spotted by the dagoes aboard the rest of my ships, and—"

"A risk I must take, sir."

"Don't interrupt, I detest that. I was about to say, I shall create a diversion." Watkiss beamed. "What d'you think of that?"

Halfhyde nodded. "A good idea, sir. But divert with care, if you please."

"You may leave it to me." Captain Watkiss went down the gangway, not hurrying unduly and never mind the urgency: captains did not hurry, it was undignified, a common seaman's mode of progress. The gangway was whipped away almost from under his very heels; and when he turned to salute his brave fellows every man had his back to him. Fore and aft, ropes were cut and the shoreside ends dropped into the water to trail down from the bollards: there was no time to put an unberthing party ashore. In hurt dudgeon Captain Watkiss strutted along the jetty towards *Venomous;* he was still wearing his grotesque long shorts and on the wings of a strong breeze they acted like sails to speed his progress. Halfhyde, on the bridge, moved to the standard compass as the reports came in from fore and aft that everything had been let go and no lights showing anywhere.

"Main engines dead slow astern, Mr Sawbridge."

"Dead slow astern, sir."

"Close up the guns' crews—quietly. I want complete silence along the upper deck."

"Aye, aye, sir."

"Wheel five degrees to port, Mr Sawbridge."

"Wheel five degrees to port, sir." The ship's stern began its swing off the jetty; Halfhyde ordered more port wheel as his engines continued giving sternway. From up the line of British ships a great hullabaloo started; a report came to the bridge from aft that there was much light and men were running along the jetty, away from *Vendetta.* Halfhyde grinned, and met

Sawbridge's questioning eye. He said, "That's Captain Watkiss diverting attention, and evidently succeeding."

"What'll he be doing, sir?"

"That is known only to God and Captain Watkiss. He may have fallen into the water in our interest." Halfhyde watched his ship's head carefully; when he had swung right round and his bows were pointed for the entrance and the open sea beyond, he steadied the course and put his engines slow ahead. The night was dark; with luck he could fade into it for long enough, and preferred to ghost through the waters in the hope of attracting no attention, rather than make a dash for the entrance at high speed. So far, at any rate, luck was undoubtedly with him: he was off the jetty and under way and the port stood quiet before him, and peaceful, the gangway lights from de Valdares's battle squadron showing distantly from up the harbour. Towards the entrance more ships loomed, black shadows in the night peppered with light from the ports and from the quarterdecks. A sound of music drifted: aboard one of the ships a guitar was being strummed. From another as Halfhyde nosed along came gusts of laughter, probably from a ward-room where the liquor was running free. Halfhyde grinned to himself: often enough in past history strong drink had dulled the watchfulness of those who should have known better!

They cruised down harbour, a little faster now, totally unmolested: this was luck that could not last. Someone, somewhere in the port, must surely be keeping a proper watch; somewhere there must be a vessel detailed, as would have been the case in any British port with a naval presence, for the duties of guardship. The guardship's officers would be more or less obliged to remain sober and not indulge in distracting revelries; and there, if not before, would come the moment of danger.

Halfhyde stood tense, almost fearing to breathe in case some sound should alert the Spanish. There was a monumental silence throughout the ship, broken only by the engine sound below and a swish of water along the side plating. Not a man spoke; such orders as were necessary were being passed in whispers, the repeater bells from the engine-room to the bridge were silent; engine orders were passed when necessary by voice-pipe.

"We're going to get away with it, sir!"

Halfhyde suppressed sudden anger. "No chickens, if you please, Mr Sawbridge. And keep silent." He lifted his telescope, scanning the emerging entry for the tenth time: the darkness was holding yet, though for how much longer before the moon sailed out was a matter for guesswork, hope and prayer. Halfhyde licked his lips, finding them suddenly dry; but as they came down the straight channel direct now for the harbour mouth his heart leaped with joyful triumph. Already he saw himself passing into the open sea to turn for Cape Tinoso under full power, clear away for Gibraltar. He was using his telescope to search the seas beyond the entry for some sign of a British presence when he heard the voice, a voice kept low but calling urgently from immediately below the bridge: "Captain, sir!"

Halfhyde leaned over the guardrail. "Yes?"

"Sir, there's—" The man had no need to finish: his words were cut into by a report from the bridge lookout and in the same instant Halfhyde saw it also: a black shape moving out from the northern side of the harbour, a vessel standing directly into their path. At the same time the moon came out from cloud cover, bathing Cartagena in harsh, silvery light.

Now there would be no mistaking their intent to escape.

"Stand by guns' crew!" Halfhyde called. "Mr Sawbridge, engines to full ahead and I'll take the ship."

"Aye, aye, sir." Sawbridge passed down the engine order, then stepped away from the standard compass. Halfhyde watched ahead minutely: it looked as though the encroaching vessel meant to lay herself slap across the outward channel to block him in. "Mr Sawbridge, your chart. Where's the most water—ahead or astern of the Spaniard?"

"Ahead, sir, as she lies at this moment, but there's not much—"

"How much?"

"Two fathoms maximum, sir."

Halfhyde swore. "As I thought! It's not enough—unless I can shift the fellow."

"By gunfire, sir?"

"It would be more prudent not to, Mr Sawbridge, but I am not a prudent man. By gunfire if necessary, but I may be able to squeeze past. He'll not risk putting his bows into the mud himself!"

"He might, sir. His object's to stop us, nothing else."

"Yes, by God, you're right." Halfhyde's eyes narrowed as he made a quick mental calculation of possibilities. "It'll have to be gunfire. Mr Sawbridge, tell the captain of 'A' gun he's to be ready to open on my order and put a shell across the Spaniard's bows. I—" He stopped as a signal lamp began flashing from the ship ahead. "Yeoman?"

"Aye, aye, sir. Signal reads: *stop instantly or I open fire, sir.*"

Halfhyde laughed savagely. "So he fears my ram, does he! Mr Sawbridge, 'A' gun to open at once."

On the heels of his order, there was an orange flash from below the bridge, followed by a surging, acrid-smelling cloud of gunsmoke, and a blast of heat accompanied by the sharp crack of the cordite charge in the six-pounder. Seconds later a spout of water, clearly to be seen in the moonlight, came up right ahead of the Spaniard. As the sound of gunfire echoed back across the port, something happened far astern in the upper reaches: two flares shot skyward, twin whooshes of high-travelling flame that came down again in a shower of colour, and simultaneously the scream of a steam siren was heard.

"What was all that, sir?" Sawbridge asked in wonder.

"Captain Watkiss, I shouldn't wonder, creating another diversion a little late. Or possibly the port signal for the general alarm." There was a brilliant flash now from ahead; Halfhyde and Sawbridge ducked instinctively as the shell whined over the bridge. Meanwhile the gap was closing fast and any more shells must smash right into *Vendetta*'s superstructure. Halfhyde clasped his hands behind his back and stood straight, four-square to anything the Spaniard might care to send. It was all or nothing now, total defeat or total victory, and victory it had to be. Reports from aft indicated that the harbour was coming alive; lights were showing and vessels were moving down fast towards the entry in *Vendetta*'s wake. The ship sped on, raising a wind by the speed of her passage, a wind that sang through the ropes and wires of her standing rigging like an orchestra, and there was an immense vibration in her plates as the engines climbed towards full power to send her on like a bullet.

Suddenly there was a shout from Halfhyde: "The Spaniard's aground for'ard, I believe! She went a shade too far . . . Mr Sawbridge, what are the soundings astern of her?"

"One and a half fathoms, sir, no more."

There was an oath from Halfhyde. He was about to order "A" gun to open again, and to aim this time for a hit, when he checked himself and stared ahead, frowning. With little more than half a mile to go to open water, and a quarter of a mile perhaps from the grounded vessel, the Spaniard's shape was altering: gone was the long, lean line, fading into a bunching as of a ship beginning to come stern-on. Halfhyde gave a shout of triumph and called to the torpedo-coxswain at the wheel. "Cox'n, she's swinging her stern round and is virtually in irons with her bows nipped. I'll leave it to you to bring me round her counter!"

"Aye, aye, sir."

"Keep close in—nothing to port."

"Nothing to port, sir." The torpedo-coxswain stared in concentration and sent an almost automatic stream of tobacco-juice from a corner of his mouth to the deck. There was no spitkid handy, but a seaman boy would be scrubbing-out if Mr Halfhyde brought them through this . . . At his side Halfhyde prepared to face possible collision or grounding at speed and sent the bosun's mates piping round the ship in warning to all hands to brace themselves. Then, as the distance closed, another hazard was seen ahead, moving out towards the channel: another warship to add her steel sides to the task of closing the exit.

Halfhyde bent to the engine-room voice-pipe. "All possible revolutions even if you sheer the holding-down bolts." He straightened and spoke to the torpedo-coxswain. "Once again we have a gap, Cox'n, and this time by God we're going through!"

Chapter 14

THEY SEEMED TO MOVE like a rocket, cleaving through the exit channel: Halfhyde prayed that his high speed in shallow water would not have its very possible effect of putting his stern down to touch bottom and enfold his thundering screws in the mud; but while they moved, they lived, and would live to save the Queen.

Expertly handled by the torpedo-coxswain, *Vendetta* rushed down upon the strip of water between the grounded vessel and her oncoming sister. As they passed the stricken ship, keeping close in accordance with the order from the bridge, Halfhyde heard the scream of metal as the plates scraped together. *Vendetta* seemed to twist a little under the glancing impact, but kept on going. Seconds later she was thrown heavily away to starboard as her flying bows smashed across the stem of the second ship. The torpedo-coxswain wrenched the wheel and sent her back on course with no slackening of her speed, and she raced on past, heading clear and free into open water. Halfhyde turned to look aft: by now the second ship, flung aside by the impact, had turned through something like one hundred and eighty degrees and lay sluggishly across the channel, her bows pushed into the mud and her stern tucked into the original ship's side amidships. Effectively, Cartagena was blocked to all inward and outward movement. Halfhyde, as his ship raced away, stared back towards the port, which was a mass of lights, some moving, some stationary. He had it in mind that the great guns of the fortress might yet open; but as time passed they remained silent. No doubt the Spaniards were unwilling to risk the condemnation that would follow upon the actual bombardment of the British flag at sea . . . Halfhyde spoke warmly to the torpedo-coxswain.

"Well done indeed, Cox'n, a brilliant piece of work and you have my deepest thanks. We're safe, and free . . . the hour's late, but not too late. I'm instructing Mr Prebble to splice the mainbrace." He stepped back from the binnacle. "Take the ship, Mr Sawbridge. There's no Fleet to be seen, so you'll lay off a course for Gibraltar, if you please."

"Aye, aye, sir."

Halfhyde rubbed his hands together, briskly. "We should enter by dawn. In the meantime, once the rum's been issued, I have work to do. A message to Mr Prebble, if you please. I shall wish to see the Spanish plain-clothes officer in my cabin. I think he may be somewhat rattled, and thus may be induced to talk!"

The Spaniard was indeed rattled and seemed not to know whether it was better to stand on his dignity as a shanghaied government official, or to cringe respectfully to the perennially victorious, if heretical, British in the hope of pacifying them. The man, whose name was Jose-Pedro Garcia, had been instructed from birth by a devout mother that the British were wicked, were beasts, and boded no good for Spain. Jose-Pedro Garcia had been fed, as it were, along with his mother's Catholic milk, with the dreadful fate of the Most Happy Armada under the glorious Duke of Medina Sidonia, and knew all about the savages of Scotland and Ireland who had put brave Spaniards to the sword, the club and the knife in the back when the survivors had staggered ashore from shattered galleons in search of food and shelter; he had been fed with tales of the terrible Duke of Wellington who had broken the Spanish armies, of Admiral Lord Nelson who had smashed the Spanish Fleet—his instruction went even as far back as Drake who had entered the great port of Cadiz and burned the fine vessels of the King of Spain. Britain stood, the world's bully, rejector of the word of His Holiness the Pope. Now he was in their hands and steaming, to pile insult upon injury, to the naval base of the usurper at Gibraltar, as integral a part of the land mass of Spain as was Portland of Great Britain . . .

From a chair in the cuddy, he looked furtively up at Halfhyde. He spread his hands and answered Halfhyde's question. "I am sorry, Captain, I do not know."

"Or won't say. You are a *politico*. You must know the facts."

"I am not of exalted rank. I am a humble person, a humble servant of the Queen Regent."

"Yet you are sent to arrest the man Stanley."

"*Si, señor.*"

"Then you know his crime—so much, indeed, you have said. You speak of it as murder. I wish to know the circumstances, all of them, and quickly. Do not insult me by saying you are not aware of the circumstances. I shall not believe you, and I shall dig out the information."

Eyes peered up sadly, scared. "Dig, *señor?*"

"Dig, yes. If you have beads, say them now. I am an impatient man, and the fortress of Gibraltar looms. Before that there is time for keelhauling, or hanging from the masthead, or—"

"*Señor,* you joke, you make play with me. Such barbarous times are past!"

Halfhyde nodded. "Which is not to say they can't be revived, or could be if I had the proper gear aboard, which I have not, and can't have makeshift gear ready in the time available. However, I have other things."

There was a sharp intake of breath. "What things, *señor?*"

"A gunner's mate," Halfhyde said indifferently, "who served in the old sailing navy, and who has great dexterity in wielding nicely lead-weighted cat-o'-nine-tails that can rip a man's flesh to bloody shreds in five minutes. If I give the word, you shall be handed back to the Queen Regent of Spain a mass of quivering butcher's meat fit only to hang in a warship's beef-screen." He loomed over the wretched, terrified Spaniard, looking dangerous and determined upon cruelty. "Now, you shall tell me, shall you not?"

"*Si,*" Jose-Pedro gasped, "*si, si si!*"

As the ship came close in around Europa Point to head up into Gibraltar Bay for the naval dockyard, Halfhyde pondered the words that had been drawn from the *politico* during the long night. All in all, it was a strange story and failed in certain important particulars to check with that of Colonel Stanley: the most significant discrepancy being concerned with the identity of the man said to have been murdered by the Queen's Messenger. He was not, the *politico* had insisted, a member of the Duke of Villanueva's household; he had been one of Garcia's own agents set upon Stanley's trail. Halfhyde had asked why a

Queen's Messenger should be trailed by the *politicos* in the first place, and the answer had been alarming.

"Because Colonel Stanley," Garcia had said, "was believed to be involved in intrigue with the Duke of Villanueva de Cordoba, and with certain other high persons, in matters likely to affect the security of Spain."

"In what direction?"

"We do not know. We know only that there had been meetings held clandestinely." Garcia had been shaking as he spoke; fear of the lash, Halfhyde had felt certain, was extracting nothing but the truth now. "The Duke of Villanueva de Cordoba is on our secret lists of those persons likely to attempt to overthrow the Regency, and establish a power of their own."

"So you are always suspicious of any . . . clandestine move he makes?"

"*Si.* That is so."

"And of those who are involved with him?"

"*Si, señor.*"

That had been about as far as Halfhyde had been able to progress; Jose-Pedro Garcia, it seemed, was acting on suspicion alone and had no hard proof; but in Spain suspicion was enough. The rest would follow later, after an arrest had been made. Without being precise, Halfhyde had probed in regard to possible events, originating inside Spain, that might cross the frontiers to affect the wider world; Garcia shrugged, seeming not to understand what was in Halfhyde's mind. That might have been an act or it might not; but Halfhyde, with the diplomatic considerations heavily in his mind, knew he dare not press the point too far. He had Garcia removed under guard and went himself to the bridge, where he paced thoughtfully as the ship headed south-westerly for Gibraltar. His instinct was to face Stanley with the *politico's* words, assess his reaction, and hear what he had to say: but a sense of caution warned him not to be precipitate. This affair seemed likely to be about to pass beyond the ken of a naval lieutenant, and the Queen's life was at stake, no less. Possibilities of ham-fisted interference must be avoided; in Gibraltar would be found both advice and communication with Whitehall. In the meantime, Stanley was safe vis-à-vis the Spaniards and had no further need to stoke. He had been relieved of his duties and now, clean again if blistered, he was sleeping in Sawbridge's cabin. Or had been: as the ship brought Europa abeam, Stanley appeared in his reach-me-down suit at the head of the bridge ladder.

"Good morning, Halfhyde. May I step on the bridge?"

"Of course, sir. I trust you've slept well?"

"Very well." Stanley looked around, sniffing the keen air of early morning. "A fine day."

"Yes, indeed." There was a tenseness in the air, and Halfhyde had no eyes for the undoubted beauty of the morning, the shimmering blue of the sea, the violet and gold tints on the North African hills rearing through a slight dawn mist, distantly across the strait, the white buildings, tinted now like the hills, of Algeciras and La Linea, the great brown eminence of the Rock of Gibraltar, looming huge and impregnable and as steadfast as the Empire itself. "When we enter the harbour, sir, what will your movements be?"

Stanley said, "Why, I shall seek the fastest possible transport to London—"

"But not across Spain, I take it?"

There was a laugh. "Scarcely! And talking of Spain . . . I've not thanked you properly—"

"It's not necessary, sir. I only did my duty, as ordered and expected."

"Yes, but still—" Stanley broke off. "This question of transport. There'll be a P&O liner through the day after tomorrow. I'll see the agents about a berth."

"Which, of course, a Queen's Messenger will get without difficulty," Halfhyde said. "A slow passage, however."

"Fast enough. We have time in hand." Stanley glanced at the officer of the watch and the rest of the bridge personnel, and then, warningly, at Halfhyde. "At what time will breakfast be served?" he asked.

"After we've secured, sir." Halfhyde took a look around: there was some distance yet to go for entry. He said, "But I'll come down with you now, sir, and see what—"

"No, no, I can wait—"

"A word, sir, if I may. Mr Prebble, you have the ship. I'll not be long." He turned away down the ladder; Stanley followed. By the foot of the ladder, the deck was deserted but for themselves. Halfhyde faced Stanley. "The wireless station, sir. I have mentioned it before. That is the fastest way."

"I prefer not to use it, Halfhyde."

"But—"

"My business, I think." Stanley's tone was crisp, brooking no argument. "*I* am the Queen's Messenger, not you. You have brought me out and I'm deeply grateful, so will Her Majesty be. But your part's ended, Halfhyde, or will be once I'm ashore in Gibraltar."

Halfhyde gave a formal bow. "My apologies, sir."

"Oh, that's quite all right, Halfhyde. I don't mean to be difficult, you know, far from it. My hands are tied, however.
Diplomacy's diplomacy, after all—it took me a devil of a time
to appreciate that, after years as a soldier, but there's always a
reason for everything." Stanley paused. "By the way, that government man—and the Spanish army officers, you've still got
them aboard, I gather—did anything emerge? I imagine you
questioned them?"

"I did, sir, but to no purpose."

"Ah—I see. Don't let me keep you from your duties, my
dear fellow."

Halfhyde saluted and turned away up the ladder. As he
went, he reflected that the lie about Garcia's silence had come
surprisingly easy to him: he must be learning something of the
ways of diplomacy after all.

There was an exchange of signals with the captain of the port
and with the rear-admiral commanding the Particular Service
Squadron: boats would be sent alongside *Vendetta* to take off
the Spanish personnel and Halfhyde was ordered to wait upon
the rear-admiral at four bells in the forenoon watch. Breakfast
taken, he watched the disembarkation of the Spaniards: fists
were shaken in his direction and threats were uttered as the
motley assembly went over the side, looking considerably less
brilliant than the evening before; the uniforms had been slept
in and the various places where they had been kept under
guard had left their marks in oily stains and fragments of food,
and some of the splendidly attired officers had been seasick.
Stanley did not come up on deck to watch them go; he had,

he said, seen enough of Spaniards to last him the rest of his life. He sat in the small ward-room drinking coffee and smoking an early cigar; he too had been requested—rather than ordered—to wait upon the rear-admiral, and would attend along with Halfhyde. At three bells Halfhyde's boat was called away, and left the quarter-boom to come alongside the ladder under Leading-Seaman Parslow. Halfhyde and Stanley were pulled out into the bay, where the ships of the Particular Service Squadron lay at anchor, and were piped aboard the flagship to be met at the head of the ladder by the flag captain and flag lieutenant. They were escorted by the latter to the admiral's quarters, moving along shining steel alleyways burnished by the sweat of the flagship's company, past rifle-racks, and past a sentry of the Royal Marine Light Infantry who saluted with shouldered arms as the officers passed.

They went into the day cabin to be announced by the flag lieutenant. Rear-Admiral Sir Humphrey Arbuthnot rose from an armchair: a big man, his hair, grey turning to white, almost swept the deckhead and the bulk of his broad body seemed to fill the day cabin, large as it was. He was a bluff man as befitted his size, heavily side-whiskered to give his red face the look of having been framed for posterity. A man of apparently few words, he quickly elicited from Stanley the reason behind his urgent need of a pick-up from Spain; and, having learned it, gasped and fell back into the armchair, taken utterly by surprise.

"Good God, it can't be true!"

"I assure you it is, Sir Humphrey, I assure you most positively—"

"Then what do you propose to do about it?"

Stanley said, "To reach England as fast as possible, and make all speed to Whitehall and the palace."

"Having telegraphed ahead, I presume?"

"No." Stanley shook his head firmly. "I've been into that with Halfhyde. I must report in person and must not entrust the information to the wireless station. If word reaches Villanueva or his hired assassins, the plot is likely to be switched. As matters stand, I know the facts. With my knowledge, Her Majesty can be protected and the parties to the plot arrested."

"Yes, but look here, Colonel—"

"I must insist, Sir Humphrey. I have diplomatic reasons as well for doing so. I am not permitted to say what those reasons are."

"I understand that, of course." The rear-admiral got to his feet and prowled the cabin like a restless, anxious bear. "Well, you're the principal in this, Colonel. I must abide by your decision. What can I do to help?"

Stanley said quietly, "I ask two things only, Sir Humphrey: first, your complete silence; second, transport to England. I would like to embark in the P&O for Tilbury the day after tomorrow, and it would assist if you would instruct the agents to make room for me without asking questions."

"It shall be done." For a moment the rear-admiral's gaze rested on Halfhyde, thoughtfully, then he turned back to Stanley. "There's the question of your accommodation. I'll be glad to offer you the hospitality of my flagship until the P&O enters."

"Thank you, but I'll not trouble you. I'm well acquainted with Gibraltar," Stanley said. "I shall find accommodation without difficulty."

"I think you should guard your person, Colonel."

Stanley laughed. "I'm accustomed to doing that!"

"No doubt—no doubt."

"If I could now be put ashore, Sir Humphrey, I'll make my arrangements. Perhaps Halfhyde—"

"No, I'll provide you with a boat myself, Colonel. I wish words with Halfhyde, who has left his senior officer in an unfortunate predicament in Cartagena, I rather fancy!"

There had been a hint of amusement in the rear-admiral's tone when he had referred to Captain Watkiss. Once Stanley had departed he said, "I've had tidings from the Mediterranean Fleet, Mr Halfhyde, and was on the point of sailing my ships to lie off Cartagena when your ship was reported by Europa. How will Captain Watkiss be faring now, d'you suppose?"

"Angrily would be my guess, sir," Halfhyde answered with a straight face. "I think, if I may say so, we should act to make his position easier."

"Have you a suggestion?"

"I have, sir. It is this: that the Spaniards whom I took should be released across the frontier into Spain, and that the Spanish authorities in Madrid and Cartagena be informed by an immediate despatch that Colonel Stanley left Spain with me. This they'll assume in any case, so nothing's lost unnecessarily—"

"But it will make the detention of Captain Watkiss a pointless exercise?"

"Exactly, sir. Once the facts have been confirmed, then to detain British ships any longer would be highly dangerous."

"I agree, and will see to it. Now there's another point: Colonel Stanley's transport to England."

"Yes, sir, and there also I have a suggestion to make: my ship is faster than the P&O."

Sir Humphrey laughed. "You take the words from my mouth, Mr Halfhyde! It will be easy enough to detach you from Captain Watkiss, since the matter is in any case a *fait accompli*. I wished, however, to put it to you in Stanley's absence."

There had been some curious quality in the rear-admiral's tone.

"I see, sir," Halfhyde said. "May I ask why?"

"You may. But I'm sure you have some ideas of your own?"

"The wireless station, sir?"

"Yes, Mr Halfhyde, the wireless station. Up to a point his reasons are sound enough, but with Her Majesty's life in the balance . . . no, no, if it were I in his shoes, damn it, I'd cable Whitehall and to hell with the diplomatic niceties or whatever it is! And as it happens, that's not all."

Halfhyde raised an eyebrow. "Not all, sir?"

"Not all by a long chalk." The rear-admiral moved to his roll-top desk and opened it. He took up a sheet of paper, waved it at Halfhyde, and said abruptly, "Stanley told us, did he not, that the threat to the Queen's life would come whilst she was at Balmoral, and that she was to leave for there in . . . eight days' time from today?"

"That's right, sir."

The rear-admiral waved the sheet of paper again. "Mail from England reached us yesterday, by the outward-bound P&O. I have a letter from my sister, who's a lady-in-waiting to Her Majesty. The Queen leaves Windsor in eight days' time for Scotland, Mr Halfhyde, but not for Balmoral. She is to stay at Inveraray Castle, on Loch Fyne, with His Grace the Duke of

Argyll. This news was intended to remain a secret from the general public, but has been communicated—many days ago, I stress—not only to the government but also to the Embassies in Europe, who have a need to know the whereabouts of Her Majesty at any time."

Chapter 15

THE WORD FROM WINDSOR was not of necessity significant, but was strange: Stanley should have been aware, before cutting his connections with the Embassy in Madrid, of the altered plans of Her Majesty. Taken in conjunction with Halfhyde's report of the interrogation of Garcia, it raised serious speculation; so much so that Sir Humphrey Arbuthnot preferred the Queen's Messenger to proceed to England aboard a warship where he would be under supervision and less of a free agent than aboard a liner.

"Will you inform him, sir?" Halfhyde asked.

"I will. I'll have him told to report aboard my flagship for further consultation, and then have him sent across to you. When will you be ready to leave?"

"The moment I've taken enough coal for the Channel, sir."

The rear-admiral nodded. "Then I'll act with despatch, and you shall sail without further orders as soon as you're ready with Stanley aboard."

"Aye, aye, sir. And—will you cable Whitehall, sir, or not?"

"To the extent that I shall notify the Admiralty that Colonel Stanley is on his way to England, yes. No further than that. I'm on unsure ground, to be frank, and I'll not risk breaking diplomatic procedures in case we're both wrong. As it is, you'll reach England in plenty of time."

Halfhyde was pulled back to the inner harbour and his ship in the grip of a growing concern. Stanley's integrity had not been wholly impugned, but now there was more than a vague mistrust; yet the rear-admiral was playing a cautious game—and could well be playing with the fire of the Queen's life by not sending a fully informative cable to the Admiralty at once. Halfhyde scowled across the brilliant blue water towards the great Rock with its barracks and bastions, its parade-grounds and its high gun emplacements facing across the neutral ground towards Spain. Across the water the sounds of martial music came to Halfhyde, the sound of the pipes and drums as a Highland battalion paraded at Red Sands . . . from here of all places, from one of the nearer outposts of Empire, the Queen would expect loyal salvation and proper forethought, yet the great god diplomacy was making cautious civil servants of them all!

Coming alongside, Halfhyde climbed to his quarterdeck and was met by Prebble.

"We sail for the Channel the moment coaling's finished, Mr Prebble, and there will be no shore leave. We're to be Colonel Stanley's escort. He'll re-embark shortly." Without further words Halfhyde turned for the hatch leading down to his cabin, frowning, deep in unwelcome thoughts still. Within fifteen minutes he was on the bridge to take *Vendetta* alongside the coaling berth, with his engineer under orders to bunker to the full capacity of sixty tons. At economical speed *Vendetta* would have a range of some three thousand miles—much more than enough for the voyage to Portsmouth Dockyard, enough to permit of a higher speed in the urgent situation. With in fact only a small quantity of coal consumed since their last bunkering, the operation was quickly completed and as *Vendetta* moved off the coaling berth with the deck hoses and scrubbers and squeegees washing down, a boat from the shore was seen making out towards the flagship with Stanley in the stern-sheets, now dressed respectably in a suit of white linen that he had presumably bought ready-made from one of the tailors' shops in Waterport Street. Soon after this boat had gone alongside the flag, it was seen coming off again and making for *Vendetta*. Halfhyde went to the accommodation-ladder to meet his passenger personally.

"I understand I'm to give you passage, sir. Welcome back aboard."

Stanley, whose suit fitted where it touched and looked uncomfortable, grunted. There was an impatient look in his eye, and perhaps something else as well. "Quite unnecessary really."

"Faster, sir."

"And a damn sight less comfortable than the P&O . . . not your fault, Halfhyde, and I don't mean to be rude, but I think Arbuthnot's panicking a little, to be frank. However, there it is."

"Yes indeed." Halfhyde moved to the guardrail and looked down at the boat's crew from the flagship: it was no more than a passing fancy, and unsubstantiated; but in the stern-sheets were a gunner's mate and two seamen in gaiters, and they had the look, unmistakable to naval eyes, of an escort. Halfhyde had a shrewd suspicion that those men would have prevented Stanley from going anywhere other than *Vendetta* had he tried to browbeat the boat's coxswain into putting him ashore . . . Halfhyde turned and met Prebble's eye. "Is the ship ready to proceed, Mr Prebble?"

"All ready, sir."

"Thank you. Pipe special sea dutymen, if you please, and hands to stations for leaving harbour. We sail for Spithead and Portsmouth Yard in five minutes' time."

Halfhyde's guess, back in Cartagena, had been a good one: Captain Watkiss had indeed fallen into the sea in the performance of his diversionary duty, and had caused an astonishing amount of consternation. The Spaniards had by no means wanted to lose a post captain of the British Fleet in such a manner, and had rallied round with ropes and ladders and lifebuoys notwithstanding sundry low-voiced comments from the lower deck that now was the time to let the old bugger sink: Captain Watkiss, floundering and gasping like a landed salmon, was pin-pointed, contacted by swimmers who fastened lines, and drawn in to the jetty. In the hoisting process his head was swung hard against unyielding stone, and he became unconscious. He was in this state for some while, and came to in his bunk where, feeling ill, he decided to stay until he was fit, a decision with which the Spanish doctor attending him concurred. On the third day he rose again and ascended to his quarterdeck, telescope in hand, and was met by his first lieutenant.

"Ah—Beauchamp."

"Good morning, sir." Beauchamp saluted. "I'm delighted to see you better, sir, delighted."

"Thank you, Mr Beauchamp. I am lucky to be alive."

"Yes, sir."

"The damn fool who allowed my head to bang into the wall while I was being rescued. Put him in the report."

"The report, sir?"

"Yes, Mr Beauchamp, the report." Captain Watkiss prodded disagreeably with his telescope. "Pull yourself together, for God's sake—"

"I—I can't do that, sir. Put him in the report, I mean—"

"Can't, can't?" Watkiss's face went a dangerous red. "What damn use are you, may I ask, Mr Beauchamp, if you can't obey my orders?"

"The man was a *Spaniard*, sir."

"Eh?" Watkiss's eyebrows went up. "Oh. Yes, I see, quite, a Spaniard." There was a momentary silence. "You're saying it was a *Spaniard* who saved my life?"

"I am, sir."

"H'm. Decent act for a dago, but then, as I remarked once to Halfhyde, they do respect rank. Well, you certainly can't put a dago in the report, never heard—" He broke off. "What's this?"

He pointed with his telescope and Beauchamp turned. A Spanish officer, all sky-blue and gold, was approaching the gangway. Seeing the officers on deck, he stopped, bowed, saluted, and bowed again. Watkiss regarded him suspiciously. The gilded personage called up, "I come aboard, yes, please?"

Beauchamp looked at his captain. Watkiss said irritably: "Oh, tell him he can, yes!"

Beauchamp passed the message. The Spaniard came up the gangway to the salutes of the naval ratings and of his own armed guards. "Good morning, Captain. I bring messages from the fortress commander, and from the admiral of the port also."

"What are the messages, pray?"

"A hope, a sincere wish, that you are no longer sick."

"Correct. I'm not. And by God I'm—"

"And more, Captain." The Spaniard spread his hands, smiling

with pleasure in good news. "You are free to leave Cartagena. Your ships too, all of your ships. They may all go."

Watkiss stared. *"What?"*

"Captain, the freedom of the sea is yours. You have been our guests—"

"Guests? Guests my backside!" Captain Watkiss's face mottled and his telescope came up threateningly. "Held under duress —captive against my will—damn insult to the British flag and Her Majesty the Queen . . . *what is it,* Mr Beauchamp?"

"I advise some caution, sir—"

"Oh, balls, Mr Beauchamp, don't be impertinent." Watkiss swung back upon the now disconcerted Spaniard. "Get off my ship, sir! Get off it this instant!" He shooshed at the surprised officer with his telescope. "Go away before I clap you in arrest, and take your damn sentries with you! Mr Beauchamp?"

"Yes, sir?"

"See this person over the side. Make a signal to my commanding officers—general from senior officer: *you are to repair aboard immediately.*"

"Yes, sir."

"And make ready in all respects for sea, Mr Beauchamp. We sail within the hour for Gibraltar." As though nothing untoward had happened over the last few days, Captain Watkiss turned and strutted importantly up the ladder marked "Captain Only," making for his navigating bridge. He stared out across the harbour and at his flotilla, now freed from the hand of Spain. His chest swelled: he hadn't done too badly, he had upheld British honour, and all his ships were safe—and Stanley was away, thanks to his handling of the situation . . . Thinking of the Queen, he brought out his great maroon handkerchief and blew his nose hard. To his ears from the flotilla came cheering and happy shouts as the word spread that they were about to sail for Gibraltar; and from somewhere aft aboard his own ship a raucous voice was raised high in happy, bawdy song:

Be I Pompey,
Be I buggery—
I belong to Fareham.
That's where the girls
Wear calico drawers
And I be the bugger
To tear 'em.

Captain Watkiss glowered, and opened his mouth to shout for Mr Beauchamp. Then he closed it again, and began tapping time with his telescope. He had a fine ship's company, brave fellows all, let them have their well-earned relaxation for a few minutes. Why, those stout tars had helped the dagoes save his life!

Three days out from Gibraltar: Halfhyde, staring at restless seas, grey and windswept, from *Vendetta's* bridge, thought with a degree of wistfulness of the warm blue waters of the Mediterranean now far behind him. Carnero Point, Tarifa, Cape Trafalgar, Cape St Vincent, they were all well behind him now, landmarks of a sailor's progress home. In the turbulent Bay of Biscay after passing Finisterre he had been forced to reduce his speed. His bows were slicing into great waves that ran horribly across the heavy swell that surged in from the North Atlantic to give the ship a corkscrew motion. Colonel Stanley was lying in his bunk, no doubt praying for death's deliverance from utter misery as the ship gyrated and shuddered to the weight of water dropping aboard and to the sudden released thunder of the racing screws as her stern lifted clear of the sea for them to spin like tops. There was a desolate grey overcast and a lash of rain borne down upon them by the wind, the wind that was now blowing up to gale force and howling eerily through the rigging like a devil's lament.

The foul weather seemed a fit background to Halfhyde's bleak thoughts. Stanley had been uncommunicative until the worsening seas had rendered him wholly speechless; his mood had been dour and withdrawn, and Halfhyde was more and more convinced that something had gone wrong for him, and that that something was the fact of his being aboard a warship. Yet this didn't quite make sense: if Stanley was up to some sort of jiggery-pokery, then the fact of going to England aboard a warship would really make little ultimate difference. Halfhyde had no option but to land him in Portsmouth, after which he would be a free agent in any case. But Stanley nagged continually at his mind: the Queen's Messenger was hiding something, and it might not be merely the exigencies of diplomacy that was making him do so.

Halfhyde, remaining on the bridge while his command laboured through the Bay of Biscay, stood wedged in a corner by the flag locker, staring ahead at endless masses of grey, spume-covered seas, at water breaking over the gun-shield before the bridge to be tossed back along the wind to drench everything in its path. Amidships the seas washed aboard as the vessel rolled, surging across to slide away beneath the guardrails on the opposite side, or flow aft to sweep along the quarter-deck. Every now and again *Vendetta* rose to the tops of the great long wave-crests, and paused for a moment as though grounded upon a mountain peak; and her personnel could look right down the side of that sheer mountain before she fell away again, down into the depths of the water-valley with the mountains on either beam, and the wind's song weirdly cut off by the huge solid walls of water so that for a space there was a kind of comparative quietness with little but the engine sounds to obtrude.

As the day darkened into evening, Prebble came up the ladder. He fought his way alongside Halfhyde and asked, "Shall I relieve you for a spell, sir? I've had sleep enough."

"Thank you, Prebble, but no. You have your own watch to keep."

"Then when I'm on watch, sir, why not take the chance to get some sleep?"

"My duty's here with such a sea running. I'd be happy enough for the ship to be in your hands, but . . ." Halfhyde shrugged: as a seaman, Prebble would understand well enough. He changed the subject. "I've spared a thought or two for the good Captain Watkiss, Prebble. I trust the Spaniards have let him go."

"Yes, sir. I've a feeling they may have been glad enough to do that, in the end. He's not the man to make life easy for his captors!" Prebble turned as he heard feet on the ladder. "Bodger, sir."

"With my supper, I trust."

"Yessir." Able-Seaman Bodger, miraculously with a white napkin over his arm and an unspilled plate, covered with a second plate, on a tray, steadied himself in front of Halfhyde. "Supper, sir, best galley corned beef stew, sir, plenty o' gravy, spuds, greens—fresh aboard in Gib, sir—cocoa. Not in the stew like—separate. All right, sir?"

"Wonderful, Bodger. The same for Colonel Stanley?"

Bodger grinned. "Not bloody likely, sir, beggin' your pardon, sir, it's all the other way with Colonel Stanley, up rather than down—"

"All right, Bodger, I'd sooner not know the details."

"Very good, sir. Eat it while it's 'ot, sir." Bodger deftly removed the plate to reveal a congealed mess. He brought a knife and fork from his pocket and, bracing his body, held the plate for Halfhyde to eat from. Then, looking away over his captain's shoulder, he said, "There's something funny about that there Colonel Stanley, sir."

Halfhyde stared, then looked down at his plate. In a casual tone he said, "It's not your job to pass comment, Bodger, nor to take tittle-tattle from one of your gentlemen to another. Is it?"

"Well, sir, in a manner o' speaking like, no it's not. Sorry, sir."

"I'll overlook it this time, Bodger."

"Yessir. Thank you, sir. I thought as 'ow you might, sir, seeing as . . . we get to 'ear things like, sir, on the lower deck."

"I'm not unaware of that. What do you hear, in particular?"

"That Colonel Stanley's a Queen's Messenger, and 'e's going to Pompey to save 'er life, sir. An' we all wish 'im the best o' luck, sir." Bodger reached again into a pocket, keeping hold of the plate with one hand. "This isn't a case o' hearing, sir, it's a case o' seeing. Seeing this, sir. Under his pillow, sir. It fell out like." He held out a piece of paper that fluttered madly in the gale. Halfhyde took it, held it steady and read with difficulty in the fading light. He saw some writing in the Spanish language and a set of numbers in groups of five, some fifty groups all told. The 7s were crossed like Fs, in the continental fashion. A code? If so, what sort? Halfhyde frowned, folded the paper and held it safe in his fist. There were various commercial codes, and this could have been passed to Stanley during his brief sojourn ashore in Gibraltar, perhaps by one of the business houses in Waterport Street. And if so—if Stanley had received a message, one that could have come from Spain via the wireless station—then he could as easily have despatched an outward one as well if he had wished to make contact with anyone in Spain . . .

Halfhyde handed the paper back to Bodger. "You're a most wicked fellow, Bodger, and much to be condemned."

"Yessir," Bodger said deferentially.

"Not too much, however. Take the paper—protect it from flying away on the wind or I'll have your liver out—take it to my cabin, Bodger, and make a careful copy and place it in my desk. Then take the original back to Colonel Stanley's cabin, and restore it. I take it Colonel Stanley needn't see what you're doing?"

"Correct, sir. Colonel Stanley, 'e 'asn't seen nothing since the weather come up, sir."

Halfhyde nodded. "And keep your mouth tight shut, Bodger."

"Aye, aye, sir, tight as a virgin's you-know-what, sir."

Chapter 16

THEY CAME thankfully out of the bay, leaving Ushant away to starboard and finding kinder weather as they came round into the Channel: seamen had no fear of the elements, but a degree of comfort was always welcome. Spirits improved and men lost their ill-used look as they went about their duties. Halfhyde was able at last to snatch some sleep, leaving the ship in Prebble's hands as they came up between the Bretagne peninsula and the Lizard, first landmark of English soil: but his sleep was not to last. As *Vendetta* brought the Eddystone Light abeam to port, a steam launch was seen hurrying out from Plymouth Sound with her signal lamp winking out *Vendetta's* call-sign.

The yeoman of signals reported to Prebble: "Request you to heave-to for despatches, sir."

Prebble nodded, ordered the engines to stop and bent to the captain's voice-pipe. Within a couple of minutes Halfhyde, rubbing the sleep from his eyes, was back on the bridge. The launch was closing fast and fifteen minutes later was coming up aft to be met by a seaman standing by on the quarterdeck with a boathook, on to which one of the launch's crew hung a leather bag. When this had been brought inboard, the launch lay off to await the response from Halfhyde. The bag was hurried to the bridge; Halfhyde opened it and brought out a sealed envelope which he tore open.

He read, but offered no comment. "I'm going below, Mr

Prebble," he said. "I'll be back directly. There'll be an envelope for the launch to take into the sound."

He went down the ladder fast, sliding on his hands along the rails; in his cabin he brought out the copy made by Bodger of the apparent code groups found in Stanley's possession, scrawled a concise report on a sheet of ship's writing paper, and sealed the two documents into an envelope which he addressed to the commander-in-chief, Plymouth, and marked "Urgent and Most Secret." Leaving his cabin he took the envelope to the quarterdeck himself and handed it down to the midshipman in charge of the steam launch. "There will be no one to take ashore, Snotty, and the explanation's in the envelope," he said.

"Aye, aye, sir." The midshipman saluted, stowed the sealed envelope and headed back for Plymouth Sound. Halfhyde returned to the bridge.

"Engines half ahead, Mr Prebble," he said formally. "Wheel fifteen degrees to starboard."

"Half ahead, sir, starboard fifteen." Prebble's response was equally formal, though he was consumed with curiosity underneath. *Vendetta* came round to the reciprocal of her former course for Portsmouth, heading back to come once again below the Lizard. When she was steadied on her course, Halfhyde ordered the engines to full ahead. "We turn up round the Lizard and the Wolf Rock, Mr Prebble, then north into St George's Channel."

"Aye, aye, sir."

Once the Longships Light was away to the south-east and *Vendetta* was standing clear of Cape Cornwall, Halfhyde had words in Prebble's ear below in his cabin. "I am obeying part

of my orders, Prebble," he said, "and disobeying another part.
The part to be obeyed you may tell the ship's company: my
orders for Portsmouth are in abeyance—so much must be obvious—and instead I am ordered into the Firth of Clyde for dis-
posal by the captain-in-charge of the coastguard for the Clyde
District."

"The Clyde, sir?"

"Yes. I read your mind, my dear Prebble, since Loch Fyne
connects with the Clyde and Inveraray is on Loch Fyne—but
remember that the threat's existence was not known ashore at
the time my fresh orders came. As a result of a report that I
sent ashore by the launch, that will be known by now, but not
until now—unless the rear-admiral in Gibraltar changed his
mind. It's possible Whitehall may simply have felt that to have
a shallow-draught vessel of her Navy handy might be appreciated by Her Majesty, threat or no threat, and we are chosen.
That's all."

"Yes, sir. And the disobeyed part of the orders?"

Halfhyde grinned. He said, "I was ordered to put Stanley
aboard the launch, and I did not do so."

Prebble's lips formed a whistle that did not come: on board
ships at sea, one whistled only for a wind. "That'll not be popular, sir."

"A situation I'm not unaccustomed to," Halfhyde said evenly.
"If you want to know why I made the decision, it's because I
prefer to have Stanley where I can keep an eye on him, as
indeed did the rear-admiral. He's a wily bird, Prebble, and a
forceful one, and I fear the ways in which he could manipulate
matters to his advantage once he sets foot ashore. While he is
aboard, he is inhibited, is he not?"

"That's true, sir." Prebble frowned, his open round face troubled. "What do you suspect, sir? Is it that Colonel Stanley's involved himself, against the Queen?"

"You have it, Prebble. God alone knows what his motive might be, but a deal of hard thought about all that has happened leads me to believe it's his hand that's to be turned against her. I propose to hold him aboard until Her Majesty's safely back in Windsor Castle."

Prebble gave a gloomy shake of his head. "I foresee trouble, sir. If he's to be held away from his crime, why, afterwards it can never be pinned on him!"

"Good God, Prebble, do you wish the Queen to die so that her assassin can be hanged?"

Prebble coloured. "Of course not, sir. But if he were allowed to commit himself—"

"And perhaps succeed in the process! No, Prebble, my way's the better one, I promise you. In the meantime, Stanley's to be well watched, though not too openly and not by way of arrest at this stage."

Stanley's face was like granite. "Look here, Halfhyde. I was under the impression I was to be landed at Portsmouth, and now—"

"My orders were cancelled by C-in-C Plymouth, sir. I had no option."

"I see. And may I ask where we're going now?"

"To the Firth of Clyde, sir."

Stanley's control was good. "The Clyde. A damn long train journey to London!"

"Or Balmoral, sir?" Halfhyde asked, with a lift of an eyebrow.

"Why Balmoral?" There was no hint in Stanley's tone that he was in any way aware of the change in the Queen's plan.

Halfhyde said, "The Queen in residence—"

"Yes, yes. But it was never my intention to go myself to Balmoral. Whitehall's my aim, to inform the proper persons. You're acting against the Queen's safety, Halfhyde—"

"No, sir." Halfhyde shook his head and kept his gaze full on Stanley, and his own tongue in his cheek as he went on: "I sent word ashore by the vessel that brought my change of orders—"

"You did what?" Stanley's voice had risen sharply.

"I made a full report to the Commander-in-Chief for onward transmission to the proper authorities. You may be assured, sir, the Queen will now be safe."

Stanley half rose from his chair in Halfhyde's cabin. "The devil she will be! God damn you for an interfering pest, Halfhyde! By God, your career shall never survive this if the Queen dies!"

"If the Queen dies through a fault of mine, sir, it would not deserve to, but she will not, I assure you." Halfhyde paused. "Perhaps you'll explain one thing that has puzzled me through-out, and the more so now. Why must your report, so vital to the Queen's safety, be made by yourself alone and in person to Whitehall?"

Stanley snapped, "Diplomatic considerations, as I've already been at some pains to make clear!"

"Yes. Diplomacy must be the strangest of beasts, sir. And the man you killed in Spain?"

"What d'you mean, Halfhyde?"

"He was not the man you said he was, a private employee of the Duke of Villanueva de Cordoba. He was a government agent."

There was a sneer on Stanley's face now. "Garcia told you this?"

"He did, sir."

"Yet you inferred to me that he had not spoken, which says ill of you in my eyes—but no matter. Garcia is a liar."

"Possibly." Halfhyde shrugged. "I wasn't impressed with the man, though I believe fear kept his tongue on the path of truth at least some of the way. Do you not think, sir, it's time *you* entrusted me with the truth . . . or shall I say, the full story of this matter?"

"It's not your concern, Halfhyde." Stanley's face was livid; his mouth had thinned to a pencil line, closing like a rat-trap. "It's a matter for Her Majesty's ministers . . . you're here to put me in touch, direct and personal touch as I've said, with Whitehall and the Queen. You are a lieutenant, no more. I am a member of the Diplomatic Corps. To me you are no more than my coachman, in whose capacity you are in a sense acting, or are supposed to act. If I were you, I would think carefully about that."

"Indeed I shall, sir, and about my capacity as your boatman as well if you wish."

There was a stare. "I beg your pardon?"

Halfhyde said coldly, "The sea off Cartagena, sir. You went over the side at an unfortunate moment. I wonder why?" He paused, keeping his eye on Stanley. "A deliberate act, sir, or did you slip as many a landlubber would?"

"It was deliberate."

"Then, sir—"

"And intended to be helpful. The cutter was under fire. It was vital I should reach the battle Fleet, and being a powerful swimmer I saw more chance alone in the water. A smaller target and one that could conceivably not have been seen at all by the Spanish."

"And us to draw the Spanish fire?"

Stanley shrugged. "A risk that should have been acceptable to men of Her Majesty's Navy. The fact that I hit my head . . . that was not deliberate, I assure you." Stanley, who had got to his feet whilst speaking, stalked out of the cabin. Halfhyde sat at his desk, frowning: what Stanley had said held logic, and was in character for the man, certainly. Time would tell whether or not it was true. Indeed Stanley's whole reaction, rude though it had been, and overbearing, had been perfectly in character for an official being baulked in his duty. His anger had been natural—even proper if he were genuine. He was a convincing man, and though there were very many reasons, in Halfhyde's view, to doubt him there was undeniably no doubt about one thing: Halfhyde had been ordered to put him ashore at Plymouth and had not done so. And if Colonel Stanley was made aware of that fact, he would clearly be an even angrier man than he was now.

Halfhyde got up and climbed the ladders to the bridge, returning the salute of the officer of the watch absently. He looked away to starboard and the jagged coast of Wales as the ship approached Anglesey and the Skerries Light off the entry to the Mersey. There was a fair amount of shipping, merchant vessels inward bound for Liverpool or outward bound for distant places—great square-rigged sailing ships for Australia around Cape Horn, ships for South America, New Zealand, or China and Japan via the Sunda Strait and Singapore, servicing, as the Royal Navy policed, the world's trading routes, the routes of Empire where the Queen of England ruled and half the world lay red upon the map. Halfhyde brooded darkly, standing silent by the guardrail. There was so much at stake: had he acted over-hastily, even precipitately—even stupidly? Should not a Queen's Messenger be allowed his reservations, should he be expected to reveal all to a naval lieutenant? Yet something about Stanley stuck in the throat, and stuck hard; not in Halfhyde's throat alone, he believed, but also in that of Rear-Admiral Arbuthnot in Gibraltar. If it was the case that the rear-admiral had decided after all to make a full report to Whitehall, then his feelings about Stanley must have intensified after further thought.

Halfhyde turned from the guardrail and paced the bridge, looking at the coming and going merchant ships, looking across Liverpool Bay towards the Mersey as *Vendetta,* clear away north from Carmel Head, continued on passage for the Clyde. Then he saw a small craft, a steam launch, coming fast from the Mersey and heading to cross his track. Lifting his telescope he saw men in blue uniforms and helmets: police, looking curiously out of place on the sea. Two of them, together with a man in plain clothes of a sporting nature. A moment later a flag hoist crept to the vessel's miniature mast: a signal in the International Code indicating that *Vendetta* was to heave-to.

With a snap, Halfhyde closed his telescope: the police were the police and discretion was called for. He ordered the engine-room telegraphs to stop, and then half astern. *Vendetta,* pulled up in her tracks, sat the water like a wild swan. As the disturbed foam from astern reached amidships, Halfhyde stopped his engines finally and waited for the steam launch to come alongside aft, where men were standing by a Jacob's ladder. The two uniformed police, both of them sergeants, came aboard followed by the plain-clothes man in his Norfolk jacket, and were brought to the bridge.

Halfhyde looked them up and down. "I am on passage to the Clyde, under orders from the Commander-in-Chief, Plymouth. I hope you have a good reason for stopping me?"

The plain-clothes man spoke: by his voice, a gentleman, Halfhyde noted. "A good reason indeed, Mr Halfhyde. You seem to have ignored certain orders—"

"Who are you, sir?"

"My name's Cadogan-Goodison. I'm the Chief Constable of the county palatine of Lancaster, and I'm ordered to give passage ashore to Colonel Stanley. You'll be so good as to have him informed."

"May I ask what you intend doing with him, sir?"

"He's required for urgent consultations in London, and time is short. You will be good enough to send for him instantly."

There had been no option; Colonel Cadogan-Goodison, whose military rank had emerged when Halfhyde had sent for Stanley to come to his cabin, produced his credentials and announced that he was acting under the orders of the Home Secretary himself. That was not all; he and Stanley knew each other. The Chief Constable, formerly of the 21st Lancers, had been brigaded with Stanley's regiment during manoeuvres on Salisbury Plain some years before, and they greeted each other as old acquaintances. Within half an hour of the boarding by the police, Stanley was on his way into Liverpool and the train to London. Though furious and incredulous when told that he should, had Halfhyde obeyed orders, have been landed into Plymouth Sound, he had cooled down enough to thank Halfhyde before leaving the ship for all that he had done on his behalf. "All's well," he said tritely, "that ends well."

"It's not ended yet, sir."

"No, indeed—"

"I hope your words will be found true when it is, sir."

Stanley snapped, "Everything will be done that can be done."

Halfhyde, having saluted the Queen's Messenger over the side, went back to the bridge with his first lieutenant, deep in thought. He was restless and far from happy, still unsatisfied about Stanley. Yet Her Majesty's government in London seemed satisfied, and must be assumed to know their business. The code groups that had been sent ashore in his despatch to the Plymouth Command must have been broken down by now, presumably; perhaps they had proved innocuous—in fact they must have done, unless Stanley was proceeding to London under arrest, and no warrant had been produced in Halfhyde's presence.

Liverpool Bay faded away on the starboard quarter and *Vendetta* headed up to cross the Solway Firth beyond Barrow-in-Furness, steaming through a flat sea beneath a blue sky darkening as the sun went down: a perfect day, but spoiled for Halfhyde by his nagging anxieties. Time, as that Chief Constable had said, was indeed short now. The day after tomorrow the Queen would join the royal train at Windsor station and her coaches would be fed into the network that would carry her to the railway station at the remote junction at Crianlarich in Argyll, and the long journey by most lonely roads along the upper reaches of Loch Lomond, through Tarbet and Arrochar and across the head of Loch Fyne to the great castle at Inveraray, seat of Mac Cailein Mhor, chief of Clan Campbell, Duke of

Argyll, Hereditary Master of the Queen's Household in Scotland, Admiral of the Western Coast and Isles, Keeper of the Great Seal of Scotland; and most importantly to Her Majesty perhaps, something else . . . Halfhyde, struck by a sudden irreverent and disloyal thought, laughed aloud; and then met Prebble's questioning eye.

He said, "I'm as loyal as you, my dear Prebble, but there's something we shouldn't forget!"

"Sir?"

"His Grace is the father-in-law of the Queen's daughter, Princess Louise. It occurs to me that Her Majesty's perhaps the most terrible mother-in-law in Europe!"

Prebble remained stiffly silent, and Halfhyde was aware that he had much offended his first lieutenant's susceptibilities.

Chapter 17

SHORTLY AFTER the next day's dawn *Vendetta* turned to star-board below the Mull of Kintyre and entered the broad sweep below the Firth of Clyde, leaving the great seagull-whitened rock of Ailsa Craig on her port hand. She headed up past the isle of Arran, coming across the entrance to Inchmarnock Water that led into Loch Fyne and Inveraray; leaving Garroch Head to port, Halfhyde took his ship through the Cumbraes channel to enter the firth proper and head for his anchorage at the Tail o' the Bank off Greenock. Once anchored, Halfhyde looked keenly at the sky: he fancied there was wind in the offing, and the Tail o' the Bank was no easy anchorage when the wind blew strong.

"Set an anchor watch, if you please, Mr Prebble, until fur-ther notice. And the engine-room to remain on stand-by."

"Aye, aye, sir." Prebble hesitated. "Is this just for the weather, or do you expect a movement order?"

"Both," Halfhyde answered. "As to the second part, I shall know more once I'm bidden aboard the *Benbow*." HMS *Benbow*, a first-class battleship of 10,600 tons lying at a buoy off Greenock, was the district ship for Coastguard and Royal Naval Reserve Duties for the Clyde District; Halfhyde's Navy List had already shown him that the *Benbow* was commanded by one

Captain Eustace Rooke with Commander William Ricketts as his executive officer. "In the meantime, Mr Prebble, there'll be no shore leave piped."

"Aye, aye, sir. Colonel Stanley, sir—what do you suppose—"

"I suppose nothing at this moment, Mr Prebble. I am in the dark and await enlightenment."

Halfhyde turned and went down the ladder to his cabin, a man more worried than he had wished his first lieutenant to see. The time was closing in, the time of danger that would start tomorrow. The responsibility for the Queen's life was, of course, not his; but he was much involved and he had interfered by his act in disobeying orders. If Stanley was genuine, damage might have been done and that would lie wholly and firmly at his, Halfhyde's, door. If he was not, then damage would be done by the fact of Stanley's uninhibited freedom, in which case, perhaps, Halfhyde now thought, he should have risked going the whole dangerous hog and held the police, Chief Constable and all, on board with Stanley . . .

In the privacy of his cabin, Halfhyde raised clenched fists at his own reflection in the mirror above his washstand: as ever, a commanding officer of one of Her Majesty's ships of war faced a fifty per cent chance of being wrong each time he took a decision. Sometimes to be wrong was inevitable; but in that thought there was no satisfaction whatever. Savagely Halfhyde glared out of his port at the town of Greenock and the hills of Renfrew behind: like yesterday the day was fine, with a bright sun shining down on blue water, and coastal shipping was going by, to and from Glasgow and other ports farther up the river—and crossing their track now was a Royal Naval craft with her brass-

work gleaming, a steam picket-boat coming off from the battleship *Benbow.* Halfhyde emerged from his cabin to be met by
the gangway messenger bearing word of the approaching boat.
Five minutes later he was back in his cabin with Commander
Ricketts in person.

Ricketts, a grey-haired man in his late forties, came straight
to the point. "We shall talk freely, Halfhyde. I understand there
was a coded message and that you sent it to the C-in-C at
Plymouth. It's been broken down and my captain has been sent
the plain language version by Admiralty messenger from
London."

"You have it with you, sir?"

"Yes."

"May I see it?"

"By all means." Ricketts brought a sheet of paper from his
pocket and handed it across. The originator appeared to be one
Attilio La Malfa, probably an Italian, and it was addressed to a
person named Luis Orbea care of the P&O agents in Gibraltar.
The message itself was at first sight imprecise; it referred to all
arrangements having been made for "the project" and that the
shift of venue had been notified to the parties concerned. That
was all; but with Halfhyde's background knowledge it dropped
neatly into place. Frowning, Halfhyde passed the sheet of paper
back.

"Luis Orbea, sir? Do we know who he might be?"

"A Spaniard, possibly handy by in La Linea. Or a Gibraltarian,
though I doubt it—they're loyal to a fault." The commander
paused, looking thoughtfully at Halfhyde. "Or Stanley, under a
nom-de-plume. After all, he had the coded message, hadn't he?"

Halfhyde's lips tightened. "So suspicion does rest on Stanley in minds other than my own—and not too late, I hope!"

"So do I indeed. He's coming north, by the way, and will reach Glasgow this evening—"

"In what capacity?"

Ricketts smiled. "Queen's Saviour, I rather fancy! He's asked, and been given, permission to bowl these assassins out himself—"

"Was this before or after that message was decoded?"

"After, which I agree is perplexing, Halfhyde."

"Not too perplexing. Stanley is a forceful man, and would have found a way of explaining his possession of the coded cable—which was not in fact addressed to him by name. And the fact of his being assigned to the job after it was decoded—that points to its being disregarded as evidence against him, sir."

"True. And I'm not saying I entirely agree with your views on Colonel Stanley—"

"A distinguished officer, a gentleman—from a good regiment, and rides to hounds," Halfhyde said bitterly. "Your pardon—I quote the senior officer of my flotilla. And it counts, does all that—it weighs mightily!"

Ricketts said, shrugging, "It has its relevance, one can't get away from that."

"Then I think one should try, sir. May I know what the counter-measures are, or is the Queen's safety to be left entirely in Stanley's hands?"

"Largely, yes," Ricketts admitted. "That is, as to the co-ordination of HM's defence. He knows the score—he knows these people. He has many advantages, and it appears that

HMG wants to catch 'em and not scare 'em off by large-scale troop movements, which are awfully cumbersome. The theory is, they could live to try again. If they're actually caught—"

"They hang! I concede the point, but consider it dangerous to Her Majesty, sir."

"Stanley will have plenty of support to call upon, Halfhyde, of course. A cordon's being thrown discreetly around the outer perimeters of regions likely to be visited by Her Majesty—"

"Your pardon, sir. How does one throw a cordon discreetly?" Halfhyde asked in a cold tone.

Ricketts grinned. "How indeed? In more precise terms, the idea is that troops and police will be available at immediate notice rather than be visibly deployed on the spot as it were— with two exceptions: the Black Watch is to provide a guard at Crianlarich, which is where HM's rail journey terminates, and the 1st Battalion the Argyll and Sutherland Highlanders will be on manoeuvres in the district north of Inveraray—between there and Oban on the west coast. They were under orders for these exercises long before the threat was known, and before the Queen's decision to visit Inveraray instead of Balmoral was known, too. The assassins, assuming they've acquainted them- selves with possible opposition, would be more alerted by a cancellation—and that's fortunate for us."

"Will there be a personal escort for Her Majesty when she drives out from Crianlarich, sir?"

Ricketts said, "She'll not go unprotected, Halfhyde, you may be sure." He paused. "You yourself are to be part of her pro- tection. I have your orders, which are that you'll weigh and sail from the Tail o' the Bank at midday and enter Lamlash Bay in Arran, where you'll lie at anchor overnight. Her Majesty's

expected to leave the train at Crianlarich after she has breakfasted the morning after tomorrow—she'll spend the night in
her coach, rather than face the roads after dark—"

"The coach will be well guarded, I imagine?"

"Yes, most certainly. You'll remain in Lamlash throughout
tomorrow, weighing after dark to begin a patrol across the exits
from Loch Fyne. If the assassins should have planned their
escape route by water, then that's the way they'll take, most
likely, though the sea routes out of Oban are also being covered, likewise the Mull of Kintyre. The land routes will be covered by the army."

"One thing," Halfhyde said to Prebble for whom he sent when
Commander Ricketts had returned aboard the *Benbow,* "that stands
out like a sore thumb is this: if Stanley wasn't playing a double
game, Villanueva would have called the whole thing off the
moment we left Cartagena with Stanley aboard. Wouldn't he?"

"That's likely, sir. And maybe he has."

Halfhyde snapped, "You sound like Ricketts—I put the point
to him. Damn it, Prebble, is the Queen's life to depend on a
maybe?" He paced up and down the quarterdeck, broodingly.
"I think we're governed by a set of lunatics who can see no farther than the ends of their noses! Some much more positive
action's called for!" He smashed a fist into his palm. "Damned
if I don't supply it myself!"

"How, sir?"

Halfhyde walked on. "At this moment, I see only the trees
and not the wood. The sea breezes may clear my head. It's time
to shorten in, Mr Prebble. Pipe the hands to stations, if you
please."

"Aye, aye, sir." Prebble saluted and turned away; Halfhyde made his way to the bridge. At noon precisely the anchor broke water and Halfhyde put his engines ahead, moving out from the Tail o' the Bank as the water became ruffled by a sudden gust of wind that rattled the signal halliards and blew coldly across the bridge. As the ship turned to port around Cloch Point and headed for the Cumbraes, the wind smote more strongly, battering against the canvas dodger around the bridge guardrails and sending the White Ensign out stiff as a board from its staff. Halfhyde faced into the wind's teeth, his face set, his mind roving over possibilities and impossibilities as the time ticked on towards the Queen's entraining at Windsor. Down past Toward Point by Castle Toward and on to face heavy black cloud rolling in beyond the Cumbraes: a dirty afternoon and probably a worse night was in prospect. The seas were short and sharp as Halfhyde, dropping south, made the turn for Arran and took the ship in to anchor in Lamlash Bay.

That night, Halfhyde turned in early, snatching sleep when he could before he was called on deck, as he believed he might be, should the anchors start to drag across the bottom . . . and after a night that was in truth largely sleepless although he was not sent for by Prebble, the weather was no better. It remained a strong blow, laced with rain, throughout the day; and as each hour passed Halfhyde found himself visualizing the Queen's northward progress in the comfort and elegance of her drawing-room coach in the company of her ladies-in-waiting, all of whom would stand at some risk from the assassin's hand. Halfhyde distracted himself, as decision began to form, by poring over the charts of the sea areas around Arran; and then, as once again night fell, the ship's company were piped to their stations and anchor was weighed. *Vendetta* stole out to start her patrol across the entry to Loch Fyne and the convergence of Inchmarnock Water and Kilbrannan Sound. As they reached their position, Halfhyde spoke to his first lieutenant, his mind made up.

"I'm going in, Mr Prebble."

"In, sir?"

"Into the loch, for Inveraray. There's a somewhat difficult turn at the entrance to keep in the deep channel, but once in it's all plain sailing. There's plenty of water, with the five- and ten-fathom lines running off Inveraray, and once there I shall anchor."

"Yes, sir. And then?"

"Boats, Mr Prebble, and landing-parties, seamen and stokers, armed with rifles and bayonets. The parties to land at Cairndow, on the opposite side of the loch from Inveraray and right up at its head, which cuts off a good deal of the road to Crianlarich, and if we're lucky we can cut off more by going across country to the headwaters of Loch Lomond." In the binnacle's glow he looked hard at Prebble. "You think I'm crazy. You may as well say so!"

"Sir, I—"

Halfhyde said crisply, "The time for chances has come, and for assessments that I agree may be wrong. But it seems to me that the assassins will strike on the road from Crianlarich, which is the only one that is known positively that the Queen will take during her stay—and her time known also. And I happen to know that by Loch Lomond the lie of the land is most favourable for attack. It's lonely, it's heavily wooded, and the trees grow on ground that slopes steeply to the road. The cover's excellent, and the Queen's carriage can be raked by fire from above."

"But the distance, sir! We'll never have the time!"

"We need only reach the road, not Crianlarich. Forced marching, Mr Prebble, best foot foremost!" Halfhyde rubbed his hands together. "We shall do it. I shall be off Inveraray by eleven o'clock at the latest, and the landing-parties will be ashore before midnight. The Queen won't breakfast early, Mr Prebble, and we shall have at least ten hours in hand before she leaves the train."

Halfhyde was as good as his word: once past the entrance, Loch Fyne presented no difficulty to the safe navigation of his shallow-draught TBD. They steamed without lights and in the filthy weather prevailing Halfhyde felt certain he would not be spotted from the shore; the darkness was intense, with heavy cloud overhead and not a vestige of moon to be seen. It was only five bells in the first watch, half an hour ahead of time, when the anchor rumbled down not far off the small white township of Inveraray dominated, at any rate in daylight, by the great grey castle of the Dukes of Argyll; and by eleven-fifteen the landing-parties were ashore in Cairndow—thirty seamen and stokers with four leading hands plus the gunner's mate and the torpedo-gunner's mate, led by Halfhyde himself with Sub-Lieutenant Sawbridge, all in black oilskins, all gaitered, all armed as heavily as the ship's weaponry would allow. Halfhyde and Sawbridge and the petty officers carried revolvers; the gunner's mate had brought a cutlass as well, and looked almost demoniacal in the wild highland night as he flourished it like a claymore. Though the march was not to be a particularly long one, progress as the crow flew must be slow despite Halfhyde's confident words to Prebble earlier. With a boat's compass to give them their bearings, and a large-scale map to guide them, they would have to penetrate the lonely glens below the heights of Ben Vorlich and Beinn Ime. Halfhyde's orders were few and clear.

"Keep together, march in single file and don't lose your next ahead. I'll be in the lead. Don't straggle—if you do, the gunner's mate will have your guts before he herds you on. When we reach the ground above the road, I'll make a reconnaissance and further orders will follow then. All right? Off we go, then!"

Studying his map in a lantern's glow, checking with a boat's compass, Halfhyde stalked ahead, along the high road out of Cairndow to begin with, then striking off left into the wildness of the open country. Rain teemed, and trees bent to a strong wind; it was bitterly cold, a cold that the oilskins and sou'-westers failed to keep out in spite of all manner of warm garments beneath, balaclavas, jerseys and scarves. By some miracle they kept together through the glens, by some miracle they held to the right track, as the night grew even wilder. Now and again Halfhyde rested the men for brief spells, always getting them back on their feet before they could stiffen and succumb to the biting cold.

It was a nightmare journey; as the dawn came up palely all of them looked like automatons, weary-eyed, stumbling as they put one foot painfully before the other, climbing like mountain goats, treading through the heather, through bracken, over rocks and up terrible slopes that sent them, in some cases, headlong down the other side. There was much bitter and resentful muttering, and never mind the Queen: they'd fight for her, all right, but this was different, they were sailors not farmers or soldiers.

They trudged and grudged along behind Halfhyde, who seemed to be impervious to wind and weather, mud and abominable things that tripped men up to send them flat on their faces. He appeared totally set and single-minded; aware that he could be quite wrong in his assessment, he was sustained by the certain knowledge that if his action didn't help the Queen, it could at least not harm her nor could it lessen the chances of the assassins being apprehended in an attempt to get out of the country: despite being left sadly short-handed with half her company ashore, *Vendetta,* under the capable command of Prebble, was under Halfhyde's order to return to her patrol position and resume the watch.

By morning, with time in hand, the landing-parties had reached the ground above the road running south from Crianlarich, and had the headwaters of Loch Lomond, grey and forbidding beneath an ugly sky, in view beyond. Halfhyde fell the men out for a rest, and then gave his final orders, splitting his force into two main groups, one under Sawbridge, the other under his own command. One group would extend southwards towards Tarbet and the other, his own, northwards towards Crianlarich.

"You'll move as quietly as possible," he said, "and spread out widely. Keep well back on the high ground—and watch and listen. The first man to spot an intruder will pass word back to Mr Sawbridge or myself, and every effort is to be made to ensure none of us is seen until we're ready to attack in strength. However, if any man is forced to open fire for his own protection, he has my authority to do so. If a shot is heard, all men of the group concerned will close the position it was fired from, and carry out an attack. Are there any questions? Yes, Petty Officer Thomas?"

Thomas, the gunner's mate, said, "Beg pardon, sir. By the time we can all muster, the buggers may have run for it, and—"

"A chance we must take. Once they're flushed and on the run, at least they'll not harm the Queen, and our objective's achieved in its most important part." Halfhyde added, "We must face the fact they may not be in the vicinity at all. This may be a wild-goose chase. Her Majesty is guarded at Crianlarich by a company of the Black Watch, and the assassins may not risk this area. Nevertheless, I have a feeling in my bones that they're not far off. I wish you all good hunting. You are within a few miles of the Queen. If she knew we were here, she would rest easy, putting her trust in the men of her Fleet. I know that every man will prove worthy of that." He turned to Sawbridge. "Carry on, if you please, Mr Sawbridge."

"Aye, aye, sir." Sawbridge brought a hand up to the brim of his sou'-wester in salute, and turned about. Halfhyde nodded to the gunner's mate, who would accompany his own group, and, quietly, Petty Officer Thomas detailed off the hands for their spread along the high ground. To move in complete silence was impossible: brushwood crackled beneath booted feet, twigs and branches snapped. Actually to take the assassins might well prove far beyond probability, but to set one's aim high was seldom a mistake. Halfhyde watched his men move out, one by one; then moved himself to take up his position in the centre of the line, with the rest of the ratings following on as their turns came and they were checked out by the leading hands. Making his way along towards Crianlarich Halfhyde looked down upon the ribbon of roadway running above the loch. Not often had he seen such a lonely road, full of twists and turns and almost hairpin bends where a carriage would need to slow down to a crawl: those must be the points of most danger to the Queen's life.

Halfhyde moved on as fast as he could: he found nothing amiss, no sign of human life beyond his own men. There was indeed an intense quiet broken high up by the wind sighing in the lofty treetops, and a creak from the swaying trunks below— a creak that could very well mask the small movement sounds made by the sailors; there was the occasional sound of birds, and of small scurrying animals; nothing else. Halfhyde gave an involuntary shiver: beyond Crianlarich and Tyndrum lay the desolation of Rannoch Moor that led into the dread remoteness of the Pass of Glencoe with its massive mountains often lost in mist as the clouds came down. Glencoe, and the massacre of 1692, when the MacDonalds were wiped out with the con- nivance of an ancestor of Her Majesty's host-to-be . . . this morning, as the sun struggled in vain to penetrate the leaden sky and the wreathing mists, Halfhyde could almost fancy he heard the groans and cries, the sickening thrust of knives and the smack of cudgels on unprotected heads, as though the mournful ghosts of the slain were gathering in kilt and tartan plaid to witness the death of a descendant of the Hanoverian kings . . .

All at once there came a fresh sound, and a sight to dissolve Halfhyde's fanciful imaginings: down upon the road to his right, the swish of rubber tyres on a wet surface was heard—a bicycle. On the bicycle was a fat figure in blue uniform, the trousers visible beneath the folds of a blue cape as the feet thrust vigorously on the pedals of his machine and water dripped from the brim of the helmet: a solitary policeman, some village bobby from Tarbet, hastening perhaps to add the weight of his friendly presence to Her Majesty's safety. Halfhyde watched in some amusement: great fat did not lead to efficiency upon a push-bicycle, and the policeman was puffing like a steam-engine. As the man rode up towards one of the hairpin bends he swung a leg in the air and dismounted from the machine as though to take a rest from his exertions. The helmet was pushed back and a handkerchief was withdrawn from beneath the cape; a streaming face was mopped and then the policeman's attention seemed to be caught by something of interest in the trees and undergrowth. He wheeled the bicycle into the roadside, looking upwards as he did so: Halfhyde moved on faster, cursing to himself. He had no wish for his men to be remarked, and called out to, and questioned by some interfering bobby who could give the game away.

Then the situation altered suddenly and sadly. There was a shot, followed by another, and the policeman fell, staggering towards the support of a tree and not reaching it. He collapsed by the roadside; he managed to lift an arm and put his whistle to his lips, and blow a blast, and then three figures had materialized from the trees and were dragging the man back into the cover whence they had come.

Chapter 18

HALFHYDE DIDN'T LINGER: he went down the steep slope almost headlong and out into the road, pulling himself up just short of a tumble into the loch below. He doubled along towards where he had seen the policeman fall, shouting his sailors to the attack. They had no need of his order: the gunner's mate had already led them into the area and the seamen were bunched along the top of the slope and starting to move down behind their rifles with bayonets fixed.

Halfhyde reached the spot where the bicycle had been dragged hurriedly into the trees and left half visible. With his revolver in his hand he moved forward, crouching, searching ahead. He heard the sounds as the naval ratings moved down towards him, led by the gunner's mate. He got to his feet.

"Any luck, Thomas?"

"None, sir." The petty officer wiped the back of a hand across his face. "Buggers have gone to earth . . . or made off sideways. They left the bobby, sir."

"Alive?"

"No, sir."

"I'll take a look at him. He could have been carrying a message for Crianlarich."

"Aye, aye, sir. If you'll follow me, sir."

The gunner's mate turned away; Halfhyde followed up the slope a little way, pushing aside branches that whipped back as he passed. The blue-clad body was lying on its back in the undergrowth. The head lolled; the throat had been slit from ear to ear, a horrible gaping wound. Evidently the bullets hadn't been enough. Feeling the bile rise, Halfhyde squatted and ran his hands over the body, through the pockets. He found nothing of interest.

He stood up. "Keep searching, Thomas, and maintain the patrols as ordered, right along the line. I'm going ahead to Crianlarich. It's possible we've routed the assassins, but the danger's still there and Her Majesty must be warned that they're in the vicinity."

"That'll take time, sir."

"On foot, yes! But not so long by bicycle." Halfhyde turned away and went fast back for the road, picking up the policeman's machine from its resting place. Swinging himself into the saddle, he pedalled off fast for Crianlarich and the royal train, which by his reckoning was no more than a dozen or so miles away. The exertion, for a mostly ship-bound man, was punishing, but Halfhyde didn't spare himself. He arrived at the small highland railway station in a lather of sweat and badly out of breath, a somewhat grotesque figure in his oilskins and sou'-wester and leather seaboots who was stopped by a sergeant of the Black Watch on duty at the entrance to the station under the looming shadow of the Crianlarich Mountains.

"Who are you, and what's your business here?"

Halfhyde blew out his cheeks and dismounted. "Lieutenant St Vincent Halfhyde, Royal Navy, commanding the torpedo-boat destroyer *Vendetta*, on duty for Her Majesty's protection."

"Aye, sir." The sergeant looked him over, dourly. "You'll have proof o' this, sir?"

Halfhyde opened his oilskin, showing the brass buttons with the naval crown and anchor on his monkey-jacket. "I have no proof other than the Queen's uniform, Sergeant. I must see Her Majesty at once, d'you hear—at once!"

"You'll need to state your business, sir, first to me and then to—"

"Life or death," Halfhyde said. He lifted an arm and pointed. "Down the road to Tarbet armed men are waiting for the Queen's carriage, and already a police constable has been killed—" He broke off as a tall, kilted officer approached, eyebrows raised at the intrusion. "Major, I wish urgent audience of the Queen, or at least of her guard commander—"

"I am the guard commander. And you?"

Once again, Halfhyde explained. He demanded, "Is there a Colonel Stanley here? He—"

"Yes, he's here. He's presently waiting upon the Queen, who's to grant him audience when she's breakfasted."

Halfhyde's face was stony. He said, "That should not be allowed. Stanley's loyalties are suspect."

"Really?" The major's tone was scathing. "By whom?"

"By me at least, Major. I brought him out of Spain—I was sent to meet him there. Believe me, there's no time to lose." Briefly he explained the circumstances, was relieved to see that the soldier understood his references. Sweat poured down Halfhyde's face in spite of the early-morning cold. He looked round as he heard the crunch of wheels and the clop of horses' hooves; already the Queen's carriage was moving up to the station approach. He swung back to the Scots officer. "You must let me approach the Queen. The very fact of my presence with her may deter Stanley—"

"Deter him from what, for God's sake?" The major gave a laugh of impatience. "Do you suggest he may kill her?"

"Not himself, unless he's mad. But he's not to be trusted, in my view. He may persuade her that the road's safe to Inveraray, and she may believe him—and it's very far from safe! I am the one person here who can assure her from experience of that. Are you prepared to chance the Queen's life by holding me here talking, when already a man has died?"

"A police constable, you say—"

"Murdered. Shot in cold blood before my eyes."

The Scot was clearly alarmed at the implications of the killing; something had penetrated, but he was taking his time. Halfhyde shook with his frustration, feeling that he would have to draw his revolver on the man and force him to conduct him to the royal drawing-room coach. Then the major nodded. "Very well, Lieutenant Halfhyde, your point is taken. Come with me."

He turned about and strode through the tiny booking hall out to the platform where the royal train was drawn up under a strong guard of Highland soldiers, their breath steaming in the air as they marched their posts alongside the ornate drawing-room coach and the curtained windows of the Queen's sleeping compartment. There was a smell of breakfast in the air: bacon and eggs, fish, coffee. Her Majesty, taking her ease on her journey, was currently blocking the single track from Stirling to Oban. At the platform entrance to the booking hall stood a portly man wearing a black frock-coat and a tall hat: the stationmaster, swollen with self-importance and high responsibility. The major spoke to him.

"Has Colonel Stanley boarded the train, Mr MacInnes?"

"Aye, sir, he has that. He's waiting in the vestibule of Her Majesty's drawing-room coach, sir."

The major nodded and stalked along the platform with Halfhyde at his side. Halfhyde, opening his oilskin again, slid his right hand over the butt of the Service revolver in its webbing holster. He felt a curious prickling in his spine as he approached the coach where the Queen sat; the Scots major opened the door leading into the small vestibule. Looking in, he addressed someone inside.

"I am in a quandary, sir. Certain things have been said, and I think you should hear them." He turned his head and beckoned Halfhyde closer. Halfhyde, as he moved in, saw Stanley rising from a seat.

"Good morning, sir."

"You!" Stanley's face had gone deathly white; it could have been fear or rage. "What the devil are you doing here, may I ask?"

"I ask you the same question, sir. As for me . . . I am here for the Queen's safety."

"And I also. Major, I suggest you remove this officer and send him back to his duty—"

"A moment, Major." Halfhyde's voice was loud and angry. "If you value the Queen's life, you'll place Colonel Stanley in arrest and then question him about certain movements in Spain—and in this country, so that Her Majesty can go safely to Inveraray. I accuse him of being party to a plot to assassinate Her Majesty this very day, and I—" He broke off. On Stanley's right hand a door had opened from the drawing-room coach and a lady-in-waiting had emerged, her expression frosty; and her features not unlike those of Rear-Admiral Sir Humphrey Arbuthnot.

"If you please, gentlemen," she said. "Her Majesty dislikes such shouting, and desires you to stop instantly. She wishes to know what is happening."

Stanley's mouth opened but Halfhyde beat him to it. "Ma'am," he said, "am I right in thinking your brother is the rear-admiral commanding the Particular Service Squadron, currently in Gibraltar?"

The lady-in-waiting stared. "What makes you think this?"

Halfhyde bowed. "Your looks, ma'am! You are like him in looks."

She hesitated, then smiled. "Well, you're right, he is my brother. What—"

"I am loosely under his orders, ma'am. Sir Humphrey's concern is for Her Majesty, as is mine. I wish to speak with her. The matter's vital."

Stanley was asked, politely, to step down from the coach; he went to the waiting-room accompanied by the major, who, though deferential, was clearly alert for possible trouble. Halfhyde was bidden into the royal presence. A bundle in black, an imperious bundle whose breakfast had been interrupted by unseemliness, sat with hands clasped in the lap by a wide window looking down into Glen Dochart and away north to Rannoch Moor. The expression on the face was impatient, disagreeable, as Halfhyde executed an awkward obeisance.

"We much dislike *noise*."

"My apologies, ma'am."

"Lady Fairfax recommends we listen to what you have to say, but there is little time before we leave for Inveraray." The Queen consulted a bejewelled watch hanging upon her breast. "Well, Mr Halfhyde, what is it?"

"A threat, ma'am, to—"

"Yes. It has been brought to our attention, but we are certainly not afraid. Our dear subjects would never lift a hand against us, Mr Halfhyde."

"Exactly so, ma'am. But these people—"

"Foreigners."

Halfhyde coughed. "In a word, yes. But the effect would be the same, ma'am, whatever the hand that fired the bullet. Ma'am, I am here to advise you that already a policeman has died at their hands on the road to Tarbet, and to suggest that you vary your route—for the country's sake, ma'am. You are much loved, and can ill be spared."

The expression on the Queen's face softened; she smiled and bent her head. "You flatter me, Mr Halfhyde. I am told by Lady Fairfax that you have been much concerned in looking after my safety in Spain, and I am most touched. But I shall not vary my route as you suggest."

"Ma'am, I beg—"

"Tell me about this poor constable, and how he died. I am most upset."

Halfhyde told her of the tragedy; she was indeed most visibly upset, and promised that the policeman's family would never want. Tears came to the Queen's eyes when she spoke of the man's sacrifice and his great loyalty; and she insisted that if a constable had not shirked his duty then neither would she. Her route remained; she utterly rejected Halfhyde's suggestion that she take the carriage to Ballachulish while he hastened back to his ship and sailed north into Loch Linnhe to embark her for Inveraray; this, she replied crossly and with some justification, would mean far too long a wait and would be discourteous to His Grace. She was not shaken even when a butcher's cart rumbled into the station approach, bearing the dead policeman and a triumphant gunner's mate who reported a successful search and an even more successful execution of orders: no less than six apparent Italians lay dead above Loch Lomond, and no others had been found. The Queen received this news with equanimity, saying that the route was now perfectly safe, as indeed Colonel Stanley had assured her it would be.

"Colonel Stanley, ma'am—"

"Dear Colonel Stanley is never wrong, Mr Halfhyde. Never. Such a charming man as well."

"No doubt, ma'am. I think, however, that he meant you no good on this occasion—"

"What do you mean, Mr Halfhyde?" The head was raised; the Queen looked down her nose. "No good! What does this mean?"

Halfhyde said with a touch of desperation, "I believe he was against you, ma'am. I believe he was on the side of the assassins—"

"Nonsense!" The Queen was trembling, her face ashen as she lifted a black walking-stick and flourished it in Halfhyde's face. "Such talk . . . *treason!* There is *no man* more loyal than dear Colonel Stanley!"

"Ma'am, it's my duty to disagree." Halfhyde's voice had risen again; Queen or no Queen, he was not to be browbeaten. "I go further. I suggest Colonel Stanley be placed in arrest, and—"

"No, no, no!" Each word was emphasized by a thump of a heavy rubber ferrule on the floor of the royal drawing-room coach. "It is our order, our personal order, that Colonel Stanley accompanies us to Inveraray as he wishes—"

"Ma'am, I—"

"Our personal order and there is no more to be said!"

"But—"

"Get out of our sight!" The stick was flourished again; the Queen waved her arms as though about to have a fit; then she screamed, and screamed again, quite beside herself with rage. Halfhyde obeyed her last order and backed away from the royal presence, his face furious and his own temper high at blind stupidity. As he stepped on to the platform he came face to face with Stanley, who was smiling widely.

"May I offer my sympathies, Halfhyde? I heard Her Majesty's command, as did the major commanding the guard. I assure you it will be obeyed." Stanley paused. "There's something else, my dear fellow."

"Well?"

"My congratulations on flushing the assassins. You've done excellent work, and I'm deeply grateful, as the whole country and Empire will be . . . though you came within an ace of messing up the whole operation!"

"I did?"

"Yes. The moment I saw you, I fancied you might be thrusting in a naval boot . . . it was a delicate business to be sure, and best left to the experts." Stanley turned as another man came out from the booking hall. "This is Sir James Renshaw of the Foreign Office . . . I think he'll resolve all your natural doubts." He paused, looking shrewdly at Halfhyde. "Some wise man once said that a diplomat's speech is always half-way between a cliché and a damned lie, and he wasn't far wrong. But the gentry are not corrupt, my dear fellow, they have no need to be. They have money and position already. When the gentry are no more, then you will get corruption, for all the little men will try to grow big." He held out his hand; after a moment's hesitation, still to some degree doubtful, Halfhyde took it.

An hour or so before the Queen's scheduled boarding of her carriage, the butcher's cart, pressed into naval service, took Halfhyde back to where his victorious ship's company awaited him along the road to Tarbet. Other tradesmen's vehicles came out with him from Crianlarich to collect all hands and drive them down by road to Inveraray; and in the meantime a message had gone by telegraph and semaphore to Prebble with orders to steam back up Loch Fyne and re-embark the landing-parties. Halfhyde was kicking his heels in Inveraray when the royal carriage rolled in safe and intact; and he joined the cheering of Her Majesty's subjects as the old lady came over the hump-backed bridge and proceeded in state to the great castle, Stanley by her side. Soon after this a message reached Halfhyde with word that he was to report to the castle, where he was accorded another and happier audience of Her Majesty. When he left the castle in a brougham he found *Vendetta* in sight to the southward, and after she had let go an anchor off-shore boats were sent in to pick up Halfhyde and his sailors. Boarding and going below with Prebble, Halfhyde reported on recent events.

"A simple enough story, Prebble, if humiliating to a degree! Stanley was entirely genuine, and the Spanish government blameless too."

"But the cloak-and-dagger, sir?"

Halfhyde shrugged. "Stanley had obviously to be got out that way so as not to drop any hints to Villanueva, who had to be lulled the better to incriminate himself. Hence the co-operation of certain Spaniards—the showing of the light from the shore, the buoyancy tanks in the chest—"

"But the authorities in Cartagena, and Admiral de Valdares?"

"My dear Prebble, the Spanish authorities knew nothing. Stanley was simply to be apprehended on account of that killing, the one he'd carried out after leaving Villanueva's *hacienda*, a killing I'd not myself call murder in the circumstances. And the men who were helping Stanley impressed upon him that their help was conditional upon his helping, in return, to nail Villanueva and his associates—which, I repeat, meant lulling the opposition and maintaining full cloak-and-dagger procedure, even to the extent of not revealing Her Majesty's change of plan to anyone. The secret was well kept by everyone except the rear-admiral's sister—for which we may be thankful, but Stanley was right not to broach security in the smallest way."

"I see, sir," Prebble said wonderingly. "So Colonel Stanley's really cleared?"

"Absolutely. He'd arranged for a battalion of Highlanders to cover the loch road, which was where he knew the assassins would be mustering. As a matter of fact, he'd taken the precaution of giving them the map reference himself. He was furious when he saw me, put two and two together, thought our men would muck it up—and was furious again when he heard we'd got there first. That's all there is to it." Halfhyde added, "The coded message was innocuous to Her Majesty, though not to others— the intent being further deception of Villanueva, who is about to be quietly arrested along with certain of his associates. As Stanley once said: all's well that ends well, Prebble."

"Yes, sir. And us?"

"We shall receive acclaim on our return to Portsmouth, I don't doubt. Currently, we're invited to partake of His Grace's hospitality. Two watches—officers and ratings—two parties on successive nights, and a presentation to Her Majesty of all hands of the landing-parties." Halfhyde wagged an admonitory finger. "Not too celebratory! We weigh for Spithead and Portsmouth in the early hours after the second of the parties."

Captain Watkiss, upon his arrival at Gibraltar many days ear-lier, had obtained permission to take his flotilla home to Portsmouth in the wake of *Vendetta;* making Spithead, he had sought information and had been informed that in case of fail-ure to protect Her Majesty Halfhyde was patrolling off the entry to Loch Fyne in order to apprehend any after-the-event assas-sins should they attempt escape via the waters outside the loch. Watkiss had immediately weighed once more, had informed the commander-in-chief, Portsmouth, that he was proceeding north for Scottish waters, and had steamed arrogantly out from Spithead to follow the course taken by Halfhyde. And on this particular bright morning, in the wide sweep where Kilbrannan Sound met Inchmarnock Water, he felt that his action had been wholly vindicated: his roving telescope had brought up a sailing dinghy beating out of Loch Fyne and his sharp eye had recognized Colonel Stanley in the stern-sheets.

He stood transfixed; his thoughts ran riot. The rear-admiral, back in Gibraltar, had imparted alarming tidings and in Watkiss's mind Stanley was now more than suspect. One thing stood clear: Stanley was making good his escape, and that could mean only the one appalling thing: the Queen was dead. Watkiss, his face solemn, removed his cap.

"Mr Beauchamp."

"Sir?"

"The damn plot . . . it's been brought off under Halfhyde's blasted nose." Captain Watkiss extended his telescope towards the dinghy. "Out there, in that boat, is Stanley!"

"I doubt if—"

"Damn your doubts, Mr Beauchamp, call away the sea-boat's crew and lowerers of the watch and arrest that man Stanley." Watkiss lifted his telescope again. "There's someone with him. An accomplice, a damn Italian or whatever it was. I shall arrest them both! Yes, what is it, Yeoman?" he added testily.

The yeoman of signals saluted. "*Vendetta* ahead, sir, approaching down Loch Fyne."

"Indeed!" Watkiss sniffed. "Mr Halfhyde is a little late in his pursuit, I fear! We shall see, shall we not, Mr Beauchamp, what he has to say to this, and how he will explain to the nation how he came to let Her Majesty perish!"

Beauchamp stared, wide-eyed. "Her Majesty, sir?"

"The sea-boat, Mr Beauchamp, why have you not obeyed my orders?" Watkiss sounded truculent. "Hurry, man!"

"Aye, aye, sir." Beauchamp went down the bridge ladder to the upper deck. Captain Watkiss turned his attention to the sailing dinghy and scowled: Stanley was waving an arm in some sort of greeting—sheer impertinent effrontery! When the sea-boat had gone down on the falls and taken the water, Watkiss ordered his ship to alter course towards Stanley. As the sea-boat was pulled alongside the dinghy some kind of altercation took place; but orders were obeyed, and the dinghy was taken in tow of the sea-boat and brought alongside *Venomous*. The two occupants climbed a Jacob's ladder to the quarterdeck: from the bridge Captain Watkiss studied them triumphantly: the second man was no dago, so much was certain, but it was likely, if deplorable, that Stanley had British accomplices. There was a lump in Watkiss's throat: he was very conscious of the vital part he was playing in apprehending the ringleader of the Queen's assassins. He called to his yeoman of signals: "Yeoman, make to *Vendetta: you are to repair aboard immediately.*"

"Aye, aye, sir."

The signal lamp began clacking out the order. Captain Watkiss's mind roved ahead: this sad moment, this veritable end of an era . . . why, his flotilla's seamen might well be called upon to provide a guard for the body! The Queen could not be left to the Scots, she had been Queen of England. No doubt she would be conveyed south by the train—on the other hand, he, Watkiss, was on the spot, and would be honoured indeed by the dreadful duty of a sea escort to the Nore and the Thames . . .

Hearing feet on the ladder, Watkiss turned. "Ah, Mr Beauchamp. It's likely we shall have a state function to perform and we shall acquit ourselves well when Her Majesty's brought aboard. Seamen in gaiters, chin-stays, sennit hats, rifles and bayonets—why always leave ceremonial to the army, Mr Beauchamp? The gunner's mate shall—"

"Sir, I—"

"Hold your tongue, Mr Beauchamp, I am pondering." Watkiss paused. "I take it Stanley and his accomplice are in most safe arrest?"

"Sir, there has been—"

"Damn—"

Beauchamp raised his voice, his face scarlet. "Sir, the other person in the boat is His Grace the Duke of Argyll!"

"Stuff-and-nonsense, Mr Beauchamp, the *Duke* wouldn't . . . *what did you say?*"

Beauchamp repeated his words, and added with forbearance, "They were going fishing, sir, in the waters off Arran. Her Majesty is alive and well, sir—thanks to Mr Halfhyde."

"What?"

Beauchamp made his report again. Watkiss's mouth stood open like that of a landed fish. "You're sure?"

"I am certain, sir, quite certain. I—"

"Thank you, Mr Beauchamp, you may hold your tongue." Watkiss stared up Loch Fyne, his face a deep red. He was shaken, and badly. Delighted—naturally—that Her Majesty was apparently safe. But Stanley: memory was stirring most awkwardly. Back in Gibraltar—given the rear-admiral's views as given earlier to Halfhyde he had searched his conscience and, mindful of his own career, had added some fairly damning observations upon Stanley's past behaviour that he had suddenly seen in proper perspective—proper, that was, as he had seen it at the time, in the rear-admiral's presence. Now those observations seemed only too likely to rebound . . . Captain Watkiss suddenly attacked his first lieutenant. "Why the devil did you not report this before, hey—instead of—of hanging about like a curate round a bishop!"

"Sir, with respect, you—"

"Hold your tongue, Mr Beauchamp, what a *useless* first lieutenant you have turned out, to be sure! Good God! The Duke!" Watkiss bounced up and down his bridge for a moment, then turned again upon Beauchamp. "My apologies to them at once, d'you hear me, at once! A dreadful mistake, Mr Beauchamp, I—no, wait. That won't do." He pummelled his head. "I fancied they were in trouble, they looked as though they were, did they not . . . and the waters round here are notorious for sudden gusts of wind—the sky's full of it, you can see if you look—very treacherous." He paused again. "The arrest, Mr Beauchamp, did you make an actual arrest?"

"No, sir—"

"Thank God! You acted very properly, Mr Beauchamp, and nothing's to be said about arrest." Captain Watkiss was bouncing resiliently and triumphantly back to command of the situation. "I've saved them a damned unpleasant experience, have I not—you shall tell them that! A safe passage back for them, back to Inveraray. It's fortunate I arrived here in time to be of assistance, by God, and I shall expect to hear from Mr Halfhyde why he didn't proceed to their assistance himself, do you understand?"

"Yes, sir—"

"Tell the ward-room steward to prepare a nourishing meal, and brandy. And Mr Beauchamp . . ."

"Sir?"

"Belay the order to *Vendetta*. I shall have private words with Mr Halfhyde later. I'm damned if I want him aboard just now."

Captain Watkiss stared dourly across the water towards *Vendetta*, feeling a stirring of unease as he reflected that the wretched Halfhyde might well cast stones into his placid pool of maritime assistance.

THE LORD RAMAGE NOVELS

of Dudley Pope

This popular series by renowned naval historian Dudley Pope traces the Royal Navy adventures of Nicholas Ramage, the eldest son and heir of the tenth Earl of Blazey. Lord Ramage and his equally colorful crew serve with humor, audacity, and distinction during the wars against France and Spain, through furious sea battles, shipwrecks, secret missions, daring land rescues, and the attentions of a surprisingly large number of handsome and spirited young ladies.

"Not even C. S. Forester knows more about the routine and battle procedures of the British Navy in the days of Nelson. . . . **a grand tale written with panache, glitter, and awesome authority**—one can only rejoice."
    —*The New York Times*

"The first and still favourite rival to Hornblower."
    —*Daily Mirror*

"An author who really knows Nelson's navy."
    —*The Observer*

Ramage
    0-935526-76-5 • 320 pp., $14.95
Ramage & the Drumbeat
    0-935526-77-3 • 288 pp., $14.95
Ramage & the Freebooters
    0-935526-78-1 • 384 pp., $15.95
Governor Ramage R.N.
    0-935526-79-X • 384 pp., $15.95
Ramage's Prize
    0-935526-80-3 • 320 pp., $15.95
Ramage & the Guillotine
    0-935526-81-1• 320 pp., $14.95
Ramage's Diamond
    0-935526-89-7 • 336 pp., $15.95
Ramage's Mutiny
    0-935526-90-0 • 288 pp., $14.95
Ramage & the Rebels
    0-935526-91-9 • 320 pp., $15.95
The Ramage Touch
    1-59013-007-3 • 272 pp., $15.95
Ramage's Signal
    1-59013-008-1 • 288 pp., $15.95
Ramage & the Renegades
    1-59013-009-X • 320 pp., $15.95
Ramage's Devil
    1-59013-010-3 • 320 pp., $15.95
Ramage's Trial
    1-59013-011-1 • 320 pp., $15.95
Ramage's Challenge
    1-59013-012-X, 352 pp., $15.95
Ramage at Trafalgar
    1-59013-022-7 • 256 pp., $14.95
Ramage & the Saracens
    1-59013-023-5 • 304 pp., $15.95
Ramage & the Dido
    1-59013-024-3 • 272 pp., $15.95

The complete 18-book series of Lord Ramage novels is now available in bookstores, or call toll-free to order or request our free book catalog: 1-888-266-5711.
Visit the McBooks Press website: www.mcbooks.com

The Privateersman Mysteries

In his exciting six-volume series, David Donachie re-invents the nautical fiction genre with his smart, authentic, action-filled shipboard whodunits set in the 1790s.

When Donachie's hero, Captain Harry Ludlow, is forced out of the Royal Navy under a cloud, he becomes a privateersman in partnership with his younger brother James, a rising artist with his own reasons for leaving London. Together, intrigue and violent death take more of their time than hunting fat trading vessels.

The Privateersman Mysteries

"Not content to outflank and out-gun C.S. Forester with his vivid and accurate shipboard action, storm havoc and battle scenes, **Donachie has made Ludlow the most compulsively readable amateur detective since Dick Francis' latest ex-jockey.**"

—*Cambridge Evening News*

"High adventure and detection cunningly spliced. Battle scenes which reek of blood and brine; excitements on terra firma to match."
—*Literary Review*

To request a complimentary copy of the McBooks Press Historical Fiction Catalog, call **1-888-BOOKS-11** (1-888-266-5711).

To order on the web: **www.mcbooks.com**
and read an excerpt.

Order the complete series!

THE DEVIL'S OWN LUCK
1-59013-004-9 • 302 pp., $15.95

THE DYING TRADE
1-59013-006-5 • 384 pp., $16.95

A HANGING MATTER
1-59013-016-2 • 416 pp., $16.95

AN ELEMENT OF CHANCE
1-59013-017-0 • 448 pp., $17.95

THE SCENT OF BETRAYAL
1-59013-031-6 • 448 pp., $17.95

A GAME OF BONES
1-59013-032-4 • 352 pp., $15.95